## PRAISE FROM READERS AND CRITICS

### *The Lawnmower Club,* RED SKY SERIES/BOOK 4

"*The Lawnmower Club* is a story that blends metaphysics, psychology, and cerebral anatomy into a humorous romp through northern Michigan. Author Evans shifts his writing gears like a British racing car climbing Pike's Peak, varying his delivery style from the fast pace of a Captain Marvel Comic to the penetrating look into our souls in a Bronte novel. His improbable utopian view of a world in harmony seems logical and achievable by the time the reader comes to the end of this intricate and amusing story...."

—DAVID THOMAS, RETIRED HEALTHCARE EXECUTIVE AND UNITED STATES MARINE

### *When Strangers Meet At Devil's Elbow,* RED SKY SERIES/BOOK 3

"Small, heartwarming coincidences bring together a group of people who find love outside their comfort zones...an uplifting tale about human connection, random acts of kindness, America's heartland, and love. *When Strangers Meet at Devil's Elbow* shines in empathy and grace through well-crafted characters."

—INDIE READER

"Northern Michigan is the perfect setting for a plucky group of characters reinventing their lives and forming community. The 'rules of ice fishing' and how they apply to life in general are reason enough to read this enjoyable book."

—JANET TROTTER, ARTIST

## *Out of the Inferno*, RED SKY SERIES/BOOK 2

"*Out of the Inferno* examines life, love, and cancer. Randy Evans documents the years he and his wife battled cancer, touching on everything from treatments to travel...his descriptive prose and powerful imagery (Evans needed a wheelchair to move the enormous stack of Laurene's medical files from room to room) drive the story home."

—KIRKUS REVIEWS

"*Out of the Inferno* is an eye-opening, honest memoir written by an author whose wife lived and died with cancer. Rarely have authors whose partners died taken the time and effort to put their experience on paper for the rest of us. The powerful writing forces the reader to feel the good, bad, and the horrific while uplifting the reader with lessons learned. This unique book fills a gap in the cancer literature. I love this book."

—DR. THEODORA ROSS, M.D., PH.D., CANCER GENETICIST, DIRECTOR, CANCER GENETICS PROGRAM, UT SOUTHWESTERN MEDICAL CENTER, DALLAS, AUTHOR, *A CANCER IN THE FAMILY*

"What happens when cancer takes center stage? Randy Evans bares his soul and shares his and Laurene's story and the aftermath of that story in a very engaging book. He combines down home Texas culture with a running commentary on lessons learned, all within the context of a trip through hell (Dante's Inferno). But he continues on, out of hell, and into a new life. A powerful story."

—LINDA YARGER, MEDICAL LIBRARIAN, UT MD ANDERSON CANCER CENTER, AND BREAST CANCER SURVIVOR

"A beautifully written memoir filled with stunning stories, terrific insights, and first-hand advice. I laughed and wept, openly and honestly dozens of times."

—WADE ROUSE, INTERNATIONAL BESTSELLING MEMOIRIST AND AUTHOR OF *THE CHARM BRACELET* AND *THE HOPE CHEST* WRITTEN UNDER THE PEN NAME VIOLA SHIPMAN AS A TRIBUTE TO HIS GRANDMOTHER

*Red Sky Anthology*, RED SKY SERIES/BOOK 1

"As well as the poignant and painful, there is also the uplifting in Red Sky Anthology. In total, offering a variety of poetry, short stories, drama, memoir, and two novel concepts, Evans demonstrates a writer in control of multiple genres, each providing insight and understanding for introspection."

—GLEN YOUNG, PETOSKEY NEWS AND REVIEW, TEACHER, WRITER

"Those of us who know and appreciate the lakes, forests and wildlife of northern Michigan can identify with a cottage deck in fall, smell of wood smoke in the air, an autumn boating excursion, an April snow that leaves tree trunks 'whiskered with wind-whipped snow,' trillium breaking through in the spring."

—ANNE KELLY, JOURNALIST AND FREELANCE WRITER

# The Lawnmower Club

A NOVEL

RED SKY SERIES
*Book 4*

# RANDY EVANS

Copyright © 2018 Randy Evans, Ph.D.
ISBN-13: 978-1546859659
ISBN-10: 1546859659

Little Traverse Press, Bay Harbor, Michigan
All rights reserved. No part of this publication may be reproduced, stored in a retrieval system, or transmitted in any form or by any means, electronic, mechanical, recording or otherwise, without the prior written permission of the author.

Printed on acid-free paper.

The characters and events in this book are fictitious. Any similarities to real persons, living or dead, is coincidental and not intended by the author.

First Edition

*BLOG: randyevansauthor.com*
*Literature & Fiction>Humor & Satire>Humorous*
*Literature & Fiction>Contemporary*
*Literature & Fiction>Literary*

*In memory of Harold Bruce Custer (1900-1977),
my grandfather, who loved to cut grass*

*Grandfather smiled in his sleep. Feeling the smile and wondering why it was there, he awoke. He lay quietly listening, and the smile was explained. For he heard a sound which was far more important than birds or the rustle of new leaves. Once each year he woke this way and lay waiting for the sound which meant summer had officially begun. And it began on a morning such as this when a boarder, a nephew, a cousin, a son or grandson came out on the lawn below and moved in consecutively smaller quadrangles north and east and south and west with a clatter of rotating metal through the sweet summer grass.*

—**Dandelion Wine by Ray Bradbury (1920-2012)**

# Contents

| | | |
|---|---|---|
| *Chapter 1* | The Cougar | 1 |
| *Chapter 2* | The Cart Shed | 7 |
| *Chapter 3* | After Mona | 17 |
| *Chapter 4* | The Social Worker | 27 |
| *Chapter 5* | Swallowing The Moon | 51 |
| *Chapter 6* | It Takes Two To Tango | 61 |
| *Chapter 7* | Mallard Pond | 79 |
| *Chapter 8* | Fathers And Sons | 85 |
| *Chapter 9* | Hope From Feathers | 101 |
| *Chapter 10* | Near Miss | 115 |
| *Chapter 11* | Manhattans And Peanuts | 123 |
| *Chapter 12* | Halfway Happy | 129 |
| *Chapter 13* | Inside And Outside | 137 |
| *Chapter 14* | Making Music Together | 149 |
| *Chapter 15* | Noise Like Music | 157 |
| *Chapter 16* | Warming Up | 169 |
| *Chapter 17* | The Bookcase | 183 |
| *Chapter 18* | The Wolf Moon | 191 |
| *Chapter 19* | That Dog Won't Hunt | 201 |
| *Chapter 20* | A Momentary Hero | 211 |

| | | |
|---|---|---|
| *Chapter 21* | Lawn's Early Light | 223 |
| *Chapter 22* | Zitzelberger's In Paradise | 241 |
| *Chapter 23* | So Silent | 253 |
| *Chapter 24* | After The Tree Falls | 267 |
| *Chapter 25* | The Keyhole Bar | 279 |
| *Chapter 26* | Spring Mowing | 291 |

| | |
|---|---|
| About the Author | 303 |
| Acknowledgements | 305 |
| Reading Group Guide | 307 |

# 1

# THE COUGAR

*M*Y GOD, THE COUGAR thinks. *It's almost heaven.* Six in the morning. In the red light of an August dawn, beautiful and brutal, the cougar, nine feet from head to tail, soft-foots the woodsy edges of a golf course fairway. To trembling creatures of the forest, the tawny predator looks like a never-ending procession of sun-flecked fur. His long upturned tail thrashes brush under blue-green spruce boughs, his new territory, savannahs of open fields and marshes, inland lakes and rivers, and large tracts of hilly forests, perfect in every way, except for the nonstop thrumming of lawnmower engines.

The cougar raises an eyebrow as he looks east beyond a stand of cedars, where the unfathomable noise starts at first light and doesn't stop until just before sundown, six days a week. Sunday stays silent as deep forest. Monday mornings, the unnatural lawnmower sounds once again disturb the primal stillness.

*Randy Evans*

Wanted by the law for nipping the heels of a jogger who happened to be a dental hygienist. (The cougar had noticed her excellent gum health when she turned and opened her mouth to shriek *"AIEEEEEEEEEEEEEEEE!"*), the cougar had escaped cops and dogs the winter before, immigrating from Wisconsin to Michigan in search of a better life. Passing through the old mill town of Escanaba in the moonlight, he had scampered through hundreds of miles of frozen streams, rivers, and lakes, wood patches of pine and birch; strolled through hedges and lawns of small towns, trailer parks, and abandoned fishing camps; napped between rows of snow-whiskered corn stalks; slinked past a wolf pack in Hiawatha National Forest, all the time, keeping the sand-dunes on the northern shore of Lake Michigan to his right—once running through the headlights of a car that nearly hit him.

Below the town of St. Ignace, he arrived near the point where Lakes Michigan and Huron join. He crossed the frozen waterway to the edge of a current-whipped, river-like channel, a sluice of icy gray water. Paddling against the sideways current with all his might, he swam to the other side, ambling ashore on Michigan's Lower Peninsula near Wilderness State Park, where no mountain lions had been known to live or breed since 1906.

The rich land provides the large predator with an abundant supply of rabbits, woodcock, turkey, porcupines, raccoons, coyotes, deer—and numberless chipmunk, his favorite snack when he wants a little something. The nomad cat could have ranged deeper into state park land nearby, but the sure source of easy prey keeps him in this unfamiliar 30-square mile territory, a clandestine Garden of Eden—but for the unnatural and incomprehensible noise from a small army of lawnmowers.

The cougar stares in the direction of the racket. His ears flick forward. His neck cranes. He smells gas fumes and engine oil. His eyes lock onto a band of humans huddled over noisy machines, riding across wide expanses of green grass. His muscular body tenses to high alert. He launches terrible hisses in the direction of the lawnmowers, showing his teeth and his own superb gum health, the last thought of the dental hygienist he'd recently attacked in Wisconsin. (He had merely tackled and gripped her leg in his jaws until the girl screamed. Only a few drops of blood.)

*Why did she wear red running shoes? I hate red. Now humans want my hide.*

Animated by flashing light against a blurry backdrop, the unfortunate encounter had been recorded on a trail cam. Wildlife biologists recorded the incident and gave the cougar marquee status at national meetings accompanied by speeches about LION-HUMAN INTERACTIONS. They wrote him up like an outlaw pursued by vigilantes, but the cougar had vanished into the stillness of the Wisconsin North woods.

The 150-pound feline crosses a dirt road, runs across a field of dry grass, and over an embankment. He's light on his feet and lightning fast, a splendid specimen of lithe beast hood. In a state of ennui, he drops into a depression of underbrush. Even at this distance, the clattering of lawnmowers rumble over the fields like tanks on a remote battlefield. The mechanical sounds of rotating metal encroach the cougar's world as strange and treacherous. The sounds disturb his thinking—makes him twitch when he's awake and whimper when he's asleep. He wants either supreme quiet or the sounds of nature.

There is a magical intelligence behind his face and eyes. Unlike the more limited consciousness of other animals, the super-cougar's mental abilities excel beyond the guesswork of scientists, both a gift and burden. Or maybe he's not unique, just slightly more gifted and burdened than the rest of his species. Who knows? In addition to an amygdala programmed to fight or flee in the presence of life-threatening danger, he possesses a cerebral cortex with the gifts of reflective thought and problem solving, the burdens of negative emotions, the capacity to suffer beyond pain, and the fragile pursuit of happiness in the face of imminent death.

The cougar knows his place in nature. He knows that the lawnmower guys must be special animals—two legs not four, neck held vertically not horizontally—like two-legged bears. All the while he tries to breathe through the strange barks from the upright bears, and the disquieting machines. He summons positive thoughts. He thinks how the rebound of whitetail herds in North America has supported his independent lifestyle. His muscles relax.

The lone cougar lives in an abandoned landfill site, two miles from the golf course. He circles back and uncovers a fresh deer carcass protected with deadfall limbs, a kill from the previous night. He reposes and settles into the leftover deer, his head dipping, his jaws casually tearing and chewing, but he eats without the usual pleasure. He feels stressed deep inside his white underbelly.

*It will do me good to roam,* he thinks. He jogs on the nature trail nearby, and drinks swirling algae-speckled water from a creek. Wind rustles sweetly in the trees and calms him.

The cougar returns to his daybed in the landfill. He stretches and yawns and closes his eyes for a morning catnap. Little lives scurry around him, playing chicken to see who can come closest. The critters never get used to seeing him. The cougar is as strange to them, as the lawnmower riders are to the cougar. A brave chipmunk pitters close by. The grumpy cougar swats at the chipmunk but misses.

During his whimpering dreams, the cougar runs with explosive speed, and pounces with vampire bites to the necks of the lawnmower riders like he's sinking his teeth in a juicy rabbit. The thrill of a tooth-and-claw ambush stirs through his best nighttime reveries. During the daytime, the unrelenting noise infuriates the cougar. Could he stalk and crouch close enough for a sneak attack? The golf course's expanse of cut grass provides no cover.

He decides to hunt. His life would be so empty without quarry—the blessing and curse of a natural predator.

## 2

# THE CART SHED

MY GOD, LEO thinks. *I must be the luckiest man on the planet!*

The late-August sun rises red, as Leo Zitzelberger watches his lawnmowerians, bent and stiff, fused to their tractors in the crisp morning air, their breath steaming little clouds and their machines puffing smoke, as if men and machines run as a single unit, on common fuel and a shared soul. Like an admiral glassing fleet maneuvers of ships at sea, Zitzelberger watches from the deck railing of his clubhouse. He admires the wavy contours of freshly-trimmed rows of grass, the fairways of the formerly bankrupt golf course he now owns. When Leo Zitzelberger had purchased the run-down country club, the banker said how proud he must be, and Leo said yes, he surely was.

"Do you golf?" the banker said.

"I hate golf," Leo replied.

Wearing a loosely-knit gray cardigan, a brown-and-green plaid shirt, and moss-green pants. (He looks like he dresses himself in the dark, which is what he does.) Zitzelberger yawns and stretches his long arms and legs. He pours a cup of lukewarm coffee. He yawns again—his yellow teeth jutting out from shrunken gums, a periodontist's nightmare. He removes a blueberry muffin from a paper doily, his favorite snack when he wants a little something. He tears away a piece of muffin from its stretchy top and pops it into his mouth. The taste is not nearly as good as the muffins that Mona, his deceased wife, had baked from scratch on Sunday mornings.

Remembrances of Mona come less frequently these days. He no longer feels like a stray animal. He's staging a comeback. The change of locations has helped. For a long time after she died, his consciousness had been split between *before Mona* and *after Mona*, but his lawn mowing club has offered him a secondhand life, not as good as the first one, but acceptable, tolerable, and digestible, like a day-old blueberry muffin.

As Zitzelberger finishes the last crumb, he remembers an important task. *Oh, yes, a would-be lawnmowerian has applied for membership.* He must interview him before the first shift—one of his duties as owner and founder of club.

Zitzelberger carries his large body over to what used to be a cart shed to speak to the applicant and inspect his lawn tractor. Shambling east into the morning sun, he drags his shadow like a black cape—like a character created for a novel. A healthy 70-year-old except for bulk, his feet leave large footprints in the sandy soil. He passes a boxlike, glassed-in sign, the kind you find displaying the sermon topic in front of a country church.

## *The Lawnmower Club*

The sign reads NO CHILDREN! NO PETS! He pauses and bows his head before entering the dim light of the cart shed, as if he's stepping into the tabernacle of a sanctified sect. He smells the sweet incense of grease, gas, and mildew.

In some ways, he's like a priest. He leads a celibate and solitary life, dedicated to cutting grass and maintaining his independence. He stands over six feet tall with a hatchet face and large steel-colored eyes. His sharp chin looks like the toe of a Western dress boot. When he walks, his arms swing like the steel bars of a chain saw. To people in town he looks fearsome—mothers pick up their children when he lumbers down the sidewalk. Dog owners heel their dogs. Boys throw stones at him.

In Zitzelberger's mind, the perfect town would be one with a few shops along brick-red streets, a large grassy village green with a flag pole, and very few people. The only sounds would be the snap and tug of the flag, and the clink of the pulley against the flagpole. He doesn't fall in the category of a people person; a poll of the locals would support this. Many of the town people hold grudges against him for losing their vehicles. When they failed to make their payments, Leo knocked on their doors, repossession order in hand, and hauled away their cars with his tow truck, brandishing the catchy slogan, PUTTING PEOPLE BACK ON THEIR FEET. Only popular with bank collectors and finance companies, people who hate him dot the county like dandelions on an otherwise perfect lawn.

Zitzelberger wants to make sure the new member is a good fit—that he possesses true lawnmowerian values—a love of grass, respect for machines, and a do-it-yourself mentality. He only wants people as members who never tire of making perfect rows and running their machines. And people who don't want to turn the club into anything else. If a prospective member asks, "What else can we do with our membership besides cut grass? Could we have picnics with our family, play horseshoes, or camp on the grounds?" All knockout factors. He only wants members who want to mow—who are obsessed by grass cutting, who don't even daydream while cutting, because nothing can be more engaging or satisfying or exciting than mowing in neat rows.

Now he walks catlike by lawnmowers at rest, and wrecks of other machinery that members could not part with when they lost their homes: weed eaters, hedge trimmers, power edgers, leaf blowers, uprooted sprinkler systems, log splitters, air compressors, de-thatchers, front-end loaders, and spreader attachments. Zitzelberger, uncharacteristically empathetic, has no rules about storing extra equipment as long as the cart barn has room. *Men need their machines,* he thinks.

Each lawnmowerian has a dedicated work space where members can place their workbenches like altars. On peg board above the benches, t squares hang like crosses, and socket wrenches lay on top like communion candlesticks, everything necessary for maintenance on their mowers. Zitzelberger doesn't allow family photographs or trophies or service club plaques. No pinup calendars or other ephemera clutter the sacred space, but yellowed diagrams and posters of lawnmower

## The Lawnmower Club

engines and mowers are fine, or clipboards of maintenance records and dog-eared instruction manuals. If someone has a non-mowing hobby, from woodworking to building model ships, Zitzelberger says, *"YOU CAN PLAY WITH THOSE THINGS AT THE SENIOR CENTER!"* He allows no drinking or smoking in the cart shed. He wants members to focus on the purity, simplicity, and dedication of grass-cutting.

He stalks quietly up behind the prospective new member, as if preparing to scare the bejeezus out of him, which is exactly what he intends. He wants to catch him off guard, a test for healthy reflexes. *"LOOKS LIKE A SCAG!"* he speaks in a low rumble like the sound of distant thunder.

He develops a good first impression of the machine. It looks clean and oiled, a V-Ride with a Stripe Roller. Zitzelberger had read about this bright new orange model—a Cheetah 61-inch zero-turn rider with a fast, air-cooled 36-horse-power engine.

The prospect turns to Zitzelberger and tries not to act startled. "Yep, I've always had Scags, every model they ever made: Turf Tigers, Tiger Cubs, Saber Tooth Tigers, and the Wildcat—now that was a great cutter. But this new Cheetah is the best! Runs up to 16 miles per hour!"

As he moves his hands with love over his lawn tractor's steering wheel, the new member grins a gold tooth at Zitzelberger. Zitzelberger raises his eyebrow, but decides to smile back, even though he regards smiling as weakness. He parts his lips as if he's opening a wound.

"Mow for a living?" Zitzelberger says.

"No, but like most of the folks here, I live to mow. I'm a residential mower, but I have always wanted commercial grade equipment—needed to keep moving up, one model, one make at a time. Kept buying bigger properties for more grass to cut. Then my kids moved me into an old folk's home surrounded by lousy, neglected landscaping. I'm sure you can imagine the torture—confining a *lawn man* to a place surrounded by an unkempt yard. I sat by the window looking outside all day, and couldn't stop thinking about my tractor, sitting unused and unmaintained in my daughter's garage. Sad. But then I heard about this place—what a great idea! *YOU'RE A SAVIOR OF SORTS!*"

Zitzelberger detects a tone of self-pity. He hates expressions of either positive or negative emotions. Happy or sad equally offend him.

"I don't care to hear people's sob stories, and I don't regard myself as anyone's savior," Zitzelberger interjects. "I need members to help pay the bills, so I can live the way I want to live. You're not the first man to lose his home, and you won't be the last."

Zitzelberger locks his eyes on the new member like a predator about to take prey. The new member's eyes widen white like broken eggshells.

"I get that, completely," the prospect says, trying his best to take in Zitzelberger's every blink and syllable.

"Good, because I want people who pay their dues, keep their assigned shifts, and run their machines properly without

## The Lawnmower Club

damaging the turf. This isn't a church or a bridge club. We're all here to mow, and I want people who know what they're doing."

"Now, go ahead and tell me a little about your mowing history, since I have to evaluate you, but I don't care to hear about your past. Some of the members may want to trade stories with you about the good or bad old days, but I'm not interested in what you did way back when. To my way of thinking, memories are like a rotten-smelling mower bag of old clippings."

The prospect's face freezes, his body trembles, and his skin turns the color of parchment.

"Now I can tell by the look on your face that you think I'm coming on too strong," says Zitzelberger. "But I'm merely making myself clear, see. *MOW HERE NOW!*—that's my motto. So, go on now. Just the headlines—like the front-page of a newspaper."

The prospective member clears his throat like he's about to make a life or death statement. His entire body tilts backwards, away from Zitzelberger. "I do think I can make a lawn look better than the next guy—I take good care of the blades and the deck. But I like the ride of a big mower the best, like whiskey on water. And the latest technology, of course, unless they get carried away. Can you believe they're making robot mowers now?"

The man had spent so much time in the sun that his face and arms are covered with sun damage and scars from melanoma surgery. He gives Zitzelberger another please-like-me smile.

"Well, I've heard remotes work for steep hills and ditches," Zitzelberger says, "but I like to haul tail on an incline myself. I hate hedge trimmers and weed eaters. I hate shrubby lawns. I like grass right up to the foundation. Pure grass, green grass, that's been cared for and cut by someone with skill. Not everyone can afford a big house, but everyone can have a well-tended lawn. I like to walk around a lawn in my bare feet and feel fresh clippings in between my toes."

The applicant glimpses a hint of encouragement in Zitzelberger's eyes. "You'll see...I'm not at the end of my mowing career," he says, "someday, I want to get the 72-inch Scag with a bigger engine—maybe used if it looks like new and passes a compression test."

"Check the maintenance records," Zitzelberger cuts in. "Make sure you have the receipts, especially for new parts. You need lawnmower parts for two reasons—replacement parts for normal use of the machine, the other reason, carelessness and neglect. You must know the difference...I bet you know that."

"Sure 'nough." The two men achieve a beginner's level of mutual respect.

"Well, you pass. I'll let you into the club next Tuesday, after your check clears. Now, here are the ground rules. Even though this is no longer a golf course, I want it to look like one—green, lush, manicured. I'll expect you to keep your shift. When you ride, keep your balance, avoid spinning your tires, and if you dig into muddy spots or standing water, let me know. Another thing, report busted sprinkler heads—I have some boys who can replace them, but I've gotta know."

## The Lawnmower Club

"Thanks for letting me in!" the new member says like a supplicant at the pearly gates. "You'll like my mowing style. I'm a good chopper, and keep the clippings cleared from under the deck. I started out with a push reel mower when I was a kid. In the '50s, I bought a Briggs and Stratton on a Cooper aluminum deck (back when they built 'em in the USA)...later used the engine to run my son's Go-Kart. My son ran it into a creek. He drowned...but I fished out the engine (it was under water for nine hours, hydro-locked!)...still runs on the first pull...have the owner's manual, too. In the '60s, I upgraded to a 1962 Toro Reel with a Wisconsin engine. I know it's an art form—like the other grass cutters here. *MOWING IS A JOURNEY WITH NO DESTINATION.*"

"Yep," says Zitzelberger, "I admit that's a nice statement, even though you dredged up a bit of the past, which I just told you holds no interest to me. But think about it...this used to be a golf course crawling with people who shirked their yard work to play an impossible game that does violence to grass. Now let me remind you one more time, no more stories about the past or about journeys and destinations, at least not to me. But I'm sorry to hear about your son."

"He would have grown up to be a great mower," the new member says. "But for now, my prayers have been answered."

"If prayer did any good, they'd pay people the big bucks to do it, and we'd all get drop-kicked ass-first into paradise," Zitzelberger say. "Fat chance of that! And yet, this sound of running lawnmowers, hear it now, this view of grassy green fields of cut grass, is sorta holy."

# 3
# AFTER MONA

ZITZELBERGER relishes his life of freedom living at the The Lawnmower Club. He bought the property at a bank sale after Mona died. He sold LEO REPO, and his wife's business, MONA LEASE-A-CAR. He listed their home. He couldn't stay around the place any longer with Mona gone. The house had felt deserted. As the months passed, the light bulbs popped and fizzled out one-by-one. He didn't replace them. His insides felt like the burnt-out bulbs looked—a black residue at the bottom of a glassy, bulbous enclosure. The first lights to go lit the spaces where he and Mona had spent the most time together—the family room floods, the florescent lights in the kitchen, the bedroom lamps—until after sundown, he sat in the dark.

The night Mona died had been dark from a dome of clouds that hung over the yard all day, filling the whole day with gloom and cool, even after spaces of blue broke through. Even though he worked outside from morning to evening, there always seemed to be one more thing to do before Mona called him in for dinner. After he went inside, they would eat mostly in silence. When they did talk, controversial subjects were out of the question. Zitzelberger had been raised not to argue at the dinner table or risk a beating by his father. So, Mona and Leo conversed politely in private, like they were sitting in a restaurant where all could hear. Mona was a meat and potatoes cook, and Zitzelberger liked what she fixed. Eating and talking were too much for him, so he concentrated on eating. It hadn't always been that way, but after so many years, their marriage had drifted into a mutual silence. Mona was like the air he breathed. The air didn't need attention, and neither did she, at least that's what he thought.

At sundown, Zitzelberger noticed that Mona hadn't called him in for dinner as usual. His yard had nearly disappeared against the fast-dimming sky. He barged through the screen door yelling for her. Mona was nowhere, until he found her at the bottom of the basement stairs, lying on her back with a broken neck and no heartbeat. Why she had decided to go to the basement he had no idea. He called an ambulance. He had never been so distressed. When they wheeled her away, he began to miss her with an ache that would ache every day.

And with Mona's passing, the comfortable division of labor they had shared crumbled. He had to either take care of everything on the inside as well as the outside, or choose to ignore certain things. He chose to ignore the inside—the inside of the house, and the inside of him. He spent most of the time on his front porch or in the yard or his detached garage. He tried to

## The Lawnmower Club

walk away from his past like it had belonged to someone else, but it remained there, except for Mona.

During the months after Mona's death, his vibrant green and well-tended lawn provided his sole consolation. If he had been zealous about lawn care before Mona died, caring for his lawn grew rapidly into an obsession. He sat on his porch all day, guarding the lawn and glaring at passersby when he wasn't directly tending it. When he left to do errands, he stuck a large sign in the turf—KEEP OFF MY LAWN!

A mean streak in his personality rarely surfaced while Mona had lived, and outbursts quickly faded when Mona kindly said, "Now, Leo..." But after Mona, Zitzelberger couldn't seem to back off his meanness, because deep inside, he wasn't happy with himself, and this angered him and caused him to be short with the people that he couldn't avoid. He had to do something different. He wanted to live in a new way, but he didn't know how. He simply knew there had to be something better.

There was something better. One day he drove by a large FOR SALE sign posted in front of a golf club, an old club with large oaks, cottonwoods, maples, and poplars lining the fairways. He observed the wide, neglected fairways, the grass overgrown with tall weeds, the sand traps littered with fallen limbs. At that moment, he decided to form a club for people like himself who loved to cut grass but had lost their yards. Now every day except Sunday, the same. Mowers arrive at first light to mow in two-hour shifts. For a thousand-dollar initiation fee plus a thousand in annual dues, the mowers mount their riding machines, stabled in the old cart barn, and mow their assigned fairway plots. With 27 holes and four mowers per fairway, one day per week, his total membership of 100 has reached capacity in less than a year.

Zitzelberger can't believe his good fortune—his whole world filled with the mellifluous hum of engines, the sweet fumes of lawnmower exhaust. From the clubhouse, he keeps his eyes on his members raising little dust clouds, sitting fixed on their mowers. The mowers look straight ahead like the terra cotta warriors of a Chinese emperor.

Zitzelberger laughs at the sight, because he feels like royalty, like a benign monarch: *"I'm the King of Geezerdom! My subjects get to ride out the tail end of their lives on big grass-cutting machines!"*

Zitzelberger loves to walk from one end of the vast pole barn to the other for his daily inspections. Every model and make of lawn tractor sits in neat rows from one end to the other: front-mounted engine models with side discharges, zero-turn radius mowers with rear-wheel steering, big rear baggers, and heavy-duty tractors. As he walks by, members ask him questions about starters, switches, carburetors, governors, oil and gas leaks, spark plugs, mufflers, crankshaft repairs, and blade sharpening. He interprets instruction manuals like a holy man reveals the truths of sacred texts. As long as people stay on topic, he enjoys his rounds. He's even patient when members use words like doohickeys, gizmos, gewgaws, or widgets to describe lawnmower parts.

## The Lawnmower Club

In the beginning, the members want to have meetings to make rules and air grievances. Zitzelberger hates meetings. One of the members in particular has a personal agenda. Hazzard Pembrook, a fortyish third-generation resorter, wants to impose a dress code to restore the decorum of the old days when his parents owned the property as a private haven for rich golfers. "Proper mowing attire is as important as proper grass-cutting," he says. "You need to ride in style. Other people can look like slobs, but not a crackerjack grass lawn mower man."

Pembrook constantly studies the dress of people around him for signs of bad taste and indecency, people whose membership applications would have been rejected by his father who had golfed in tweeds and knickers, who dressed for dinner until the day he died, and who told Pembrook when he was a boy to never wear anything that looked like it could be purchased in a department store.

"*LOCALS!*" his father would say haughtily as he looked at new applications. "Why do they bother apply? They're not our kind of people."

Pembrook mows in a wool sports coat with arm patches, canvas hunting pants, and high-laced boots. He listens to Bach on a headset. He lives alone in a rambling Victorian mansion across the street from the club, where stand-up mirrors appear in every room like Stations of the Cross. He's a trust fund baby. His father was a trust fund baby. He wants to be the mirror image of his father—not his grandfather, who worked for a living. His grandfather made money in the railroad business, and portraits hanging on the walls in Pembrook's house show a tiny man hunched over from carrying bags of cash to the bank. Pembrook has never worked for money. He doesn't like to get his hands dirty. He always wears gloves.

Pembrook regards his well-maintained, comely lawn as a status symbol, a way to distinguish the upper class from farmers who need their land to grow crops, a way to make neighbors with lesser lawns look inferior and proletarian by comparison. Also, as a single man recently divorced, he thinks, *with an immense lawn I feel more marriageable.* He also likes the security afforded by a large lawn, where intruders lack the benefit of cover, and predators cannot mount sneak attacks.

"I can see Wisconsin from my house, almost," he says. "I feel safe knowing what may be coming from afar. In this wild section of the country, who knows what may be lurking under the cover of wilderness? Perhaps native peoples once occupied this sacred hill, where they could see pirates, missionaries, mammoths, and catamounts approaching, as did the ancient guards who looked out from their watch towers to Inner Mongolia, ever vigilant for raiding nomads and drug traffickers, about to storm the Great Wall of Korea...why is it so dark? Oh, yeah, I have my sunglasses on."

Living across the street from the club, Pembrook has a lawn service do his own yard. He had joined The Lawnmower Club, because he wanted something manly to do during the day. Lawnmower engines flummox him, and other than a Shop-Vac that he has never used, he avoids machinery of any kind. He

## The Lawnmower Club

had also joined the club because of his happy memories there. Looking across the street at the club from his porch, he thinks, *the clubhouse and the rolling hills sweep me back to better days.* His family had owned the property through his childhood, the best stage of his life. In the summertime, he used to hang around the clubhouse, and practice putting and chipping along with other junior members. He never developed enough coordination to be a golfer, but he liked the ambience of the place.

He still longs for those halcyon days when lazy children were tolerated in the privileged class he represented. "Those were my days of splendor in the grass," he would say fondly during occasional summer cocktail parties on his expansive front porch. When he made the statement, he would look across to the acres of fairways with wistful eyes, a look he occasionally practiced while facing one of his stand-up mirrors.

Rory Finnegan, another member, serves as Pembrook's foil. A large man with red hair, he grips the wheel of his lawn tractor one-handed, with the grip of an Olympic wrestler, which he once was. The other hand holds a fly swatter, and slaps away at flies as he mows. Like two boxes of cement, his large feet rest hold down the mower housing. He smokes thick black cigars, and mows shirtless in grass-stained shorts, his torso front and back, hairy as a bear.

Finnegan made his money as an independent construction contractor, and has little respect for the so-called upper classes. He regards Pembrook with the disinterested respect he applies to all people. Finnegan knows that Pembrook regards a man like him as too blue collar, but he doesn't care. He prefers to mow early in the morning when he can hear every part of his machine singing like a chorus grinding out "When Irish Eyes Are Smiling."

Harold Peter Custer, a retired automobile mogul, prefers to mow barefoot in his pajamas with a wide-brimmed straw hat. Like most of his fellow members, he regards lawn mowing to be a fine art. He gives frequent advice to others: "You need to cut when the grass is dry," he says in his raspy voice. "I don't care how big your machine or what make or model, wet grass sticks and clogs a grass cutting machine, and puts extra strain on the parts."

Custer sings as he mows: *"The breeze is a-blowin, the grass won't stop growin, oh, mowin the lawn, mowin the lawn, it's what I gotta do, listen to the sound, rev it up, take it down, it's what I gotta do, mowin the lawn, mowin the lawn."*

Custer had lost his driver's license when he turned 85 because of an unfortunate accident. He coincidentally killed a hunter and a deer when he veered off the road while eating a fast food burrito. He arrives for his mowing shift in a chauffeured sunflower yellow limousine with six wheels—long, sleek, fast, and low to the ground. His chauffeur reaches into the back seat with both arms and pulls Custer to a standing position, where he remains stationary until he gains his balance.

A descendant of the famous general, Custer surveys the mowers riding their machines, like he's looking for Lakota Sioux and Cheyenne warriors about to attack. He's the man

*The Lawnmower Club*

with the most money, and he has the biggest machine— a John Deere four-wheel drive model 8800 Terrain Cut with a 42-horsepower diesel engine and five floating decks. "The cutting decks reticulate to hold the contours of the ground," he says proudly. "By George, they use one of these on the National Mall in Washington, D.C!"

Other issues arise among the lawnmowerians: standard bench settings for cutting height, number of cuts per yard, safety training and protective gear, bagging and dumping practices, and security for the lawnmower shed. Zitzelberger has no interest in democratic processes within his world. He didn't become founder of the club to hear squabbles. The last straw—someone proposes a social membership for non-riding walkers. Zitzelberger tells everyone that there will be no social members, and that he has decided to schedule the next club membership meeting in five years, hoping he'll die first. He loudly informing the members, *"MEETINGS ARE TOTALLY NOT HELPFUL."*

After the new member interview, Zitzelberger returns to his porch slider to keep an eye on his computer screen, which displays little red rectangles, each one representing a mower moving across a map of the golf course. He watches two rectangles working the edges of each fairway. He loves the new cloud-based farm management software a sales rep sold him, technology to track moisture content by area, topsoil and subsoil pH. He keeps detailed logs of field activity—de-thatching records, re-grassing projects, slow-release fertilization, weed, insect, and varmint control, sprinkler maintenance, and damage repair areas (no longer caused by cart tracks, ball marks, golf shoes, or temper tantrums). His love of grass, thick grass with strong roots, drives his eco-friendly approach. He doesn't use phosphorous, or anything synthetic. How can you poison something you love? He plans his improvements while sitting in the bathroom, alongside his bibles, *Month-by-Month Lawn Care* and *The Encyclopedia of Turf Management*.

After a full day, Zitzelberger moves to his bedroom on the second floor of the clubhouse. Liza Fitting, an irritating social worker, has troubled his sleep lately. She had given him an independent living assessment, for what she said was his own good. She wants to place him in a retirement home called Mallard Pond, for who knows what reason. She had first left a yellow sticky note on his back door saying that he could no longer live in his home. He looks up at the ceiling, wishing the visit was a distant memory, rather than something that had happened a few days earlier. The scene of their meeting keeps looping through his head like a lawnmower without a rider.

At times like these, when his guts had been in tumult, and his brain had kept cycling negative thoughts to hell and back, Mona would tell him to lie down. She would take his head in her lap and whisper words that fell on him like gentle rain. And her fingers, soft as flower petals, would stroke his forehead, and rub his crown, until he fell into dreamless sleep.

# 4

# THE SOCIAL WORKER

ZITZELBERGER SIZZLES burgers on his charcoal grill, while Jimmy Buffet's "Cheeseburgers in Paradise" plays on his old stereo. Blue smoke rises skyward and sifts sunlight like a peace offering to another day in his self-made, do-it-yourself paradise. He munches on a handful of stale potato chips and listens to the pleasant hiss of fat dropping from the hefty burgers onto the hot white embers.

Satisfied that the burgers are on their way to perfection, he melts into his leopard spots print lawn chair. The canvas enfolds him like the skin of a cat, like someone has sewn him in. He puts on his drug store reading glasses and reads a story in the local newspaper with the pages flapping in the wind. He mouths what he reads, as if words of his own making are the only words worthy of trust.

"*SHRUBBERY!*" He reads an article about the benefits of living in a retirement community. Shrubbery happens to be

Zitzelberger's favorite curse word, particularly when he's in high dudgeon.

"There are so many things to hate about shrubs," he had told a club member. "Shrubs scratch and poke people, shrubs hide robbers, and bring deer up to the house. Hedges obscure your view of what may be coming. People trim and fuss with shrubbery to impress their neighbors when they should be maintaining their lawns. Grass right up to the foundations, that's what I say. I feel the same about flowers, except shrubs are worse! Shrubs and hedges are a way to divide people and turf—without shrubbery, we'd have fewer wars!"

Liza Fitting barges into his backyard with the results of her independent living assessment. She drags a rolling backpack through the gravel. Liza has high cheek bones and a prominent nose, her lips covered with too-red lipstick. She's tall and thin as a shadow, and her long legs seem to go high up, making her look stork-like. Even though she's only twenty-five years old, she looks frumpy and old. She wears her dark brown hair topped off in a bun like a ball of yarn with loose strands twiddling in the summer breeze. Her frizzly hair bun looks shrubby to Zitzelberger. An oversized vintage sweater drapes her body like a tea cozy.

Zitzelberger looks at her sideways with the stiff neck of an old man.

The girl with the bun doesn't give Zitzelberger a chance to react. In a nasal voice, she launches into a prepared statement, hunching over her clipboard. Zitzelberger doesn't know

*The Lawnmower Club*

what to make of her. He's never felt comfortable around women, and ever since losing his wife, he's lived deep down in the company of men.

"YOU!" snarls Zitzelberger. "WHAT ARE YOU DOING HERE?" A frazzled Zitzelberger unwraps himself slowly from his cocoon.

The social worker looks over the top of her black boxy glasses that are falling down her nose, then looks back down at the clip board, thick with rumpled papers, "Mr. Zitzelberger, my name is Liza, Liza Fitting. I'm here to help you. You haven't returned my calls, so I decided to come by. I have the results of your independent living assessment. Do you remember? The assessment was ordered by the county in response to telephone calls from concerned parties."

She paces back and forth like a zoo animal.

Liza knows she's on shaky ground and uses the "I have been ordered" phrase to add weight to her statement. Hazzard Pembrook had called the county, saying he was concerned about a destitute neighbor living across the street in an abandoned clubhouse. He portrayed Zitzelberger as an eccentric hermit who couldn't take care of himself. Pembrook can't get over the loss of the club his family had owned for most of its long history. "Even though we had to sell the place...I feel like I still own it in my heart," he would say to people with sad eyes, squeezing out a practiced tear or two.

It was at the club that Pembrook had his only brush with honest work, when his father suggested that he caddy. As soon as young Pembrook discovered that a golf caddy was required to walk long distances while carrying other people's luggage like a bellhop, he used his ample allowance to hire his own bag carrier. His father relieved him of the position at the request of the head of the golf committee who complained, "I sliced a tee shot deep into the woods, and said to your son, 'Boy, go find my ball." You won't believe what he said. He said, 'Sir, you have no idea what dangerous predators may be lurking in those far-away woods...and besides, don't you find looking for lost balls a bit plebeian?' When I insisted, he sent another boy to look for the ball. I couldn't hit another shot squarely for the rest of my round. I started thinking about wild animals in the woods, and about the missing golf ball that your son refused to retrieve, and the other boy never found. He threw me off my game."

Pembrook did his best to describe Zitzelberger as feeble and inept. "The man's at least seventy, but he looks a hundred with his saggy neck folds," Pembrook had said. "He doesn't look healthy, you know, more like a corpse in a casket, and he doesn't know how to match his clothers, and he never goes out in public, where his rough edges might be smoothed out through public intercourse. I can't begin to fathom his eating habits. Oh yes, it's my civic duty to report him like the Good Sumerian did on that road to...I can't remember. I got it—the road to Damask... oh no, that's not right. I'm thinking of my blue curtains and matching polyester bedspread."

"Mind you, I have no ulterior motives...only pure selfless regard for others. But do let me know when you remove him,

## The Lawnmower Club

because I would like to take the property off his hands. The proceeds could provide funds for his care...although he's not long for this world. Oh, Damascus...the Parable of the Highway to Damascus, that's it...you know, in the New Testament...or maybe the Testament before that."

Pembrook sees himself more as an honorary proprietor than as a member of The Lawnmower Club. He doesn't feel he belongs to the general category of the club's lawnmowerians—he's more refined and genteel. He doesn't live to mow like the others. But mowing is something he can do, as long as his machine doesn't break down. He's not mechanical—his family had always hired people to do that sort of thing.

As Liza talks, Zitzelberger's face turns puffy and gray like a rain cloud that's about to burst. He looks up to the sky as a rain cloud floats over their heads. *"Um, hah, I bet I know who called the county...yeah, I bet I know who... I'll be sure to give him a piece of mind. You bet I will!"*

"Confidential." Liza hunches back down over her clipboard. "Now, after my first meeting with you, I did an assessment. Your score indicates that your independent living skills are far below what is required to live here on your own. Mr. Zitzelberger, you need assistance."

*"WHY?"* asks Zitzelberger. He rises too abruptly from the sling chair and topples over into a heap. His drugstore reading glasses fall off. He knocks over a wrought iron table by the grill, spilling potato chips onto the ground, and also a sweating stack of processed yellow cheese, and his man-sized spatula

and tongs. He sits on the ground with his legs raised in the air. Sheets of newspaper blow away like scattering geese. A downpour seems imminent. Zitzleberger looks pissed off. He blames his embarrassing fall on Liza Fitting, as well as the scattering of his newspaper, and the change in the weather. If his burgers don't turn out, he'll blame her for that too.

"As I said, Mr. Zitzelberger, you scored below the acceptable limits on what we call ADL's. When you live alone at your age, you are always one step away from disaster. You might have conked out. It's a good thing I'm here to help you up." She bends over to help him up. "You okay?"

"*I CAN GET UP ON MY OWN*...and I wouldn't have fallen if it hadn't been for you caterwauling around my property like a wild animal. Now what did you say about an ADL?"

"An ADL is a series of scales for activities of daily living. An ADL takes about 15 minutes to figure. I learned how to do it in school with case studies and role plays. You have serious deficits in hygiene, food preparation, dressing, paying bills, and housekeeping. In other words...you're a mess."

"Do you live alone?" says Zitzelberger.

"At the moment, yes."

"And how are you doing on your independent living scales? You look you need more meat on your bones."

"This is about you, Mr. Zitzelberger, not me. I am the ASSESS<u>OOR</u>, and you are the ASSESS<u>EEE</u>." In truth, Liza is not doing much better.

## The Lawnmower Club

Zitzelberger raises his bushy eyebrows and looks at her closely. "I thought living long enough might put me in a special category, one that gives me a pass on monkey business like this. How do you think I survived this long? I do just fine on my own, and besides, you work for the county, don't you? Well, I pay taxes for the services I need like snowplowing the roads, but I don't need your services. *NO-SIR-REE-BOB!* I don't need your help, now move along and—*DON'T SCREW WITH MY LIFE!*" Zitzelberger has never learned the art of polite conversation. He hedges neither his lawn nor his speech.

Leo Zitzelberger stands before her in a state of self-indictment, wearing his moth-eaten cardigan buttoned crookedly, a faded and ripped blue canvas shirt, and grease-stained khaki work pants. He stands in front of a stack of unpaid bills on the dirty picnic table behind him, while putrid odors drift through a kitchen screen door, unhinged at the top.

"You don't have to yell at me. I'll have you know I'm very sensitive to criticism," Liza says. "I don't see why you don't let me help you. It's for your own good, you know. You should trust me, because I'm a social worker."

"*SHRUBBERY!!*" Zitzelberger says. "Why should I trust you just because you're a social worker? You want to funnel me into a nursing home. I wouldn't fit in there. I have never fit in anywhere. *THAT'S WHY I LIVE HERE!*"

"Mr. Zitzelberger, you're looking at me like you think I'm nuts. I'm serious. I've reviewed your file with my supervisor, and we both agree that an intervention is necessary. You need professional care."

"*Oh yeah...well who's going to take care of my club?*" he says. "*Tell me that!*" He makes a wide sweeping motion in the direction of the fairways. "*I won't let anyone take me away from here... OVER MY DEAD BODY!*"

"I'm surprised at you, Mr. Zitzelberger, because my psychology textbook says that people your age become more agreeable and compliant." Big fat raindrops splatter on the grill.

"We only get angry when we're intimidated. You're the one to blame. You're making me mildly insane. Now, be a nice girl and go along and bother someone else."

"You'll live longer in a controlled environment. You need to imagine yourself into a retirement home."

"You have to have a reason to keep living," he says. "If I do what you say, and let you put me in Mallard Pond, I'll die in a matter of weeks," he snarls like a wild animal. His overlarge dark eyes look fearsome underneath his bushy eyebrows and his brow furrows. His fists clench and his back muscles tense like he might pounce on the slight, young social worker.

Suddenly he thinks what Mona would say if she were standing beside him, "Now, Leo, calm down. This young lady's only trying to help." Of course, if Mona were here, a social worker wouldn't be coming around. Mona was the kind of all-purpose wife a man dreams of having. With their cozy little home, he took care of the outside, and she took care of the inside. Why did she fall down those steps?

## The Lawnmower Club

Liza continues, "Mr. Zitzelberger, you don't have what we call a social network. Without close daily connections, you'll die sooner alone than living in a place like Mallard Pond with others. Mallard Pond has all kinds of fun activities like balloon volleyball, a bus to take you shopping twice a week, and a Pit Bull therapy dog named Pal.

They also have wonderful drugs for agitation. In a matter of hours, you'll never want to be out of there, go outdoors, or go anywhere!"

*WOULD YOU PLEASE LEAVE ME ALONE!*

"Mr. Zitzelberger, don't be mean to me," Liza sneezes. (She's allergic to grass and her face turns splotchy.)

*"YOU'RE SNEEZING ON MY BURGERS!*

Zitzelberger turns his back on her. His burgers are getting overdone. He picks up sweaty slabs of Velveeta from the ground and drops them on the burgers. Over the smoke and grease, Zitzelberger smells a lingering scent of mothballs from Liza's consignment store clothes. *"ARE YOU GONE YET?"* he says without looking.

"I'm going, Mr. Zitzelberger. But I'll be back. *I HAVE A JOB TO DO!"* Liza shakes all over.

Zitzelberger's face goes completely red, but mutes his voice to a low growl. "Do your job somewhere else." The cheese has melted off the burgers, and the blackened patties look hard as hockey pucks.

Liza runs away quickly, bumping into a free-range grocery cart filled with Zitzelberger's deposit bottles, her bun bobbing, looking white in the outdoor light like large bunny tail. Tears trail from dark eyeliner over her pale face. She hasn't eaten a good meal in days, and the gusts of cooking smells from the grill are marvelous. She thinks about saving up for her own grill.

To live all alone and work a thankless, low-paying job depresses Liza. Her parents are both dead, and she has no brothers and sisters. She doesn't seem to fit anywhere. She wishes she had friends. Not a whole social network like her textbooks say she should have, but simply a few good friends. If she had friends, she could complain to them about Zitzelberger. Oh, how she would like a cheeseburger!

Rain falls on Leo. Rain falls on Liza. Rain falls on the just and the unjust, but who knows the difference?

Waking from his midmorning nap, the cougar ranges out for a morning snack. Roosted turkeys drop down from the treetops like they've been thrown out of a low-flying plane. They enjoy safety in numbers. Unlike the cougar, the turkeys live in a community with what Liza would call strong social ties. *It's too easy*, the cougar thinks. He decides to chase a runner—*more sporting*. Blood, bone, feathers, and flesh. So tasty.

He's a lone ranger alone in the wild, more than animal, less than human. Independent living is all he knows. He roams the range like a character in a Classic Western. He's destined for an untimely death in the wild from too much civilization. If

## The Lawnmower Club

he only had a mate to care for and protect, it would give his life meaning. *Subsistence. All I do is subsist. Such a shallow idea. Negative thinking. You're going to have to stop that.*

The cougar sinks into a depression in the middle of a field filled with yellow, gold, and melon daylilies. An unnatural hint of hamburger smoke and an essence of moth balls lingers in the air. He opens his mouth to get better whiffs. The incessant combustion of lawnmowers, as intrusive to the world of the cougar as the nasal voice of a social worker to the world of Zitzelberger's back yard, drives him crazy. Raindrops fall on the cougar. Lifting his nose to the rising wind, he inhales the world around him. The turkey has not been enough. Perhaps a chipmunk or two?

Zitzelberger straightens up the clubhouse and pays his bills. Even though he has no intention of reading them, he buys impressive magazines like *National Geographic* and strategically places them on the kitchen table and his nightstand, in case he receives more unannounced visits from do-gooders like Liza Fitting. He intends to stay out of Mallard Pond, or any other place where he has to depend on others.

What he wants most out of life is to be left alone. He improves the grounds of the former golf club—sells the triplex mowers, since he doesn't need to close-cut the greens, and unloads everything but what is essential to maintain his mowing club—the rest of the greens-keeping equipment, bunker rakes, golf ball washers, water stations, yardage markers, fairway signs, golf shop merchandise, and beat-up vending machines. He sells the golf carts, save one for himself.

After running a car repo agency for 40 years, Zitzelberger has finally found his true calling. Who would have thought that his lifelong pleasure, cutting grass, riding back and forth in neat rows, would be the source of his salvation? Rarely admitting to good fortune, if he could sing, he would sing, if he could write poetry, he would write poems—however, his mind is seldom baffled by higher pursuits. He tries not to think further about Liza Fitting, although he has occasional nightmares about hordes of social workers invading his property, harping about his lack of independent living skills, saying we're here to help you.

Instead, Zitzelberger mows. He keeps his own patch of lawn near what used to be the eighteenth hole. It's big enough for a two-hour ride. Touching the electric starter on his Toro 48 Professional 8000, he rolls out of the cart shed and onto the lush green fairway. The engine hums a symphony. With the belt drive engaged, he smells the mown grass exhale as it blows from the blade tips and sifts into the high-capacity collection system. He reaches his optimal ground speed at seven miles per hour.

Sometimes, when Zitzelberger moves up a slope, he might see cloud mountains moving across the sky at a casual pace, or on a turn, he might notice the bristling leaves on the ancient oak tree rising over the clubhouse, but for the most part, the

## The Lawnmower Club

natural world goes unnoticed and unappreciated. Even the sun might as well be a yellow filling station sign.

The attractions of nature are not important to Zitzelberger. He's never been sentimental about what he refers to as scenery. He's never had a happy response to the natural world— too untrimmed and wild. Even the tick tick of raindrops falling from one leaf to another in gentle rain irritates him. Neither does he associate the green tangy smell of cut grass with happy thoughts of past summers and weekends or the pleasures of boyhood. He grew up in a poor neighborhood in a small house with a dirt yard that he tended by making straight even lines with a rusty rake. Somehow making those neat lines made his topsy-turvy life more orderly.

Zitzelberger has never seen the Atlantic or Pacific Oceans, and only winks of the Great Lakes. In his land-based slumbers, a vast continental sea of green grass fills his best summer dreams, and old snow fast-melting into grass fills his best winter dreams. His travels have been limited to the up and down rows of grass, enough to circle the earth many times. The history of the human race, to Zitzelberger, consists of man fueling his machines, cutting grass as the grass grows back, week after week, year after year—waging war on an encroaching environment, while forces of nature fight back, in attempts to flourish and restore an earth before man. He's a lone cat in a hostile universe, a reverse environmentalist, who sees the natural world taking over fragile humankind. That's all he knows.

Even if Zitzelberger saw the shape of an angel in the clouds, he would think that the angel had appeared for someone else, not him. But he never thinks of God or angels or otherworldly things, or anything positive or good. He mows.

Liza Fitting persists. She doubles her efforts to move Zitzelberger to Mallard Pond. In the gloaming light of evening, she hides in a strand of river birches, and looks for Zitzelberger with her low-light binoculars, hoping to catch him acting helpless and neglectful, hoping to witness some catastrophe that will prove her right, and give her cause for rejoicing, see evidence of forgetfulness, or something else broken or missing in his house or his head.

Placing Zitzelberger in Mallard Pond has become Liza's obsession. Clearly, she has jangled her mind with too much coffee and not enough food. She has no one to help her place Zitzelberger in perspective. Why can't she move on, as Zitzelberger suggested, and bother (or help) someone else? Lots of other people might appreciate her assistance. At some level, she knows that she's the one who needs help. But Liza, like Zitzelberger, regards asking for help as a sign of weakness. If a social worker offered to help her, she would refuse. She lives alone and blames her parents for everything. *Why did they have to get themselves killed?*

## The Lawnmower Club

Only a few blocks away from her house, a teenaged Liza had been writing an essay in her diary about how she hated her parents, when she heard the crash and sirens through her bedroom window. The car had been rammed right in, and split in half. It was totally smashed up and burned. A flatbed tow truck hauled it in pieces to a gas station parking lot in Liza's neighborhood. She received a call from her Aunt Hertz who had been working the night shift at the hospital. Her aunt told her everything would be okay, but Liza had no idea what that meant. On the way home from the hospital where her parents were pronounced dead, she passed the wrecked car. Her aunt was driving, and Liza insisted that they stop to see. Blood had exploded all over the twisted metal of the car's remains and dripped from the spattered wreckage. Tiny blood pools blistered on the asphalt. She screamed. She couldn't handle the blood.

Above all, she couldn't handle being cut loose from her parents at a time when she had spent her days and nights resisting them on every little detail of their efforts to control her life. She had been abandoned by her enemies. How could they have been so careless as to be hit by a semi-truck at the most dangerous intersection in town? Didn't everyone know you had to be careful? Look both ways? Isn't that what they had told her to do? How could they get themselves killed without giving her any warning? At the hospital, a nurse had given her a plastic bag with cash and her father's watch. She placed the bag in her backpack, and carried it on her shoulders, unopened for years.

Liza had been the only child with only a single aunt in town. Her aunt had not been much help, because she had problems of her own. So, Liza finished high school, living at a girlfriend's house. Her girlfriend's parents let her do pretty much as she pleased, but nothing pleased her. She not only blamed her parents for her unhappy life, but anyone else who happened to cross her path—especially adults. One Saturday night the police busted her for underage drinking. She had downed a six-pack of beer in the back seat of a boy's car. When her girlfriend's father yelled at her, she ran away. After she lived in her car for a few weeks, she made an appointment with a social worker.

The well-dressed social worker had said, "I'm your social worker. You can trust me." The way she said, "I'm your social worker," impressed Liza, like someone on high had assigned her or given her magical powers—like an angel. Here was a confident, professional woman, not that much older than herself, who wore a beeper on her hip, and seemed to know practical ways to fix people and their problems. She wore her hair in a neat bun.

From that day, Liza decided to go to college and become a social worker. She hit the books and received a scholarship.

The day she graduated from college, Liza opened the plastic bag and took out her father's watch along with a lumpy pile of twenties, tens, fives, and ones. She put the watch on her bony wrist and took herself out for a graduation dinner with the cash. She ordered a chicken quesadilla and beer. If she couldn't fix her own life, she could get paid for fixing other people's lives—in an air-conditioned office with her own desk. And she would look cool wearing a Motorola beeper and her father's Timex watch. Before a mirror, she practiced saying, "My name is Liza, Liza Fitting. I'm here to help you."

The cougar reaches the upper level of his noise tolerance. He wants to stop the noise, but he knows from his Wisconsin experience, that harming humans can result in harassment or worse—getting chased by cops with dogs, darts, or bullets. He still rues the day when he attacked the dental hygienist in the red running shoes. Even though he had just nicked her in the heel, he knows that to return home to Wisconsin would be suicide. He has a better plan, one that will allow him to stay unmolested by the lawnmower guys in his new home territory. First, he wants to chew on his idea. Silent Sunday, a quiet time for reflection. He watches a ruffed grouse trot by, but decides to let the bird pursue its own happiness. Instead, he brunches on his endless supply of chipmunks, a guiltless pleasure.

Monday mornings, Rory Finnegan looks forward to riding onto the wet green turf of a summer day. Waking before dawn, he arrives ahead of time, to take the first shift on his Gravely ZT. His voice sounds like gravel as he speaks softly to the machine.

He full throttles the choke and presses the automatic starter button. Ignition and take off! Exiting the pole barn, something doesn't feel right. He returns to the barn, opens his metal tool chest, removes his deck leveling gauge, measures the deck side-to-side and front-to-back, checks the oil level, engages and disengages the mower blades, checks the anti-scalp rollers, the belt tension, and the tire pressure.

Finnegan wipes his hands with a shop towel and hikes up his trousers to block the breeze on his plumber's butt. He remounts the mower and restarts the engine. As he stutters out of the pole barn, he feels more confident about the machine, but still feels vaguely uncomfortable, like his inner self has wedgies.

Not one to have premonitions, Finnegan thinks maybe he's just having the occasional bad day. He feels uneasy in the mower seat. Perhaps a cigar will help? He stops the Gravely and lets the engine idle while he nips off the end of a thick torpedo-shaped cigar. He lights up with a propane lighter, and then chugs along towards his assigned mowing area. Warmed by the rising sun, he removes his red tee shirt and waves it in the air to taunt Pembrook who mows nearby. He loves to insult Pembrook's stuffy sensibilities. Pembrook can't stand bare-chested mowers. Finnegan thinks Pembrook is jealous, because Finnegan has a visible ribcage, and Pembrook's body looks boneless like a rabbit.

Zitzelberger sits on the deck buttering his toast. He's about to breakfast on scrambled eggs and two large slabs of crispy bacon. As a hedge against hunger, he has placed a box of

## The Lawnmower Club

Frosted Flakes on the table in case he needs more food to top off the meal. Zitzelberger looks at the cheerful Tony the Tiger on the cereal box. The tiger wears a bright red bandanna around his neck. Zitzelberger reads the caption on the box, and thinks, *another G.R.R.REAT! day in paradise.*

He pours a cup of coffee, and looks at his computer display of the property, the only news he cares to see. He looks again, mildly puzzled. The red rectangles are moving across his computer screen like large insects, except one that appears to be stationary. He checks the space. It's Finnegan's patch of grass. He can see the area from the deck. Finnegan's mower appears as a small, black speck.

"*GEE WHIZ!*" he says out loud. He had talked to Finnegan before about relieving himself in the open. He grabs his binoculars with the idea that he might catch Finnegan in the act. He has few rules, but the acid from urine leaves brown spots in the grass. Zitzelberger spies Finnegan's lawn tractor, turned upside down. "*WHAT HAPPENED?*"

Finnegan's machine moves so fast that he tips over. Finnegan tightens his wrestler's grip on the steering wheel, but has come to a rest under the skyward-facing wheels. His lumpy grass catcher lies detached, a few yards away, like a dead animal. Nearby, a red tee shirt settles on the ground. He feels a warm trickle of blood on the back of his neck. He feels woozy, totally surprised, like he had the year before, a deer had hit his truck, a brown bolt in his peripheral vision.

*Randy Evans*

Zitzelberger sees Pembrook rushing, all jackrabbity, towards the club house. Pembrook cannot believe his eyes. He thinks, *could this mad scene be a figment of my imagination?* As he approaches the clubhouse, Zitzelberger hears his shrill voice:

*"A wild animal has attacked Finnegan—four legs, swishing tail, like a lion or a tiger or a panther of some sort! Finnegan's so hairy, the predator likely thought he was a bear. Maybe now people will listen to my suggestions for a dress code. Sure, I could show off my sharply carved torso, too, but mowing half naked is not only ungentlemanly, it's dangerous! I don't know whether Finnegan is dead or alive. Or perhaps somewhere in between... you know, injured. Oh my God, I'm out of breath. I must be close to a cardiacical event. I've sweated my clothes. I need to go back to my house and change into something more presentable. I must uphold my reputation as the fashion icon in this small town! Sometimes I walk the streets of downtown looking for people who look like me. Sadly, I find no one."*

The cougar rises before first light on Monday morning, resolved to solve the lawnmower problem that has climbed to the top of his TO DO list. His instinct to attack has overwhelmed his sense of self-preservation. Although God has equipped him with deadly force, he has elected, at least for now, to be guided by Shakespeare's Sonnet 94: *"they that have power to hurt but will do none."*

# The Lawnmower Club

The cougar does not need cover. A kill requires cover. A good scare requires visibility. He cat crawls through the swamp to the near edge of the fairway and sees a hairy human yelling and waving a red shirt like he's a matador, the smell of cigar smoke, and lawnmower fumes fill the air.

The cougar breathes in deeply and produces a baritone test growl. *A bit too much vibrato.* He throws his head back, turning his ears inside out, and howls again, this time using the full capacity of his massive lungs. If the cougar had been a dragon, the pain and anger of his fiery exhaust would have burned grass off the fairways. His eyes narrow, he thrashes his tail, and his great feet begin to pump. He turboes towards the golf course at 45 miles per hour. A screech owl, a raccoon, a ground squirrel, a skunk, and a fox flee for cover, as if they had been caught on state highway pavement by a drunken pickup driver. Sadly, a nearby chipmunk croaks from cardiac arrest.

With the powerful thrust of his hind legs, the cougar leaps for Finnegan, surgically grazes the back of his neck, and flies over the mower with one long bound. Finnegan opens his mouth to scream, but swallows his cigar instead. Smoke fumes from his mouth and nose like a dragon. He wipes blood from the back of his neck, no more than the blood of a mosquito bite. Even so, he loses control of the mower, and tips over to face the sky.

The lawnmower blades spin above him until he lets go of the steering wheel to turn off the ignition. Once he swallows the cigar, he howls for help in an authoritative bass. Pembrook runs away from Finnegan with soprano alarms. The other mowers look at Finnegan in disbelief, shrugging their shoulders, talking in hushed altos, their flimsy inclinations to help a fallen lawnmowerian pass quickly. No one seems to know what's going on. "It's too soon to take action, before we know the facts," one says, like a politician after a school shooting.

Altogether, the cougar thinks he has given a well-paced performance, especially with the intricacies of the set, and the eccentricities of the mowers. Despite a lethargic reaction from Custer who would have under-reacted to an attack by Sioux warriors, the cougar had fully engaged the rest of the field in a mad fearful romp made up of musical body movement, like Spanish peasants dancing the Bolero in six eight time. He could have solved some of the coordination issues with one or two more cougars, but he had worked well within his limitations. He had scared the hell out of everyone, except Custer who let the whole fiasco pass unnoticed. The cougar felt like a finely-tuned predator, like the super being, which he happened to be.

From the wood's edge, the cougar sees Zitzelberger walk into the fairway where Finnegan wriggles out from under his mower. Having changed into a new outfit with a rugged plain shirt, hunter green pants, and high leather boots, Pembrook stumps and shouts at Zitzelberger while waving his leather patched arms.

Zitzelberger pays no attention to blurting Pembrook. He passes by Finnegan who might have needed help. He looks

## The Lawnmower Club

straight ahead, shouldering the strap of a deer rifle, heading for the tree line on the other side of what used to be the 18th Hole.

Custer continues to mow in neat lines, as if nothing has happened. The other mowers disappear into the pole barn, and promptly leave the club in a dust cloud of speeding cars and trucks, everyone stressed out, looking for a restaurant with a good bar and a desert menu.

# 5

# SWALLOWING THE MOON

ZITZELBERGER RETURNS from his foray to the woods without the cougar's hide. He paces off 150 yards and staples the Frosted Flakes box to a fence post. He uses Tony the Tiger's big blue nose as a bull's eye for target practice. He raises the gun stock to his cheek bone and takes dead aim. He fires a three-round pattern into the box, then walks to the target to examine his marksmanship. *All three right in the nose,* he says to himself. Tony's still smiling on the box cover. Zitzelberger notices the cartoon tiger's human-like finger pointing to the blue sky. *It's plain silly and against nature to give animals human-like qualities.* The bullet holes look like nostrils on Tony's nose.

The cougar attack has threatened Zitzelberger's utopia. The Lawnmower Club shuts down until further notice. He calls the Department of Natural Resources to report a cougar sighting. He's angry. He wants action. The whole situation defies his understanding. God created man to rule over nature and to beat it into submission like an unruly child. That's why you mow a lawn—to keep the grass from getting out of control. That's why you kill animals who threaten your lawn and livelihood. Unnatural acts must be punished.

*I spent all my money from the repo business to buy the golf club, and something like this happens! I thought only a few cougars lived in the UP, not bothering anyone. Very strange. But I'm not going to let some dumb animal get in the way of my happiness I'll put an end to him. I've got a business to run. I have to get the mowers back, or I'll be ruined. Why can't wild animals leave humans alone?*

Zitzelberger has imagined a bankrupt golf course into a personal paradise—his own personal paradise. He has reinvented the world to his own liking. He has turned his imagination into a new reality.

The cougar imagines a world before man and wants the world to be nothing but deep forest.

They are both stubborn about what they want. Both unrealistic. What they want most out of life is to live their lives, without interference, in their own way. Zitzelberger goes inside the clubhouse to rest from his unaccustomed exercise. He sinks into a beanbag chair that expectorates Styrofoam beads from an open seam, with a long sigh.

Hearing Zitzelberger's shots prompt the cougar to think about death and mortality.

## *The Lawnmower Club*

I need to be honest with myself. This was a stupid thing to do...if only the limbic impulses in my brain stem wouldn't be so dominant. If only my hearing wasn't so sensitive. The only solution is to go farther away from people, deeper into the woods. There I would have a better chance to die of natural causes. The world would be a better place without people and their cutting machines.

He edges away from The Lawnmower Club, and fades into pine shadows. The wind in the trees ,and creek water over rocks, soothes him. The disquieting cacophony of the lawnmowers lessen. The cougar drops down in deep grass, amid the sounds of natural silence, amid the buzzing and humming and chirping of insects in the grasses and bushes, their pleasant noise rising out of everything growing on the earth. A few geese honk as they fly south. He sleeps off his worries.

By early autumn, the fairway grass grows out of control. Only Custer continues to mow. Finally, even Custer gives up. Less than two weeks after the cougar attack, he runs his lawnmower up to a grassy knoll, and mows his last patch of grass, while hordes of wild geese circle blatantly, with triumphant war cries. He returns to the cart shed where an unnatural, sepulchral quiet greets him. Dark and cold inside, the overhead lights flicker yellow. He chokes off his mower, slides the creaky door shut, and wonders why everyone has disappeared.

Liza Fitting knows something's up. Pembrook tells her, "I keep hearing a voice from outer space telling me to restore the club to its rightful owner...that would be me. The voice may be the word of God...I don't know. Anyway, Zitzelberger must go!"

Liza's snooping activities around Zitzelberger's property remain unabated. The TV weather reporter announces the second full moon of August, a blue moon on the thirty-first—a perfect night for her undercover investigations. She knows that she will prevail over Zitzelberger. Eventually, she will catch him seriously neglecting himself, and presto, she will have him committed to Mallard Pond. "I bet he can't even button his shirt sleeves," she smiles.

This evening, she plans to collect samples from his trash bin to document poor eating habits, and other indicators of his threadbare way of living. She'll look for fast food containers, pizza boxes, expired canned goods, soda bottles, discarded coupons for fruit and vegetables, and anything else inconsistent with the Mediterranean Diet. She will look for dental floss, the absence of which could indicate poor oral health. And of course, evidence of alcohol and drug abuse—beer cans, liquor, wine bottles, pill bottles. She hunkers down, and hides behind Zitzelberger's pile of stacked wood. She notices painted numbers on each stick, so Zitzelberger will know if any are stolen, she surmises.

Low to the ground in the dark, Liza feels strangely serpentine, like a snake has taken possession of her body. Her obsession to control Zitzelberger's life has put her over the edge. She locomotes from behind the wood pile to the back of the clubhouse with slithering movements, thrusting her body side by side, creating snaky curves in the dirt. She feels like she's in a dream where her anima expresses unfathomable power in the form of a large, black snake. (The night does strange things to people.) Emitting loud hisses, she slides towards the clubhouse.

Earlier the same day, Zitzelberger decides to take his shotgun and hunt for rabbits. He thinks gunfire will help keep predators away. He's still sore about the incident. He hasn't seen a soul in days. He misses the mowers and wants them to come back. As he moves through the remnants of an old apple orchard nearby, a woodcock flushes out of the brush, about twenty yards in front of him. It's not woodcock season, but Zitzelberger shoots reflexively. The close shot blows the poor bird to smithereens. Blood, bone, and feathers lie everywhere. Zitzelberger gathers what's left of the bird in his large hand, and stuffs the bird, guts and all, into the back game pocket of his hunting vest.

After an hour of no rabbits, he returns to the clubhouse. He's hungry from the exercise and thinks he might visit the local grill for an olive burger or fried perch. He goes inside to grab his wallet and truck keys. Outside, the night is empty and quiet—only the full moon in the sky. As he turns to exit the clubhouse, Zitzelberger hears a strange sound from his backyard. He looks outside his back door and sees Liza Fitting slithering on the ground by his trash bin. He recognizes her immediately by the shrubby bun on top of her head. He grabs his shotgun and runs out. He points the gun at Liza with an iron gaze. *"All my troubles began with you!"* he says. *"Why are you on the ground?*

He can't believe his opportunity. He has Liza Fitting under his control. She looks like the child he never wanted. Liza and the cougar are his main enemies, with Pembrook a far second. He can shoot them both, but either way, he could end up in jail. He grabs a length of rope. Liza looks like hell—coiled up and covered with dirt, bloodshot eyes, her loose sweater stained with grass, burrs and sticks clinging to her, snaky-looking strands of hair sprouting from her bun. The binoculars hang around her neck like a noose.

Liza knows this could be her doom. She uncoils and rises up from the ground into a yoga sitting pose, tries to pay attention to her breathing, and avoid thoughts that might distract her, like *I'm going to die soon.* Zitzelberger tells her to stand up. He points to the woods with the double barrel of his gun. She wobbles forward silently, already grieving the damage this may cause her career—if she lives. Zitzelberger marches her to the wooded fringe of the 10th Fairway, into the the deeper woods, and past an abandoned barn that has fallen in on itself. He ties her to a tree. He wants to leave her over night to give her a good scare. Liza bleeds from cuts and scrapes, and the fresh scent of blood fills the moist evening air. He tightens the rope, so she can't escape.

## The Lawnmower Club

*"OWWW, OWWW. YOU CAN'T DO THIS TO ME!* Liza cries with a momentary surge of confidence. *"You want a wild animal to kill me. You're going to leave me here to be eaten alive, and all I wanted to do was help you! You won't get away with it. You'll get caught, and then you'll lose your precious club, and even Mallard Pond will reject you—if you don't go to jail. You're making a big mistake, mister. You're old and tired, and your decision-making ability's impaired. I knew something was wrong with you!"*

Zitzelberger moves his unkempt head close to hers, and stares at her with the untrimmed hedge of his eyebrows. In the silvery moonlight, his eyes look like ball bearings. He smiles and turns his back on her. He leaves her in the dark, and slowly stalks towards the clubhouse. Not accustomed to feelings of guilt, Zitzelberger senses a mild discomfort like indigestion. He thinks about what he had just done to Liza. He thinks about the cougar, prowling somewhere in the night.

*I'm a really bad man. What if the girl gets eaten by the cougar? What if she dies of fright? No, what I did was wrong, wrong, wrong. And besides, I'd never see The Lawnmower Club from prison... I think I'll return to the clubhouse for a little bite of something, and then go back and let her loose. She'll think I've come to finish her off, but I'll tell her to get off my property, and never come back. If she complains to anyone, I'll say she's making up hysterical stories.*

Meanwhile Liza struggles frantically against the rope until she exhausts herself. *If I get out of this alive, I'm going to get Mr. Zitzelberger into big trouble. I may have nightmares from this. I may need help if I survive. I'm a sorry-looking mess. There's blood on my sweater. I have no budget for dry cleaning. I don't like people to help me, but after this, I'll have to see a therapist for sure.*

The cougar has difficulty sleeping under the glaring light of the full moon. His long form lays in the grass like a sculptor has cut him from a block of stone. He dreams fitfully. Liza's cries wake him. He rises to his feet. A human scent is tall in the air with the smell of blood, and he notes, and a hint of mothballs. The cougar finds Liza tied to a tree like a rag doll. She mutters about unresolved issues with her father and mother. He moves closer and gazes at her with his dilated big cat eyes. Liza opens her eyes, and with her heart beating like a frightened chipmunk, she faints. Lucky for Zitzelberger, she has a strong, healthy heart.

*This doesn't look like a mower guy,* the cougar thinks. He's in enemy territory, but she doesn't look like an enemy. She looks like a swamp bird...unappetizing. The baffled cougar's cerebral cortex has not evolved to develop well-defined categories or other high levels of thought, but the girl does not appear to be prey. A tall gun-toting man, on the other hand, falls in the flight or fight region of the cougar's well-developed cerebellum. The cougar sniffs at Liza for five or six seconds. Liza wakes up, feels the cougar's cold nose on her hand, struggles to speak, but faints again.

# The Lawnmower Club

The cougar cocks his head and moves on like he's passing on a dish at a progressive dinner. He smells fresh-killed game in the air, fresh-killed woodcock. Through the trees, he observes Zitzelberger lumbering in a straight line back towards clubhouse, his gun pointed to the ground, his back turned to the cougar. A red plaid hunting cap rests on his head, and under his hunting vest, his canvas coat falls from his shoulders like a sheet of iron.

The cougar sees feathers and a bird foot sticking out of the back of Zitzelberger's vest. The cougar tenses his hind legs as if preparing to leap, which is exactly what he's about to do. Zitzelberger registers an uncomfortable feeling that something's wrong, something closing around his throat like the jaws of a large wild animal, which is about to happen.

I shouldn't feel bad anymore. I'm going to let the girl loose. Why should I feel bad? After tonight, I'll never see her again. I'll have a little snack in the clubhouse, and then I'll go back. Sometimes you have to use a little harmless treachery to teach people a lesson. Before I go out again, I think a little shot of whiskey might pick me up.

*FIGHT RESPONSE!* The cougar loses his peripheral vision. His large jade eyes focus on Zitzelberger's back. He becomes all lungs and legs—a killing machine in a fur coat approaching the speed of a fast sports car. He doesn't give Zitzelberger a sporting chance— doesn't circle and face him down, or give him a warning growl. He leaps roaring high into the night air, and opens his jaws as if he might swallow the moon. Unlike the harmless nick he had given Finnegan, he breaks Zitzelberger's neck. Zitzelberger jitters on the ground. The cougar howls in triumph. Liza slumps against the tree, awake and worried about how she will ever get the blood stains out of her clothes. Like the attacked dental hygienist from Wisconsin, Liza screams bloody murder. *"AIEEEEEEEEEEEEEEEE!"*

Across the road, the roaring and screaming wakes Pembrook. He rolls over in bed. Living at the edge of civilization, he expects unusual sounds in the night. But he can't get back to sleep, so he climbs out of bed, and walks over to his bedroom window. With all the strength he can muster, he raises the reluctant window, and looks out through his blue damask curtains. Fresh air rushes in, along with human-like and animal-like sounds from the woods.

# 6

# IT TAKES TWO TO TANGO

PEMBROOK DECIDES he must investigate. Unlike a professional emergency responder, he's not sure what to wear. He settles on an outdoorsy mix of plaid and corduroy. He runs into his bathroom to fetch a box of band aids, and into the kitchen for latex gloves. He looks in the hallway mirror to check his appearance, and runs awkwardly into the woods, trying to follow Liza's screams. He finds her bleeding from scratches, and splotchy with mosquito bites. A knotted rope binds her reddened wrists.

"May I be of some assistance?" Pembrook says. "You look a bit upset."

"Please untie me."

"You don't mind that?"

"No, I think you should."

Pembrook pulls clumsily at the frayed ends of the rope. "I have never learned about knots…I dropped out of scouting after I failed to pass the Tenderfoot exam."

Pembrook never ceases to explain himself, but his logic seldom make sense, especially when he talks—like the left and right hemispheres of his brain, rocking like seahorses in an underwater current, have been bound together with duct tape.

"Here let me see...looks like I'm making progress. I'll untie this rope in no time at all. I am quite muscular, but not so much as when I had a three-month gym membership. Why did you do this to yourself? I think it would be difficult to tie a rope around your own wrist. By the scrunchy look on your face, I can detect that you have another explanation."

"Mr. Zitzelberger tied me to this tree, and left me here to die. *IT WAS LIKE A CRUCIFICTION!* Liza cries. "My name is Liza, Liza Fitting. I work for the county as a social worker. I was trying to help him."

"Oh, I know who you are. Do you remember the man who called you to complain about Zitzelberger? That would be me. He tied you to a tree for trying to help him? Sounds like the work of a mad man? He must be institutionalized at once. Tell me why that would be wrong?"

"And a cougar sniffed me like I was a glass of wine," Liza whimpers. "He turned away and left me dangling here like an appetizer no one wants to eat. Five minutes later, I heard a fierce growl from over by the clubhouse. Do you think the cougar attacked Mr. Zitzelberger instead of me?"

"Heavens, I hope not," says Pembrook, "although my mind's split on the question."

## The Lawnmower Club

"Could he be dead?" Liza says. "I don't really hope he's dead. Getting him committed to Mallard Pond gives meaning and purpose to my life. If he's dead, I don't know what would do."

"It's nice to meet someone who doesn't have a life—like me," says Pembrook. "Maybe we could meet sometime and do nothing together. I need a woman who has a high threshold for boredom."

"What are you trying to say?"

"Nothing that a preacher or judge would deem out of line."

"Are you asking me on a date? Mr. Pembrook, because you're old enough to be my father!"

"Oh, I don't know. When I look at my sharply-chiseled figure in the mirror, I forget my age. But you'd be safe as church with me. I could watch over you, and you could spend my trust fund," he says with swagger. "My parents left me a gold mine... not a real gold mine."

"Gold mine?"

"My parents left me a monthly stipend for life." Pembrook nods at his expensive hunting boots with fake humility.

"Mr. Pembrook, my aunt is more your age and she might want to help you spend your gold mine. You should give her a call. She's a nurse. It's getting cold out here."

"Oh, wow. Nurse fantasies have fueled my fondest reveries, but I should stop. I don't know you well enough to tell you about those bizarre little doozies. Here, take my coat. Do you have her number? I would like to give her a call."

"Don't bother, my aunt doesn't like people with fantasies."

"I know you're trying to brush me off," says Pembrook. " I often get shrugged, I don't know why, because I'm quite fetching. Sorry about acting so nineteenth century, trying to impress you with my vast assets. I feel another thought coming...but alas, it eludes me. Would you care for a band aid? I have several sizes. You'll have to open the wrapping, because my fingers are all thumbs."

As Zitzelberger's lays unmovable in the dark night, flies and mosquitoes feast on his body like uninvited neighbors. Chipmunks play king of the hill on his belly. Worms bide their time in the warm night soil, waiting for the right time to join the fun. Zitzelberger lies there like a drunken guest at his own party. He's comatose.

As Pembrook pulls on his latex gloves, he remembers he's about to miss the evening news. His neurons misfire, and he forgets why he's in the woods in the first place. He can only think of the CPR course he took a few years earlier for something to do during the winter. He first pokes Zitzelberger with a stick, then rolls up his plaid shirt sleeves, lamenting that he has never been able to grow hair on his arms.

He tries to find a pulse by counting in even numbers. He's proud that he can count by twos. He feels a faint heartbeat, and calls the wrong number (711) on his cell phone. "We must remove him from the woods immediately," he says to Liza who

## The Lawnmower Club

has arrived on the scene, "before he becomes a shriveled corpse, and wild animals arrive to devour him." Pembrook envisages a headline in the local paper: MAN SAVES NEIGHBOR FROM WILDCAT ATTACK. Liza calls 911.

Once at the hospital, the doctors induce a medical coma until his spinal cord or brain stem injuries can be assessed. The cougar has fractured three vertebrae in Zitzelberger's neck, but his spinal cord has not been severed, an event that would have caused death or quadriplegia. The doctors screw a metal cast onto his skull, ironically called a halo.

Zitzelberger wakes slowly, and tries to connect with whatever he used to know. He's afraid to see what's on the other side of his eyelids. He can't speak because of a tracheotomy and ventilator. Catheters and tubes stick out all over his body. Scattered knowledge falls into his consciousness like clumps of sod. He opens his eyes to see his nurse who startles him. Since he can't turn his neck, he fixes on her face, which is far from friendly, and not a joy to look at.

The evil nurse in *One Flew Over the Cuckoo's Nest* looks like a shy school girl in comparison. Hazel Hertz is a large, indelicate woman in her fifties. She has a wild gray mop of hair, a long nose, and thick glasses held together with medical tape. She's heard what Zitzelberger did to her niece, and sees him as a heinous villain, which you might say he is. Hazel feels protective, even though she hasn't helped Liza much since her parents died. She's never cared much for children.

Before he can speak a word, she says, "You know Liza Fitting is my niece, *DO YOU KNOW THAT?*

Zitzelberger asks for pain medication with a faint and reedy voice.

"Life is suffering," Hazel says, brightly. "When you get wide-awake, the pain will be much stronger."

"I hurt now."

"Of course, you do. We'll get you on something by next Tuesday, unless before then, you die, or disappoint me in any small way. And you know, I don't think oral medication will work fast enough. I'll find another way in."

Hazel takes his blood pressure and pumps up the cuff tightly, squeezing Zitzelberger's flabby arm like a tube of sausage. She hears his unfathomable heart beat backwards through her stethoscope: *dub lub dub lub dub lub.*

"What happened to me?" he says grimacing with real and exaggerated pain. He feels like a rusty old lawnmower with a missing owner's manual, a dirty air filter, a loose spark plug, a clogged carburetor, dull mower blades, and an empty gas tank.

"Your neck was broken by a cougar after you tied my niece to a tree to let her die. An emergency room doctor saved you from death, but you have crumpled cervicals. You might walk again, and but you might not. We see an abundance of nerve damage. A full recovery would be an undeserved miracle, YOU ROTTEN BASTARD!. I'm betting you'll suffer a short life under my total control. I'm only telling you this to make you miserable."

## The Lawnmower Club

"Uh-huh. How short a life?"

"If I don't cut your throat in the night, you might go on living another five years in a neck brace. Some people develop mental problems, but since you're already a psychopath, you don't need to worry. If I were you, I'd hope for an early death."

Zitzelberger ignores her grim prognosis and death threat. He has only one thing on his mind. "But if make a comeback, will I be able to ride a lawnmower again?"

"If you recover and want to risk re-injury—that's your decision, but I don't think they have lawnmowers in Hell."

"*SHRUBBERY!* If I can't mow a lawn, I'm not interested in going anywhere."

"Oh my, you're slobbering. Let me give you suction." She inserts a suction tube deep into his throat until he gags. "Great gag response—we'll do this often."

"Am I going to jail for tying Liza to the tree? You know, she trespassed on my property." He sees the lines on the IV tree, and they remind him of the rope and tree at the scene of his crime. *Should have shot her from the get go, and taken the consequences.* He sees a plug of urine going through his catheter into the bladder bag. He's miserable, and hates the constraints imposed by the rigid collar around his neck. He can't stand the feeling of complete helplessness.

"Liza's not pressing charges. You have me to thank. I told her that you only had a few short months to live, and meanwhile, the pain would trump what the law could do. Think of the time you have left as an orientation to what you can expect in the afterlife, if you have one."

"I can beat the odds. I'm going to get out of here and back to The Lawnmower Club. I just need a little rehab until I get back on my feet."

"Ha! You're not going home. Tomorrow you go to Mallard Pond where I work three days a week—so I will be there, too—ha, ha. Wait until you see the big fat pills. You won't be thinking about lawnmowers anymore, or lawns for that matter. And you'll love the view— a mud and graveled lot inside a rusty cyclone fence, lined with sickly dead shrubs, and all-season views of a toxic retention pond, where stray ducks land and takeoff quickly because the water stinks. Oh, and there's a green dumpster full of old peoples' diapers and the stuff people don't want when their relations kick the bucket, like torn lampshades, transistor radios, and aluminum walkers. You'll see it all through a drug-induced haze. Inside, it's a dirty mess. We clean the facility for the occasional state inspector, but the place still reeks from the days when the building and grounds served as a day care for cats and dogs. In all fairness, it was probably cleaner then."

Zitzelberger sinks into a deep gloom, then falls into a fake coma to buy time, to plot his next move—if he could only use his arms and legs. Mallard Pond sounds like a gateway to death, or worse. He must figure out how to break out of the place, and return to the Lawnmower Club. Nurse Rachet suspects he's faking. She pokes the bottom of his foot with a long needle.

## The Lawnmower Club

His feeling comes back too soon for his own good. *"OWWW!"* he shouts.

"Good news," Nurse Hertz says. "Every time you feel the needle, say you have a few more days to live."

"I want to ride my lawnmower," says Zitzelberger in deep panic.

"Mallard Pond has no grass," Nurse Hertz says. "But I'll be there for you, and every time you turn your head, you'll see me. Oh, please forgive my insensitivity—you can't turn your head. Now stick out your satanic tongue." She leaves the room, slamming the door so hard on her way out that Zitzelberger's medical chart falls from the bedpost to the floor with a plastic clatter.

Zitzelberger cannot abide all the medical contraptions surrounding him, the bedside supplies, and the tubes encumbering him. His rigid neck brace. He feels as if he's looking out at the world from the inside of a lawnmower engine. His hopes for a good-looking, empathetic nurse have vanished. Rather than the reassuring mechanical sounds of lawnmower engines, he hears faint, frightful electronic beeps.

Of all the many bad decisions in his life, tying a social worker to a tree was the worst.

Liza Fitting fears she has post-traumatic stress disorder, and she smarts from the cuts, scrapes, and rope burns resulting from Zitzelberger's evil deed. She's barely able to perform her job duties, but she's a total wreck otherwise. And she misses the battle with Zitzelberger. Her obsession about getting him committed had concentrated her mind, kept her awake at night watching the minutes go by on her alarm clock until daylight.

Liza has never sought help for anything in her life, but she now has terrible feelings inside—like she's wading in a swampy marsh surrounded by large creatures about to bite her. She decides to look for a psychologist. She feels frightened, anxious, and disconnected, as she did before the horrific event, but more so; in particular, she feels a sense of danger, painful memories of the rope and the tree, and the fear of getting eaten alive by a ferocious animal. She doesn't know if she will ever feel normal, of course, she has never felt all that normal before. At least before, she could fake normal.

Since there are few psychologists in town, Liza tries Skype sessions first. The online psychologist lives in New York City, and keeps running out for lox and bagels, then goes home on the subway, leaving Liza looking at a screen showing nothing more than a desktop waterfall beside a miniature bonsai tree. Next, she finds a Silicon Valley life coach who tells her that she needs to change her hair style and makeup, buy trendy new clothes, and follow the advice of Mahatma Gandhi to be the change she wants in the world. None of these internet resources provide Liza with the support she needs. Mostly, she feels depressed from too many puzzling issues in her life—the lingering fears from her encounter with Zitzelberger, her

## The Lawnmower Club

unsuccessful attempts to help people though her job, her concerns about never finding a partner, and her lack of friends who might comfort her, and say, it'll be okay, it will.

In the yellow pages of the local phone book, Liza finds Benjamin Putzkin, a local psychologist and fly fishing guide (he's listed in two places). Would he be honest and real, the answer to her problems? Liza decides to give him a try. She likes getting counseling from a person that she can see face-to-face.

Putzkin is a small, thin man in his sixties with balding gray hair, and large brown eyes. His eyes poke out from oversized black plastic glasses, with one eye much larger than the other, making him look cyclopsian. He shares a lifelong interest in psychology with his parents, who were both psychologists, European Jews who escaped to America to flee the fascist rule of Franco.

His parents sent him to therapy three days a week from the time he was twelve years old. Through therapy, he discovered a personal affinity for water. He devoted his boyhood to liquid pursuits, like fly fishing and the study of blood borne pathogens. In college, he flunked his first course in biology. He switched to psychology, and ten years later, graduated from a Guatemalan doctoral program in clinical psychology. He moved to northern Michigan after looking at travel ad filled with photographs of fish swimming in clear lake water.

Putzkin sets up a studio in the loft of an old flour factory by the railroad tracks in downtown Petoskey. He can see a silver sliver of the Bear River from his window. He finds an old chaise lounge in a secondhand furniture store, has it reupholstered with flame-retardant fabric, along with a roll cushion that serves as a head rest, upon which he places disposable paper covers. He sits in an ergonomic desk chair behind the chaise under a magnifying lamp with an extendable arm, tying flies on a small workbench where he intends to listen to his patients with positive regard in the style of Carl Rogers...or Roy Rogers. He's not sure.

Liza surprises him with her visit. His first patient. She interrupts his fly tying. Liza says she can't afford the sessions, but she needs help, so they work out a barter arrangement.

"Paint my walls and make me soup," Putzkin offers. "How about that?"

"Are you sure that would be all right?" Liza replies.

Liza paints murals for the walls of his studios, and makes soup for him three times a week. She has no artistic talent, and knows little about cooking, but Putzkin likes having her around.

Liza pours her heart out to Putzkin, who half-listens. Liza begins by talking about her body, and goes from there to her emotions. She's angry because she's too thin, and she's angry that her feet are too small. She's angry because she has been nearly unnoticed by boys while growing up, and that she doesn't have a girlfriend with whom she can talk. Having no enemies angers her, as well as having no friends. Not getting involved in much of anything angers her. Not having money to buy nice clothes. Barely surviving on a social worker's salary.

One day, she shouts from the therapy couch, "I'm angry, because I live alone."

Putzkin had been entering some boilerplate language on his theories about Liza's condition in between computer games. With this sudden outburst, he feels he needs to say something.

"So you're feeling angry?"

Yes, I'm lifelong angry," Liza says, wrinkling her forehead. "I haven't exactly had a *Zip-a-dee-doo-da*h life."

"Well, my advice to you," says Putzkin. "It's okay to be angry, but be angry at one thing at a time. If you're angry at everyone and everything all the time, you end up with rage, which can be confusing and dangerous. Dealing with one anger at a time also fits into a 50-minute appointment schedule. Times up."

Over the next six weeks, Putzkin determines that Liza is some kind of crazy, but precisely what type of crazy escapes him. He tentatively diagnoses her with a wide array of conditions, including apathy, depression, sedentary behavior, assorted neuroses, panic attacks, anorexia, fear of heights, insecurity, high-functioning autism, hypochondria, but settles on chronic muscular tension. He recommends she learn the tango to plumb the dark themes of her zombielike life. He refers Liza to Cristina, a psycho- tango dance therapist, who happens to be Putzkin's girlfriend.

Christina developed her love for tango in the *milongas* of Buenos Aires, and achieved runner-up status in the World Tango Championships. Liza tries to do the tango as a way out of her suffering. Christina gives Liza dance therapy each week at her tango therapy club in the loft of an old downtown building. Christina has tried for gender balance, but so far, the only man to show up, left immediately for the nearest bar. She starts each session with a dharma talk about dance and personal growth:

"Tango class doesn't require special clothing. If you want to wear slit skirts and strap on high-heeled shoes you may, but sweats and tennis shoes will be fine. You must have shoes. I don't want any barefoot yoga types, and please leave your body odor at home. Now let's talk tango.

"It's all about movement and expression through dance. You dance away what bothers you. That's the therapy part. No talk, just dance. The healing roots of tango will take hold of you. *THIS ISN'T A WALTZ OR THE FOXTROT, LADIES!* Love will fill the air. Just bring water bottles to class for hydration, and if you're feeling bad in any way, stay home.

"After six weeks, you will enjoy a more positive body image and higher self-concept. You will experience lower anxiety and excellent bowel health. You will stir the air with sexiness, and ooze romance when you tango with your partner, if you have one.

"Now everyone warm-up—bend those knees and keep your spines straight, place your hands on your hips, look to the right and look to the left. Move those hips to the right and left, stand on one leg and swing the other, now lunge, lunge, lunge. Okay, take a cleansing breath...that's enough. *LET'S DANCE THE TANGO!!!*"

## The Lawnmower Club

In the beginning, Liza looks upon her sessions as exercise. But in the process of learning to walk backwards (the class contains all women, so she has to follow as well as lead), she develops a fluid feeling that pleases her. And the act of embracing provides a physical connection to others that has been sorely missing in her life. Her brain shoots off staccato sparks of joy, and endorphins romp through her body like playful dolphins. She arches her neck, and lets the beat and rhythm of the slow, melancholic music carry her away. She learns the lyrics to her favorite tangos—tragic love stories. As her technique becomes more aggressive and rhythmic, she emerges from her self-limiting world. The therapy works. Her dark side, that she manifested as a slithering snake on that fateful night when Zitzelberger captured her, blossoms into a strength. She's inspired to get out more, to use her newly-discovered dark side, to have more fun and go on dates. Maybe she will do something awful, and land in jail for a night or two in the name of personal growth?

One night after class, Liza and Christina drop in for drinks at a grill with high ceilings and a long dark-wooded bar. A bearded young man sits next to Liza drinking a beer. He's tall and rugged, a jeans-and-lumberjack shirt kind of guy. He looks across at her with steel-blue eyes. There's something warm and active and straightforward about him. Strangely, Liza notices a faint whiff of skunk scent.

"You have rosy cheeks! Did you run to the bar?" he says.

"Just finished dance class," Liza laughs. "I'm learning the tango."

"So yeah, I've heard of tango"

"Most people have heard of tango."

"Looks old-fashioned and sexy."

"I guess so," Liza says. "Yes, very sexy."

"Lots of embracing," he says. "It takes two—"

"—to tango," says Liza. "But my tango club's all women. We need male partners. I need a male partner…I didn't mean to say…I meant someone to dance with."

"I teach the class," Christina interjects. "You should come. I could give you a free sample lesson."

"Not much chance of that. I don't dance."

"You could learn," says Christina. "You look very coordinated, and all you have to do is move together and stop at the same time. I bet you can do that. And you don't have to talk."

"Yeah, well I wouldn't be good at the tango then, because I like to talk."

"You could talk to me," says Liza. "What's your name?"

Liza wants to know more. He's about her age. His hair and beard are combed, and he's wearing a faded but clean light blue shirt. He's not dashing, but definitely good-looking.

"Zach Zuman. People around town call me the Skunk Whisperer. I have a varmint control business. Cover three counties. Got started with pest control in Iraq—mostly insects and rodents, but one day they ordered me to shoot feral dogs. An officer got bit on the base. They gave me a rifle, and that's what I did all day. That's how I got into varmint control."

"Why do people call you Skunk Whisperer?"

## The Lawnmower Club

"Well, for one reason, I have Sugar Bear, a housebroken pet skunk who walks on a leash. She's sensitive and intelligent like me. She's a rescue skunk, a surplus skunk from a fur farm. I love the little rascal. Sugar Bear's descented, but I give her baths once a week. I play with her, but avoid playing rough, because her sharp teeth and long fangs can damage your hands. I don't talk about her much, because people have a very limited understanding of skunks. We live in a cabin in the woods on the Maple River, just us two. I'm separated from my wife, but our separation has nothing to do with my skunk."

"I love animals, too." Liza reaches over to touch the young man's arm—an act no less daunting for her than walking across the Grand Canyon on a tightrope. She acts as if the love of an animal is one of the rarest things two people could have in common. "Maybe I could meet Sugar Bear. I'm a social worker. My name is Liza, Liza Fitting, and this is Christina, my tango instructor."

"Never met a social worker before," Zach says. "Never met a tango instructor, either."

"I help people," Liza says. "I've never met anyone with a pet skunk."

"I think it's wonderful that you that you've devoted your life to the betterment of others."

Christina feels ignored and busts up their conversation. Liza smiles at the young man before they leave the bar. He says he hopes to see her again. She smiles at him a second time, and says that would be nice.

At home in her bed, she sings the happy lyrics from "It Takes Two to Tango." *Let's do the tango... the tango...do the dance of love...there's a lot of things you can do on your own...stare at the moon...but...it takes two to tango, two to tango.*

Liza would like to see Zach again, but he doesn't call, and their paths don't cross in town. Zach walks Sugar Bear after dark. He's in the middle of a divorce. His wife has run away with a serial womanizer, who also happens to be an actuary.

The cougar loves the quiet, but now that he has time to think, he thinks himself into an identity crisis. Life in the wild has no future, especially for an animal who feels like a person. He aspires to grow beyond his circumstances. He would like to investigate alternatives. *I'm so much more than my brainstem.* Perhaps if people could understand how his brain worked, he might at least be considered on the same level as a juvenile offender for having attacked the dental hygienist. How could they have condemned him to death in Wisconsin for an honest mistake?

But he can't speak, and besides, he has no one to talk to. It takes two to tango. He falls asleep trying to remember his mother and father. He tries to smell his father, to move his body to his mother for warmth, to sleep in the crook of her neck, but they are not there.

# 7

# MALLARD POND

WHEN PAL, THE THERAPY DOG locks onto Zitzelberger's ankle, he knows that his legs are returning to normal. Pal tries to drag him out of his wheel chair. *Why are animals always attacking me?!* he thinks. He is beginning to develop free-floating hostility towards animals in the same way he regards all those in the so-called helping professions—most especially people like Liza Fitting and Nurse Hertz. He fears he may soon be assigned to a physical therapist for exercise. He can't stand exercise. He tries to block out his new surroundings by closing his eyes like little coffins.

It's mid-October, and his living space has shrunk to the confines of the Mallard Pond sitting room. The back wall faces away from Lake Michigan where a swamp sits below a high ridge. A cyclone fence surrounds the backyard, filled with trash, weeds, and scrawny shrubs. Two wide doors take up most of the opposite wall space. One side wall contains floor-to-ceiling bookcases filled with the hardbacks of dead people, and dog-eared trade paperbacks, dropped off by well-meaning donors who don't want to pulp up landfills. Angled out from the bookcases, a baby grand piano and bench sits. A large fake stone fireplace with gas-burning logs centers the other side wall. Over the mantle, a large framed picture of loons taking off from a reedy pond provides the room's main attraction.

*Haw! You'd think they could get one thing right. How hard would it be to get a picture of mallards?* The sitting room is furnished with a modest-sized free-standing TV in one corner, and a few sofas and stuffed chairs for those not in wheelchairs. Needlework ephemera ("I'm sew very happy") and artificial flowers fill the rest of the space to the point of suffocation.

Even as his physical condition improves, the mind-altering drugs administered by Mallard Pond disconnect his grasp on reality. The neurons in his brain unreliably decode sensory information—he hears ducks in the swamp outside Mallard Pond going *QUARK QUARK QUARK*, and when Pal barks, the barks sound like *ARUGULA ARUGULA*. He feels flattened like he's printed on paper, a grotesque character in some absurd cartoon. He plots every day about how he will escape from this prison where he sits shackled to his wheelchair with straps and an electronic tether. He would rather die alone in the woods like a wild animal, than slip away in an institution while watching "I Love Lucy" episodes.

Other than one other man, he's surrounded by the soft cadences of old ladies, scattered around the sitting room like pale roses in a family bible. In his muddled mind, he designs a conveyance to blast his way out of the nursing home—an armored battle lawnmower with a steel prow, tracks like a tank, a rocket launcher, and a ramming speed of 60 mph.

Liza Fitting arrives at the nursing home with a snaky new hairdo, wearing an orange tube top and short black skirt. Her branchy arms and thin legs stick out from her skirt like pincers. She wears lime green sneakers. When she sees Zitzelberger slumped and humpbacked in his wheelchair, a benign smile breaks across her face. Her therapy has worked. Her eyes glow with a new-found serenity.

She has thought about Mr. Zitzelberger. *He and I have a lot in common. We don't fit in. We're both living alone. We're both outsiders of sorts. We're both stubborn. We both want to be independent. Maybe I should have been more kind to him. I shouldn't have tried to put him away. Well, he's here now and I'm here now. Maybe I can help him, but in a different way, if my aunt doesn't kill him first. I need to talk with her.*

She realizes that she has suffered from having no protective figure in her life—no close friends, no parents, no brothers or sisters, and her aunt hasn't helped. The weight of her loneliness and insecurity had driven her over the edge. She had dumped her problems onto Zitzelberger. Now she wants to make amends. Even though he had behaved badly, she wants to give him attention. She will give him the best of her new self. Do the tango!

Leading with her body, Liza swans across the linoleum floor, then turns her head sharply to the left. She bends down and leans into Zitzelberger's face—the face she last saw sneering at her when he had left her to die, except now, his face is pale as death. She whispers to him in soft consoling tones.

At first, he doesn't recognize his former victim, then horror further whitens his ashen face. She continues her murmurs of kindness, and gives him a forgiving smile. The old man seems to be in a different category than any man she has ever known. *He looks like the kind of man who would have no pleasure tying a young girl to a tree. A big man like that needs a larger wheelchair. He looks like he's been squeezed into a can.*

Her ambivalence about him lessens after another month passes. She decides she wants to be Zitzelberger's protector—to safeguard him from people like her former self, to support his recovery, and most of all, to give him his world back again. She's a new person re-equipped with Mother Theresa's soul. She intends to save him from Mallard Pond, the very institution where she had tried so hard to place him for the rest of his life. Zitzelberger sits alone and apart from the other residents. Silence wraps him like a shawl. He looks miserable.

Liza kneels lower in front of Zitzelberger, looking into his inscrutable eyes, and says, "Mr. Zitzelberger, I want to help you, but not the way I tried to help you before. Will you—"

"You!" says Zitzelberger contemptuously. "Who are you?"

## The Lawnmower Club

"You know me. I'm Liza Fitting, the social worker. I want to help you."

*"Oh-uh. Why do you want to help me? I might have killed you."*

"Because I know I was wrong to pressure you about leaving your club. I had my own agenda. Sorry, I got carried away. I hope you'll forgive me someday. I want to make it up to you. Please let me help you?" Her face lights up with hope, an expression totally lost on Zitzelberger.

"I preferred you the way you were. You were less confusing. I have a hard time thinking or moving. Even a worm can creep along and get somewhere. But go ahead, try to help me. Be my guest! I've nothing to lose."

"What do you want?" Liza says.

*"What do I want? I want to get out of here and back to The Lawnmower Club! I need a get-out-of-jail-free card! Do you understand me?"*

*"Yes, I understand you."* Liza could see a fat tear forming in one of Zitzelberger's eyes. Liza rubbed it away with her thumb.

The cougar wakes to human voices. The golfers trespass The Lawnmower Club, trying to play a round on the former golf course, where all the fairways, traps, and greens are grown over. Their home course has closed for the winter. Wanting one more round before the snow flies, they dig out a putting cup on what used to be a green, and with a red bandanna tied to the top like a streak of evil, they stick an oak branch into the hole. The cougar hears their shouts— *"IN THE HOLE!"* *"GREAT SHOT!"* He hears a clunking sound as a golfer chips a ball too far, and on the other side of the bumpy green, it dribbles over the edge and disappears in gray pond water.

The cougar crouches low and smiling in the silver morning light. He regards the tresspassers as invasive species. He charges the field of golfers with enthusiasm—swooping like a bird of prey through fields of air. The old golfers forget about their bad backs and knocking knees. They scatter like chickens driven from a hen house by a coyote. Assorted irons and woods, along with golf balls and tees, litter the fairway.

A mixed performance—he creates mayhem in a tumbling burst of improvisation, but a bit off technically.

In horror, Pembrook watches the chaotic scene from his living room window. He calls the Department of Natural Resources.

The cougar is back.

# 8

# FATHERS AND SONS

FELIX ANGLER, CONSERVATION OFFICER, responds to Pembrook's call. In his late fifties, he's a giant of a man with coarse features and large teeth. His brush mustache sits below a crooked nose that has been broken several times in bar fights. When necessary, he disfigures his stone face with a forced smile and hard squint. He shaves his head bald to provide a snug fit to his Smokey the Bear hat. Above his weathered, reddish brown face and hat line, his skull shines white as the moon.

Angler knows, but does not admit, that a small number of cougars inhabit the northern Lower Peninsula (not the official position of the Michigan Department of Natural Resources). Angler had encountered a cougar while bow hunting several years earlier. He had disturbed a sleeping cougar who woke snarling, his sharp fangs snapping and eyes blazing like silver discs. After a deafening growl, the cougar had lurched towards Angler, then turned away and whipped his fire-hose-thick tail across Angler's leg as he launched into space. He disappeared in a whir of tree branches. Angler had thought about tracking the cat, but he decided to go for a beer instead.

Angler has worked for the DNR since he came back from Vietnam. He's about to retire with a flawless record, tracking poachers and catching fishermen without licenses. He's not great at small talk. He intends to interview Pembrook about the cougar sighting. He parks his truck on the street, and sees the large porch in front of Pembrook's house. The wicker furniture sits empty, showing off. The gingerbread trim overhead looks lavish and superfluous. As a fourth-generation local, he resents the intrusion of easy-life resort people like Pembrook, people who think they belong because they happen to have a place in the area, who think that local people like him are slow-witted, tongue-tied, and uncivilized, people who mostly run south at the first signs of winter.

Pembrook's house sits across from what used to be the tenth hole of Mashie Meadows, the name of the club before Zitzelberger bought the property. The faux Victorian house, part of the old money community of Stone Point Harbor, portrays a shabby elegance with white shingles and gingerbread trim, ample shrubs, and a high wrought-iron fence with elegant trim. The spacious three-story dwelling settles smugly beneath pine, oak, and birch trees. The closed neighborhood, three-story houses

## The Lawnmower Club

with sagging geometries standing in rows like crooked old teeth, passes property ownership from one generation to the next. Not true for Pembrook, since he has no offspring.

Pembrook feels the need to name his place to provide the correct impression, so a weathered sign hangs over the long front porch that reads CLINGSTONE. Forlorn wicker chairs line up across the porch that no one ever sits in. He no longer covers his front windows with plywood. For years, Pembrook had teed off on Number Ten, and duck hooked the golf ball through his own windows. After his homeowner's insurance failed to cover his self-inflicted breakages, he simply nailed plywood over the front windows like a Floridian expecting a hurricane.

Upon hearing Angler chime his doorbell, Pembrook totters toward the front door on bird-thin legs, after tripping over the grand piano bench and knocking into a horsehair sofa. He says excuse me to the interior of his house. He looks into a full-length mirror to check his posture. He longs to be taller. He practices his greeting smiles, having never forgotten his etiquette lessons in the sixth grade at the synagogue in his Shaker Heights neighborhood in Cleveland, Ohio. His family had attended the Episcopal church, but the country club etiquette class on Saturday mornings conflicted with his private skipping lessons—he couldn't get it—and he was in the sixth grade. The local synagogue had introduced etiquette lessons, because the youngsters, rather than sitting in prayer, were using the synagogue like an indoor shopping mall, and eating brownies in the wrong places.

Angler hears the Hertzing sound of a key in the lock, and the door opens. Pembrook greets Angler, looking up at him, curling his lips slightly with what he hopes will be perceived as an ingratiating smile. He's wearing an earth-toned herringbone shooting jacket, a tan suede vest, and khaki-colored cords decorated with little elephants. When he shakes hands, he gives Angler an extra-firm grip, but Angler's hand doesn't give, even a little.

"Good day, Officer. I have always said the DNR is a crackerjack organization. Thanks for coming over." He speaks slowly, and looks at his heavy silver fob watch, pulling it out from his vest pocket, placing it back in the pocket, taking his glasses off to make a point, putting them back on. With an air of aristocracy, he says, "You know, it's easy for people like me to forget that along with the incredible natural beauty of living in northern Michigan, we do live in the wild with wayward animals." At this moment, a fat chipmunk skitters across the porch, causing Pembrook to nearly leap out of his slippers.

Angler makes an effort at polite conversation, part of his years of human relations training, and more recently, an anger management course.

"Fine place you have here, Mr. Pembrook."

"Well, thank you very much. Some would call this house an overly-large abode for one person, but I think the place is pleasantly cozy."

## The Lawnmower Club

"You've seen a cougar?" Angler has exhausted his shallow reservoir of small talk.

"Well, yes, of course. Some people call them mountain lions, or pumas, or panthers, or catamounts, or *Felis concolor,* if I remember my Latin."

"Are you sure it wasn't a coyote?"

"Ho, ho, ho, if you tried to measure this animal in units of coyote, the beast would have been three coyotes. *IT WAS A BIG MONSTER CAT!*"

*"You know Michigan cougars are officially extinct in these parts. Most of the so-called sightings are loose pets or lone strays."*

"Well, aren't we all strays...aren't we all. You might say I'm officially extinct...a trust fund baby left on the doorstep of a changing world. I live the modest lifestyle of a country gentleman. Not many of us left. We're sort of like the Last of the Mohicans."

"So where did you see this ghost cat?" Angler risks a bit of sarcasm.

"The cat attacked us at the club across the street, and I can assure you he was no apparition."

"Club?"

"We have a club over at Mashie Meadows. My father, Milhouse Hazzard Pembrook, a machine tool magnate from Ohio, founded the enterprise in the seventies. My grandfather supplied the nascent automotive industry. He met my grandmother, an Italian countess, on the Grand Tour. Now you might ask how a family with my roots end up in this remote part of the country?"

Pembrook grabs his elbows, hoping it's the right thing to do. He looks towards the ceiling, and continues, as Angler rolls his eyes. "Daddy was a one of the original rusticators in these parts. He loved the great outdoors. He dragged my weeping grandmother up here on a train."

'What kind of club?" Angler replies.

"A lawn mowing club."

"Never heard of such a thing. Why would anyone have a club for doing yard work?"

"Well, we all like to mow lawns, so we pay to mow there. For some poor souls, it's the only lawn they have. As you can see, I have a lawn, however, mowing my own lawn wouldn't be appropriate for someone like me. As for the club, we have more members than I can count, and more than we should—standards aren't high enough. Someday, I would like to nudge the club in a backwards direction to be a symbol of the way things used to be. For example, we have members who ride mowers with their shirts off...can you believe it?"

"Good for them," says Angler. "I mow my own lawn with my shirt off. What's wrong with that?"

"Oh, never mind. Would you like to sip some Jasmine Green Tea?"

(Angler stares at Pembrook, counting to ten as he was trained to do in moments like this.)

"I'm trying to give it up. Now, please tell me more," a phrase Angler picked up in training.

"My father started out bird watching, but then took up golf and founded the club, very upscale in those halcyon days. I caddied during my boyhood without much success, and my poor vision prevented me from advancing in the sport. I seldom saw the same ball twice. My parents steered me towards scholarship. Can you believe it, they thought I might be a baby Einstein?

"After father turned up missing one afternoon while playing the course during a thunderstorm (sadly, he was never found), the remaining membership dwindled until only two members remained, an orthodontist and me. One night over cocktails, we jawed about the declining membership. We decided to close down the club and sell the property, rather than to lower our standards. After that, with each subsequent change in ownership, the place kept going downhill...such a shame."

"Sorry, but I meant for you to tell me more about what you saw?" Angler says.

Pembrook notes that Officer Angler may be losing interest in his family history, so he turns the conversation. "But all that is in the past. Please, tell me about your family background, officer?"

"My family moved to Emmet County a hundred years ago. My great grandfather was a dairy farmer, who later moved into town to start a grocery store and butcher shop. From the back of the store, he processed deer for a living until he moved into animal trapping and taxidermy. He trapped muskrats, mink, marten, now and then a bobcat, and over time, foxes interested him more and more. Now about your sighting..."

At last, the two men face each other in stunning silence. Pembrook rubs his temples, but can't squeeze out another thought.

Stretching his impersonal skills to the limit, Angler continues. "I have a wife and two sons. My wife is into professional bass fishing, my one son runs a collision repair, and the other rides bulls for a living?"

"Rides bulls?" Pembrook says. "Where does he ride them? How does he ride them? Do the bulls wear saddles? Riding a bull must take great patience."

"He rides on the rodeo circuit bareback—has a national ranking. He's broke almost every bone in his body at least once. As far as patience goes, he only needs that for about eight seconds."

"I used to do some equestrian, but had trouble staying in the saddle, because of poor balance, and a bit of trouble with coordination. Can you believe it? I didn't learn to skip until the sixth grade. That's when I stopped thinking about pursuit of the martial arts."

"Isn't skipping what girls do?" Angler says. Pembrook blanches, as if he had been somehow exposed.

"I'll have you know, I had a spouse once, but I wasn't exciting enough for her—she ran off with a seventy-five-year-old actuary, known widely in these parts as a shameless seducer. He's probably dead by now. When they first met, he told my

## The Lawnmower Club

wife that his life expectancy was 10.4 years. So I live here alone. We never had children. We didn't want children right away, and it has turned out for the best. I have never liked children because of their poor sanitary habits, and besides, they often grow up to hate you."

"Listen here—*TELL ME WHAT YOU SAW!*" says Angler, his patience spooling out like the open bale of a fishing reel. He hadn't met someone this crazy in years—not since he arrested a guy hunting bear, naked behind a bait pile the size of a dump truck.

"I observed a huge cat with paws as big as oven mitts," Pembrook says. "Like something out of the zoo. Like a slinking cheetah. The monster had a tail like a lion, claws like an eagle, and eyes like a tiger. It seemed nonchalant, in a lion sort of way. Not spooked. Not anxious. It didn't look lost. It emanated an aura of athleticism and physicality, like it worked out at a gym or played for the NFL. You should have seen its muscled forearms! Its fur was so smooth and clean. Sort of well-dressed if you know what I mean. It also demonstrated a certain cockiness, tenacious resolve...no doubt, a devoted man-eater by the way it growled and roared and howled and huffed. Had I not been a veteran, sad to say, of similar outbursts emanating from my ex-wife, the shock might have stopped my heart."

"*YOU SAW ALL THAT?* Well, if you want to bag a sample of scat or send me some track pics, I would be happy to forward the information to the Wildlife Conservancy. Those folks believe in the Michigan mountain lion. And by the way, if you ever have another encounter with a cougar—*ACT LARGE, STAND YOUR GROUND, AVOID DIRECT EYE CONTACT, WAVE YOUR ARMS, MAKE NOISE, SLOWLY BACK AWAY, AND MOVE TO A SECURE AREA.* You don't want to act like a bunny, and don't start skipping away. And if the animal does attack, fight back. Here's my card. Good day."

Liza Fitting settles cross-legged on top of a small table in the sitting room at Mallard Pond. She hovers like a humming bird over Zitzelberger in his wheelchair. She is steadfast in her resolve to save Zitzelberger. Today, she has lost the tank top, and wears something like a prom dress patterned after a shower curtain. She's on her way to her weekly tango lesson with Cristina. Liza's having trouble picking up the 2/4 and 4/4 rhythm, but Cristina flatters Liza and tells her she must have a Sufi bloodline.

"Mr. Zitzelberger, I know you don't trust me right now. I mean how could you trust someone you recently tried to kill? Most people would hold a grudge."

"I'm sorry. I didn't want to kill you," he says. "I wanted you to leave me alone—stop trying to help me. You made me awful sore. Helping people is a dangerous business, don't you think? It's like trying to cut someone else's grass."

"There now," Liza says, "but don't you agree that we all need help once in a while? In my case, I used to think I was

## The Lawnmower Club

the only one to do *everything* for me, but now I know we don't need to be alone in the world. You helped me to understand this when you tied me to that tree. I felt totally helpless out there in the dark night. But when I thought the cougar was about to eat me, I thought, *If I survive, I will help people in a different way. I'll do a better job listening to what they want. But I'll never have a chance, because I'm going to be eaten by this scary animal.*"

"That's about the silliest thing I ever heard of," Zitzelberger says. "You're talking nonsense."

"Mr. Zitzelberger, I now understand that trying to force you out of your place was wrong. I should have helped you stay where you were happy. *I GET IT!*"

"*TOO LATE NOW!*" says Zitzelberger. "Besides, I think you're trying to play some kind of trick on me."

"No, I'm not. You can return to The Lawnmower Club. *OF COURSE, YOU CAN!*"

"You think so?"

"Yes, I do."

"Well I don't think so. Now why don't you move along. Can't you see I'm busy?"

"Oh, you are so funny, Mr. Zitzelberger. Busy. You can't move. How can you be busy?"

"I'm busy thinking about how to keep you out of my life, and get back to mowing grass at my club."

"I get it. You don't think someone crazy like me can help. You think I'm an idiot. You probably don't like my frizzy hair and the way I dress. You have a bad attitude towards social workers in general, even ones with master's degrees. And my guess is you don't like women in general. Don't worry. Your insults only bother me a little."

"No, I couldn't agree more." Zitzelberger has stopped listening. He is busy thinking how he can turn Liza's momentary good intentions to his advantage. Liza has raised the possibility of his return to The Lawnmower Club. He doesn't see how. Even if his body heals, how can this naive, idealistic social worker get him back to paradise? He can't trust that she knows what she's doing.

"Please, look at me when you talk!" Liza says, fighting back tears.

*"WHAAAT?"* What are you croaking about now?"

"You're not listening," Liza replies.

*"SHRUBBERY! Why tell me this?"* Zitzelberger says. *"It upsets me to hear you* say that. You sound like Mona, my dead wife. She always whined about me not listening. That's me."

"People can change," Liza says.

"But Mona still loved me. Besides, callous helps. Callous helped me survive a crappy childhood, and succeed in a business where you take things away from people against their will. Callous helped me continue on after Mona died. Communication would have made my whole life intolerable. That's what I like about cutting grass—no talk. At least for an hour or two, you see where you've been, you see where you have to go——without confusion, decisions, or explanations, and no interruptions,

## The Lawnmower Club

no drama. It's of little use talking to me. You might as well talk to a skunk. I'm tired. Please go away."

Liza gets Zitzelberger's drift. She understands he's been through a lot. She knows she must take small steps to earn the trust of the man who tried to kill her. Before leaving, she gives Zitzelberger's shoulder a friendly pinch goodbye, which causes him to screech with pain. Her natural goodness gets her into trouble. She decides to exit down the hallway towards the parking lot. Zizelberger's comment about talking to skunks reminds her of Zach. Why hasn't he called? Before Liza disappears, she hears Zitzelberger calling her. She returns to the sitting room.

"Zitzelberger looks at her for the first time, and speaks in a soft voice, "Come back to see me."

"I'm going to my tango lesson." Liza leaves. She returns every other day.

Zitzelberger remains in the sitting room deep in thought. He begins to see Liza Fitting as a way out of Mallard Pond. She may be crazy, but it's possible that he can scam her good intentions to his advantage. He has a healthy disregard for all high-minded people like Liza, but you have to hold your nose and press your advantages. Zitzelberger's signature personal strength has always been that he cherishes little outside his own needs. His inclinations towards generosity pass quickly. Once he sponsored THE REPOS, a Little League team, but his players often missed practice, because Zitzelberger had taken away their parents' cars.

His emotionally-abusive father had said, "Son, remember to always think of yourself first, and refuse granting favors, no matter how small." When Zitzelberger's next door neighbor asked to borrow an onion for a stew, Zitzelberger refused. He had answered his wedding vows with inaudible mumbles. His repo career had been a perfect match. When people yelled at him, he replied, "Why are you mad at me? I never tried to help you?"

The day his father died, Zitzelberger decided to write down his father's last words. His father had said, "Leo, never let anyone tell you to give away your life away to some larger purpose, and if you ever think about joining a church, don't join one with a building campaign. Remember—no one person can make a difference, so don't try. Always keep your expectations low, so you won't be disappointed."

His mother would always support his father by saying, "He's right dear, you'll never amount to a hill of beans."

This pre-modern parenting style left Zitzelberger with an unmeasurably high level of insecurity, a desire to settle for small comforts, and a fervent desire to control every aspect of his modest life. His father left him a wooden Shinola Shoe Shine Kit. With a wood burning stylus, his father had etched on the side: YOU DON'T KNOW SHIT FROM SHINOLA.

## The Lawnmower Club

This unwanted and unwelcome reflection prompted by Liza, sparked rare insights for Zitzelberger, a rare occurrence. He ruminated.

*No wonder I grew up to be such a dick. No wonder I don't trust people who want to help me. No wonder I've never felt special. No wonder when the banker said I should be proud of myself for buying The Lawnmower Club, I felt strangely proud for the first time in my life. No wonder.*

*Thinking of Liza brightened his dull eyes, and the threat of a smile pulled at the corners of his mouth.*

On the edge of the woods, the cougar hears grasshoppers snapping their hind wings, rasping and scraping their legs. He also hears the soft buzz of a featherweight humming bird gathering nectar, bulking up for the trip south. The sounds of nature don't bother the cougar, because they are true and natural sounds, created by God, not man. He lays his head on his front paws face up in a salutation to the sun, his favorite yoga pose. The cougar basks in the autumn sunshine, unaware of Angler's intentions to track him down. Intuitively, he knows he needs to keep a low profile. He knows he doesn't belong here, but he belongs nowhere else.

Sometimes, he misses his father. After the cougar's mother had died soon after his birth, his father had migrated from the Black Hills of South Dakota to Wisconsin. He had lived near a coal plant, and died at an early age of emphysema. His father taught the cougar much without opening his mouth. Some nights, his father would sit still with him for hours and look at the moon and stars in animal wonderment, or in the day, at the starlight flash of mica in a rock face, the glistening water rippling through a creek, or the endless parade of shape-changing clouds. Some days, the two of them would sit for hours watching dragonflies hover over a river catching mosquitoes, or hear the fluted sounds of other species humming to each other across a marsh. His father taught the cougar how to be quiet in his body, mind, and soul. How to listen to the talk of nature and listen to its truth.

When his father signaled impending danger, they would run fast away to safety. The father and son shared a silent language. His father had groomed and touched him and taught him to stalk and hunt. The cougar knew his father's love. His eyes were liquid and kind. Sometimes at night, his father would lay on him to keep him warm. The cougar could barely breathe because of the weight, but he did not move, because the weight of love was worth bearing.

The cougar snatches the woodcock that he had let go the other day. He claws out the breasts and marinates it in old apples for dinner. He adds a side of wild greens and horseradish. He loves late-season woodcock.

# 9

# HOPE FROM FEATHERS

MRS. GNATKOZSKI PLAYS "My Way" on the upright piano, turning the pages while reaching repeatedly into her blouse to adjust her bra straps, without missing a beat.

Zitzelberger parks his wheelchair by the sitting room window and looks out on the thin morning light of late autumn to see the high ridge line behind Mallard Pond, and the endless sky beyond. Tethered to his wheel chair, he feels shackled like Houdini about to be dumped into deep water. Unlike Houdini, he has no idea how to wriggle out of his confinement—like Liza tied to a tree. He's tense as a cat. The area of his domain once measured in square miles has been reduced to the square footage of the sitting room at Mallard Pond, and the side of one bedroom he shares with an old man named Willie Snowball. Since he can't walk, he paces the floor with his defeated mind.

The scene in the sitting room behind him seems relentless and unchanging. The residents sit at odd angles, like slanted headstones in an old grave yard, their faces lighter or darker shades of pale. He feels trapped in a ridiculous reality TV show about people watching TV where the channels never change, and everyone wears diapers. He sees something reddish brown moving on the hill beyond the cyclone fence. A fox prances out of the brush and looks out towards the lake. He beds down, hiding his head in a circle of fur, protected from sleet sheeting in from the bay.

Zitzelberger has never run up against the law, never driven too fast, never beaten his wife, never gotten more than a little drunk, never smoked more than a few cigars, but he feels he's been imprisoned (he forgets what he did to Liza). He fails to appreciate his view of the distant hill with its high tree line arcing in muted fall colors against a fall sky.

He smells the foul odor of burgers cooking in the Mallard Pond kitchen. Musk oxen or yak meat, he sarcastically imagines. The hair-netted women in the kitchen who serve the food remind him of the terrible food from his high school cafeteria days. He remembers how the awful food gave him the strange hope of a future life with better food, but now he is trapped in an over-heated place, with food worse than his high school cafeteria.

Zitzelberger misses Mona's cooking—he had joked about her devotion to natural ingredients from their garden—squash soup, tomatoes in balsamic vinegar, green onions and peppers, sweet corn, eggplant ratatouille, and homemade blackberry preserves slathered on yeasty sourdough bread. Those were the

*The Lawnmower Club*

good old days, when she would call him in from his yard work to sit down for supper. Now he eats what they call mechanically-softened food.

Frieda Weatherby catches sight of him as he looks out the window. She's a retired farm woman. She has thinning white hair, and a cheerful round face, weathered and ruddy like a winter apple. With her bright blue button eyes and trim figure, she looks beautiful in her old age. Unlike the other old ladies who sit around in shabby bathrobes, pottering listlessly at made-up work, she wears a faded print dress covered by a shawl the color of strawberry shake. She dresses as if she has a future, or at least somewhere to go.

"You're think you're a prisoner here," she says. She leans over and places her hand on his forearm. Zitzelberger feels the pressure of her fingers, thumb, and palm, so gentle it doesn't hurt. It's one of the few expressions of sympathy Zitzelberger has received from another human being since Mona. He feels the warm sensation of her touch. He wants to pull his arm away and disappear into himself, but he also feels comforted for a strange moment. He wonders what she could want from him.

"You believe in God?" she says.

"Yeah, maybe. So, what?"

"Well I do, and that makes me feel like I belong here."

"No one belongs in a place like this."

"I do. I'm here for a special purpose, even though I don't know exactly why. Do you ever feel special, Mr. Zitzelberger?"

"Special?"

"Yes, do you ever feel that way?"

"I don't know. No, not really."

Frieda sits down beside him with her hand still on his arm, not saying a thing, and looks out the window with Zitzelberger. He thinks about what it would be like to sit beside her somewhere else without the other people around. For some strange reason, he feels less trapped.

After a long silence, Frieda says, "You know, when I was a young girl, I climbed trees on on my grandpa's apple farm on that ridge way up there. On a bright and chilly fall day, I stood on the ridge breathing in the apple trees, and the orange, red, and yellow of the ash, birch, poplars, oaks and maples. I could smell the drift of smoke from burning leaves. Far below me, I looked out on the Lake Michigan whitecaps. I felt a touch of a warm breeze sifting through my hair, and I stood there filled with a kind of dazzle. In that moment, I felt a certain presence of something bigger than me and the world—clear as the bright sun. That joyous feeling has never left me—a God feeling. On that glistening day, I felt God listening to me. And whenever I choose, I can go back up there in my mind and sense that presence. That's why I don't feel confined. And why I feel special." She looks at Zitzelberger with her vibrant blue eyes.

"I'm an outside person myself," says Zitzelberger. To his way of thinking, religion and shrubbery are identical—if you don't keep them trimmed back, they get out of control. A person's goal should be to do a little more than zero good, while attending to more pressing matters like making a living. Still, the idea of feeling special nags him.

After another long silence, Frieda says, "Did you know Mrs. Wilson's on a ventilator?"

"I don't know her, but I'm glad to hear she's doing better," Zitzelberger replies, thankful Frieda has changed to another topic.

Zitzelberger misses the point. Negative thoughts return. He daydreams that he has become a magician and can perform the saw-the-body-in-half trick on Nurse Hertz, and say "Oh crap, something went terribly wrong. Never mind." Frieda talking about awe and joy and feeling special disturbs him, even though he didn't catch everything she said. He feels miserable and weighted down. *I bet she thinks she's better than everyone else.*

He drifts into a dream state. He's looking up from the bottom of a lake flat on his back. He can barely see daylight as he sinks down to where everything is black. He wants to float towards the light, but he can't move. He's stuck in the bottom, and he can't breathe. The cold black around him appears as the cold black at the far end of the universe, empty of light, without hope, and other people.

He wakes to piano music banging away in the sitting room. He wants to cradle his head in his hands and cover his ears, but he can't move. He wishes Mrs. Gnatkozski possessed skills in a quieter hobby than piano playing. Fluency in braille, for example.

Frieda reads her bible. After a while, she rises and walks away from Zitzelberger to her usual sitting place. She has a slow but youthful gait. For Zitzelberger, even though she has moved a short distance, she seems a mile away. He wants to say something to her, but nothing comes to mind. He feels a slender thread of connection to Frieda. He doesn't know why. He returns his gaze to the window. He looks up to the broad hills above the bay, looking for creatures that he might see moving between the covering of trees.

Pembrook is mostly an indoors person, although he likes short stints outside to play at golf and to ride his lawnmower in style. He hasn't had much exercise since high school gym class. He's half-pleased with his sedentary life, but sometimes he regrets never having performed anything remotely heroic. Nothing even close. Most of the time he hops and skips through life, awkwardly, frightened as a rabbit on a state highway. But he has always wanted to be lauded for some high-minded act, some widely respected attainment, to provide gravitas to his life story, so paper thin with purpose. If he could jump in front of an oncoming subway and save a child (and be assured in advance of his own safety), that would be bravery enough for a lifetime.

But there are no subways in northern Michigan.

## The Lawnmower Club

Maybe he could save a drowning woman from shallow water, snatching her from the edge of a deep drop off for all to see, without getting wet above his knees. (*YOU SAVED MY LIFE!* the woman would say, giving him a wet hug, the lovely weight of her breasts pressing against him, as he stands before an admiring world, shining and magnificent.)

He decides he must conclusively prove his manhood by confronting the cougar. Unlike the first time when he ran screaming to the clubhouse and wet his tweed trousers. He looks out his front porch windows towards The Lawnmower Club. The darkening fall sky looks portentous, the clouds heavy as snow clouds. He starts planning what he will wear to stalk the cougar, and what he would like reporters to see when he captures the animal; for example, a pose with his foot on the cougar's back.

His meeting with Officer Angler was not at all satisfactory—Angler had merely visited to fill out a report. No, he must muster the courage to track down the cougar, so the lawnmowers can return to the club. Then he will wrest control from Zitzelberger, remodel the clubhouse with a mid-century modern décor, and change the name back to Mashie Meadows. He stays up late and reads Hemingway about big game hunting in Africa to bolster his intention. He says out loud, "He possessed a manic devotion to big game hunting and deep-sea fishing. And I love his wardrobe—classically elegant clothes, but durable enough to survive the dirt and grime of a safari."

He looks at the hefty fourteen-point deer mount over his fireplace, a great find at a local consignment shop. He has never hunted, not even for birds. His father's guns are in the attic, rusting with neglect, resting beside butterfly nets and croquet mallets. He decides to trap rather than shoot the cougar, a less courageous but safer option. He calls Zach Zuman, the Skunk Whisperer.

"Good Day, Zach, this is Haz Pembrook up on Wedge Wood. Look, I need you to trap a cougar for me...you know, a mountain lion. I want you to capture and kill it, then place the carcass on my porch. I'll call reporters and camera crews over for a photo shoot. Anytime in the next day or two will be fine and dandy."

"I only trap small animals," Zach says, "you know, like skunks. That's why they call me the Skunk Whisperer. I'm like the horse healer in the movie who whispers to horses, but I don't heal animals, I remove them and, most of the time, I kill them."

"Well, if you were going to trap a large animal," Pembrook says, "how would you do it?

"You don't trap large animals. You hunt them down with a dog, or you use bait or poison. But cougars are on the endangered species list. Not to change the subject, but you should probably have me come out to that old place of yours anyway. I can find varmints you don't know you have, and I can tell by talking to you, you have something in your attic—like bats, for example."

## The Lawnmower Club

"Ho, ho, ho...I get it...you think I have bats in my belfry. Well, I'm perfectly sane, thank you...but...but...do you think I have bats in my attic."

"Mr. Pembrook, I'm sorry I can't help you with the trap, but I'll be happy to come out and inspect your house. You do sound like you might have something wrong upstairs, but I can't help you there. I'm not a psychologist. Maybe you should call the new shrink in town. I hear he's a good fly fisherman."

Pembrook hangs up the phone. *There must be a way to get the cougar.* He decides to call Putzkin. If Putzkin's good at catching fish, maybe he knows how to catch a cougar. Putzkin is happy to have anyone to talk to, since he only has one client, Liza Fitting. He uses active listening with Pembrook. This technique provides Pembrook with the impression that he's talking to another person when he is only talking to himself. He takes everything Putzkin repeats back to him (what he has just said) as an affirmation of what he knows he wants to do—like a verbal mirror. Listening to himself so clearly brings tears of self-empathy to Pembrook's eyes.

"I want to trap a cougar," says Pembrook.

"You want to trap a cougar," reflects Putzkin.

"Yes, it's safe and practical," Pembrook says.

"Safe and practical," Putzkin replies.

"It's settled then," Pembrook agrees with his own words.

"It's settled then," says Putzkin.

"Yes, settled."

"Session's over. Shall we schedule another? Let's get one more in before you go after the cougar. Fifteen dollars, please, thirty if you want to pay in advance."

"Thank you so much," says Pembrook. "You're a genius at what you do, although I'm glad you're not a doctor, like you know, if I say I'm going to die, and you say, yes, you're going to die back. But I have to agree that it's therapeutic hearing my word coming out of another's mouth—somehow the words carry more weight."

Pembrook orders a large two-sectioned cage trap to capture the cougar, a trap used for tagging deer. A few days later, a large corrugated package arrives, drop shipped to his house. Pembrook decides to test the trap in his garage. Even though it's late in the day, he's so excited that he starts assembly immediately. Although his mechanical skills are limited to tightening screws to the right (or left?), he thinks the project will consume no more than a few minutes. He quickly loses interest in the instructions, skipping over the bold-faced type in the safety section. *This should be easy. It's nothing more than a box. What could go wrong?*

He finishes after midnight. Even though the sides are warped, and the contraption rocks a bit on the garage floor, he's proud of the construction. Before tucking himself into bed with thoughts of a day well spent, he decides to place bait behind the trip string. He crawls into the trap with an ample portion of his homemade Sirloin Steak Tartare. The trap door slams shut with the precision of a guillotine blade. He has trapped himself,

## The Lawnmower Club

becoming what the instruction manual describes as a non-target animal. He tries to jiggle the cage door, but he can't get out. He sits, wearing his Dolce & Gabbana white silk pajamas, pretzeled up inside the cage. His cell phone rests out of reach, above him, on his father's workbench.

Laying on his side in the trap, he has a bug's-eye view of the cold garage floor. He settles into the unreality of his situation. He may never be found. After several hours, he smells the odor of his body blending with the smell of the three-day old tartare. He runs his hands over his rough beard. He feels tired and cold and hungry. He tries to pee in a corner of the cage, but the corners are too close, and he can't stand up. He begins to eat the raw meat and contemplates his imminent death from salmonella. He should have at least coddled the eggs, but no, the Emeril recipe had called for raw egg.

He thinks hypothermia may be creeping up his extremities. Or does hypothermia go inside out? As he drifts in and out of consciousness, his thoughts focus on a fantasy rescue by a beautiful woman who opens the trap door, then slithers into the cage and rips off his stylish pajamas in a fit of passion. He jolts awake. He screams for help, but tourist season is over. No one is around. He hears a scattering of mice in a corner of the garage. The mice look at him hungrily. If he lives, he will call the Skunk Whisperer. Things get worse. His bowels let loose. He begins to have last thoughts before his imminent death.

*I wish my life had been more of a case study in the profitable use of time. Looking back on the many years of my life, the sea of human hours, knowing what little I aimed for and the results, meditating on the multitude of opportunities available in America after World War II, I can see clearly that I have accomplished practically nothing. God, if you save me, I will give up meat and become a proletarian.*

Zach Zuman's business is down, so he decides to make a cold call on Pembrook. It's Saturday night, so he brings along his girlfriend, a junior reporter for the local newspaper. Zach wears a large-pocketed game vest filled with live mice and pigeons, to make sure he finds work wherever he goes. He sees a light on in Pembrook's garage, enters through a side door with his girlfriend, and holds his nose to rescue Pembrook. Curled up like a caterpillar, Pembrook is chewing a silk pajama sleeve to stay ahead of his hunger. He greets the two of them with spasms of gratitude, paroxysms of tears, and hysterical laughter. The garage smells like shit. The hungry mice are disappointed.

The girlfriend reporter captures snapshots of coon-eyed Pembrook in the cage looking startled by the camera flash, like a cinematic ghost in a horror movie. Whisperer carries incoherent Pembrook up to his bedroom, waits for him to shower and change pajamas, and then places him in bed like a child. Before leaving the house, he plants mice and pigeons in the attic. He will call in a few days to get Pembrook on his regular client list and billing cycle. With new clients like Pembrook, he has high hopes of making it through the winter without having to flip burgers for income. More time for snowmobiling and finding a new partner (he still can't believe that his Ex left him for an actuary).

On Monday, Pembrook makes the front page of *The Review*. The headline reads, LOCAL MAN TRAPS HIMSELF. There is a picture of Pembrook looking wide-eyed out of his cage like an animal caught in a game camera. Pembrook buys camo from a sporting goods store in town. He doesn't want to be easy to spot. He begins speaking high school French, so he won't have to talk to anyone in English.

He calls Putzkin. "*J'ai perdu mon courage*," he says. Putzkin's parents gave him French lessons in between therapy appointments when he was a child, so he doesn't miss a beat, and replies in perfect French with a date and time for their appointment. Pembrook doesn't understand what Putzkin says, so he resorts to English.

"My cage-the-cougar project didn't work out."

"Yes, I saw you headlined in the paper. I'm proud."

"Proud?"

"Proud. You planned your work and worked your plan. So, it didn't go too well. You still took bold action. And you were brave to enter the cage, and brave to sit out in your garage in the middle of the night. You are becoming a new man. Let's schedule a package of ten sessions to keep you on track."

# 10

## NEAR MISS

"HELLO, ANGLER HERE. Say, I'm working on a special confidential project this afternoon, so I can't, uh, be reached...Alpha, November, Golf, Lima, Echo, Romeo, over and out." Felix Angler leaves a voicemail. (He still uses pilot jargon, even though he hasn't flown a plane since Vietnam.)

After contacting the office, Felix Angler sets up his ladder blind on the edge of The Lawnmower Club. He figures he'll get some hunting in while he looks for the cougar. He climbs the stand, pulls on his safety belt, then hoists his bow and knapsack with a thin rope. He's 18 feet off the ground and has a great view over the spindly tops of a spruce stand. He zips open his pack and pulls out a pair of binoculars with an old cigar wrapper tangled in the straps. The wrapper helicopters to the ground. He settles in about three o'clock on a cloudy November afternoon. A light wind ruffles the remnant of dead leaves still twisting on the branches of his tall poplar. He intends to write out the report on his meeting with Pembrook on his clipboard while he's sitting there, so technically, he's working.

He knows cougars disappeared from Michigan over a hundred years ago, the last one taken near Newberry in 1906. But less than ten years earlier, a hair sample taken from a truck bumper tested positive DNA for cougar. Since then, there had been eight confirmed scat samples from various locations, but no photos, no carcasses, no tracks. Angler believes the cougars are escaped or released pets, or perhaps a transient cougar from breeding areas in the Dakotas wearing radio collars, over nine hundred miles away. Angler has had no "big moment" in his career. It would be wonderful to identify an endangered species before he retires, especially one reported as a nuisance. Get his picture in the paper, have something to mention at his retirement banquet, allow him to cultivate the fine art of false modesty, and speak to local kids at high school assemblies.

He pulls his camera out of the pack, along with a Snickers Bar he saved from the snack table at a recent hunter safety course. He unwraps the candy bar and savors the crunchy chocolate. He thinks how the sound of opening a candy bar sounds in a quiet forest, compared to a movie theater on a Saturday night. Next, he cracks open a can of Bud Lite. *It's hard to have only one beer, but you have to keep your wits when you're in the wild.* He completes his preparation by spraying himself with a cover scent, but it can't begin to overcome the pastrami sandwich and garlic pickle he had for lunch, not to mention the Snickers Bar and Bud Lite. He keeps his one remaining cigar in the pack, because would make no sense to wear cover scent and smoke a cigar at the same time.

The fall colors display brilliant reds and yellows. The cougar cannot accurately discern certain features of his world. He knows the season of growing darkness brings black and cold nights broken by occasional moonlight. He perceives the coloring leaves are no longer leaves, sees them transformed into a multitude of clinging butterflies. The butterfly trees bend together in the windy autumn sky. The sun feels warm on his flank.

The cougar has stayed out of sight, living a solitary and nocturnal life. He sharpens his stalk-and-ambush skills on small game, thinks about winterizing his den, and ponders his innate persistence and motion to survive nature in this foreign land, a bit like Moses searching for the holy land, but robed in his own fur. Baggy fur skin over steel muscles. A big cat, a lion-like masterpiece of cat hood full of primitive energy, but with a brain capable of abstract thought and critical thinking, aware of humans' Neanderthal man-over-nature colonialist attitudes, his greatest dangers—man the predator and the predators of both man and beast—automobiles and trucks.

It's such a beautiful day, he decides to rise from his day bed and take a stroll. He stays undercover and moves through the large spruce stands that border The Lawnmower Club. It's super to be moving in the daylight. He stretches in a down dog pose, then opens his whiskered maw and yawns. He shakes out his long body from front to back, then snarls at a passing chipmunk. The little creature dives for cover and breathes deeply to restore its oxygen. The cougar's grumpy about the onset of cold weather and has a premonition that something's amiss in the woods.

He raises his nose in the air, and smells garlicky pastrami, brown mustard, Bud Light, a hint of chocolate, peanuts, and cigar. Must be a hunter. The birds stir and stitch through the air, and twitter to each other with hunter alert hash tags. The cougar follows the scent through the trees, keeping downwind. He sees a buck chasing a doe in the open, throwing caution to the wind, moving too fast for safety. He regards bucks as oversexed for their own good. Personally, he gets the itch for sex every other year (but when he does, look out).

Angler sees the doe first, looking backwards over her shoulder towards the buck, as if to say shoot him not me. The buck follows the doe in the direction of his stand about two hundred yards out. He softly says, "Holy shit! A big buck." The large buck moves towards him. Angler worries he smells too much like what he had for lunch, but the buck keeps coming in. The buck pees on his own legs, so horny he forgets how to whizz. Angler lets the doe pass, then when the buck is 40 yards from the stand, he pulls the bow string to full draw. He has the buck centered on his site pin, waiting for the perfect release.

The cougar sees what's about to happen. He has a moral crisis. He wants to stay unnoticed, but the buck is a beauty of nature, ten points with a massive rack, lean and healthy, just too sexed up for his own good.

The cougar approaches from the blind side of the stand, then brings up a relatively low-key growl that begins near his tail, travels through his long body, and emerges from his lungs through his wide-open maw. The arrow flies over the buck. The buck bounds out of sight. Angler falls out of the stand, and hangs by his safety strap, his fall broken by his crotch landing on successive limbs. His bow lies on the ground, along with his cell phone, camera, binoculars, and a beer can. His crotch aches like he's been hit repeatedly with a baseball bat, which he sort of has. The nylon straps compress his breathing. He faints.

Angler wakes up a few minutes later, and reaches for his cell phone, then sees it on the ground below him. It's fallen out of his pocket. Hanging helplessly, Angler is even more restricted than Pembrook had been, trapped in his cage, or Zitzelberger tethered to a wheelchair, or Liza tied by a rope to a tree.

The cougar sees the justice of what happened, but feels more than a tinge of empathy for the helpless hunter, like he might feel if he were trapped—the way he had felt about Liza

Fitting the night he found her tied to the tree. But what can he do? He approaches the base of the tree, and looks up at Angler dangling there. The cell phone's bird chirp ringtone goes off with the speaker on, startling both of them.

"Felix, I got trafficked into your voicemail. Don't you ever answer your phone? I'm up in the air about what to have for dinner tonight. Why don't you stop and pick something up on your way home? Oh, by the way, your mother called. She says, 'Margaret Jo, why doesn't Felix call anymore?' Says she's running out of light bulbs, but she supposes she can do without them, since there's nothing to do but sit around thinking about death, and it's easier to think about death in the dark. Can you believe that woman? She wants you to stop the phone service, since no one ever calls her anymore, oh, and she's running out of underpants (I have no idea why), and who knows what size she wears? The thought of your mother's panties disgusts me.

"Anyhoo, I'm in the mood for one of those roasted chickens under the heat lamps in the plastic containers by the check-out line, but ask how old they are, and be sure to smell them—remember when I was home all day with a bad chicken last year—every orifice in my body expelled greenish bits of spoiled chicken? It's taken me a whole year to get in the mood for another one of those roasted darlings. But don't get the barbecue flavor (the kind that made me hurl), get the one with herbs (and say 'erbs not herbs).

"Felix, are you there? You better not be hunting when you're supposed to be working. You could lose your job, you

## The Lawnmower Club

know, and then what would we do? I bet you're hanging upside down in your safety belt from a tree or dead on the ground where no one kind find you for days. If you're so thoughtless to make me a widow, I'll have to take care of your mother (can you believe that woman?). No one can please her, except you, her perfect son. When we got married 25 long years ago, I never thought I would have to worry about the size of your mother's underpants. I'd rather be eaten alive by a wild animal than take care of your mother. Well, let me know if you get this message, because there's nothing in the fridge, and I mean nothing. Felix are you listening? You usually say *uh-huh, uh-huh, uh-huh—* CALL ME BACK! DON'T LEAVE ME HANGING!"

*The cougar climbs the tree.*

Angler thinks he may pass out a second time. The cougar tries not to look too fearsome—does not lurch or snarl or bare his fangs, or in any way match the menace and movement of a predator. As the cougar ascends the tree, Angler prays to God that he will not be gnawed apart and eaten alive. If he escapes a horrible death, he makes a solemn oath that he will never kill an animal for the rest of his life, and he will, so help him God, become a vegetarian or a vegan (or whatever category still allows him to eat perch or walleye with fries and coleslaw on Friday nights).

The cougar bites through the safety strap, releasing Angler to the ground, then slinks away swishing his tail, fading into deep forest.

## Randy Evans

Angler decides to tell no one what happened. Who would believe him? And besides, he's not supposed to be hunting during working hours. He goes home for a nip of brandy. He forgets to buy the chicken, so his wife is pissed. But Angler's happy to be alive. He smiles and takes her out for beer and meat lover's pizza (he'll change his eating habits later). The next day, he calls his mother to discuss her underwear. After a few weeks, he has difficulty thinking about the experience as more than imaginary, and forgets about his promise not to kill animals, although he does intend to forego eating red meat every other day during Lent, and to consider vegetarian side dishes at local restaurants, unless he's out with his carnivorous buddies.

# 11

# MANHATTANS AND PEANUTS

LIZA RETURNS to Mallard Pond resolved to save Zitzelberger. Pal, the therapy dog, greets her at the door baring his teeth, and growling in low like an idling Ferrari. Liza has always been afraid of dogs, and she's heard stories about Pal, how he likes to strip shower curtains from the bathrooms and run down the hall tripping old people. He has never bitten anyone, but even when he's feeling happy and wagging his pointy tail, he looks like a fierce fighting dog, which he could be if he chose to be. Liza finds her aunt hovering over Zitzelberger's paperwork, gleefully documenting his decline, thinking up new ways to torment him and rob him of dignity. She asks her aunt how a Pit Bull Terrier can be allowed to live in a nursing home.

"No one knows for sure how Pal got here, but the story goes that when this place was a pet day care, his owner dropped him off one day and never returned. Pal remained here when the day care people left, and since the new owners wanted a guard dog, they kept him on. They only call him a therapy dog to make people less nervous. No one complains too much, since most people here don't complain about much of anything."

"He's a dog someone forgot, or more likely, left him here on purpose."

"Well, Pal has a home here for now, although we'd sell him or give him a way if we could find someone foolish enough to take him. He's sort of like one of those popular bad boys in high school. People think he's kind of cute and funny, but he's unpredictable, like when he's having a bad day, he goes after anything that's hanging or loose—he loves to rip off IV bags and oxygen lines."

"Well, dogs have to play, I guess. I've come to see Mr. Zitzelberger."

"What do you want with that old thing? Did you forget he tried to kill you?" She gives Liza a piercing stare.

"No offense, Aunt Hertz, but he is the one person in my life who has cared enough about me to hate me. Most of the time, I plain irritate people and they go away. You have to really like someone to hate them—that's what I'm thinking. Besides, if it weren't for me, Mr. Zitzelberger would still be living out at that Lawnmower Club he loves."

"He's the best living example of how helping others is useless," Nurse Hertz says.

Liza leaves the nurses station, enters the sitting room, and sits down by Zitzelberger. Pal sits outside, humped over a discarded magazine, taking a shit. She's safe for now.

## The Lawnmower Club

"Good morning, Mr. Z," Liza chirps. She thinks calling him Mr. Z might be friendlier, and save some syllables. "Were you a bit slow-to-warm-up as a child?" she plunges right in.

"What kind of question is that?" Zitzelberger says. "You keep coming back like junk mail. Did you read the news today, oh boy? He shows her the front-page headline: LOCAL MAN TRAPS HIMSELF.

"The headline makes a good point, Mr. Z. If you want to escape from Mallard Pond, you need to release mind, and stop feeling trapped, like a condemned prisoner. The first step is to let go of your regrets. I read that in a tango self-help magazine."

"I regret the loss of Manhattans and peanuts every night. It was a sacred cocktail ritual for me, like people who take communion every day in case they've committed a sin that can't wait 'til Sunday. Could you do something about that? You said you wanted to help me."

"Oh, Mr. Z, we have snacks in common! I have never had a Manhattan, but I *love* honey-roasted peanuts. This is something that I can do to help you! Don't go anywhere. I'll be right back."

"Be sure to get the right stuff. I need Tennessee whiskey, sweet vermouth, angostura bitters, and cocktail cherries. The cherries need to come with stems. And we need crushed ice, lots of crushed ice. And the peanuts need to be vacuum-packed in a metal tin with a plastic lid to keep them fresh...and check the expiration date. And oh, ah, thanks. And oh, here's some money. Jack Daniels or George Dickel will do for the whiskey. And get two cans of peanuts, because I don't like to share."

Liza pops over to the liquor store down the street, and buys the whiskey, sweet vermouth, angostura bitters, a jar of cherries with stems, and with her own money, buys a cocktail shaker. She stops by the ice machine, and brings in a couple tumblers from the kitchen. Zitzelberger pours his preferred portions (he doesn't like to drown the whiskey with vermouth), and Liza operates the shaker, giving it the number of shakes that Mr. Z proscribes. He smiles as he munches the peanuts, and takes his first guzzle of his favorite drink, topped off with two long-stemmed cherries floating on frozen chip. Like ice on a November pond," he says. He fixes another drink for Liza.

"Okay, now I've brought these 3x5 index cards," says Liza, looking luminous. "I want you to write one LIFE REGRET on each card, and what you're going to do about it on the other side of the card. I recommend four to six REGRETS and ACTION cards to start."

"I don't want to do this exercise." The warm whiskey flowing through his body helps him develop the semblance of sincere emotion. Chances are good he will enjoy his drink and peanuts without paying a price.

"Look, here, Mr. Z," says Liza with some heat, "you can slouch through the rest of your life feeling misunderstood, playing an inside joke on yourself, and eating those antidepressants like honey-roasted peanuts, but I'm not going to let you do that. So here we are, you and me." Liza can't believe the strong voice of a woman coming out of her. She marvels at herself, after one sip.

## The Lawnmower Club

"So that's it," Zitzelberger says, "you really don't care about me at all do you? I'm no more than an innocent bystander. You wanted to put me in Mallard Pond for reasons that had nothing to do with me. You were going to help me, whether I needed help or not!"

Liza shakes her bony finger at him. "You're a mean and nasty man," she sputters. "I'm taking your whiskey home with me." Zitzelberger looks horrified.

"Okay, I'll play your game," he says. "I've been desperate and lonely since Mona died, and living away from the club hasn't helped. My only regret is that my wife died, and I can't do anything about that. The only thing I can write on your index cards is that my wife died. I have no other regrets. ARE YOU HAPPY NOW?"

Frieda notices the change in his demeanor and squeezes his arm again (he's beginning to get purple bruises, because she always gets him in the same place), but Frieda says nothing more, and returns to her chair.

Liza takes another communion sip from her Manhattan and eats a handful of peanuts. She restacks her 3x5 cards, and secures them with a rubber band. "Maybe this isn't such a great exercise after all. Next time I come, let's do something fun," she says. "Maybe we can play board games or read a book or something."

Zitzelberger's sincerity stuns everyone in the sitting room, especially Frieda Weatherby. Pal comes inside with a pleased, toothy smile. He picks up a tennis ball and bounds over to Liza. Pal lives, filled with doggie joy, in a doggie paradise. He, too, has no regrets.

# 12

# HALFWAY HAPPY

THE COUGAR RANGES over the scrubby, gray fields of The Lawnmower Club, and muses how plants and animals are uncomplicated. His mutated cerebral cortex, in contrast, comes not only with the powers of cognition, but also with a bag of irony. How ironic that he loves all the natural beings, but also employs his innate predatory instincts to kill for raw meat. Buddhist he's not, but he decides to review his attachments—does he need to have such extravagant living space? Does he engage in meaningful activity, or prowl around doing nothing but being a big cat? Does he snatch chipmunks because he's hungry, or because he's crude and rapacious? Is he trying to play some romantic archetype of a mountain lion or simply be his best self?

The cougar decides to live with new sincerity. After all, he has no audience and no one to please. He works on no man's clock, and lives in a world that is perpetually in airplane mode. This self-examination makes him hungry. Backsliding immediately, he snatches a plump chipmunk like it's a honey-roasted peanut. Chipmunk chunks get stuck in his teeth. Perhaps he will give up meat for a time—maybe not all meat. A chipmunk every other day might be doable, especially if a stout vole is available. Perhaps he will find some useful employment to give meaning and purpose to his life beyond daily survival. Perhaps he could make the world a better place, especially for animals. He raises his wind-flattened face to see rags of silver clouds spinning across the sky. *The whole world hurries*, he thinks.

Liza Fitting loses her job in mid-November, laid off after five years. The county decides to cut back on social services rather than snow plowing, following the logic that if you have an abusive relationship, you need to get out of your driveway and neighborhood, fast.

Hazel Hertz, Liza's only family, refuses to help her in any way. She tells Liza that help from relatives in a time of crisis is bad for the character, and besides, she has enough to deal with at the time—a fragile relationship with a new boyfriend she recently met at a bar. He's afraid of commitment and not financially secure, due to his seasonal employment as an ice cream mixer, master fudge maker, and flower arranger. He's thinking about getting into snowmobile repair, but doesn't like cold unless it's indoors.

## *The Lawnmower Club*

Liza's finances are simple. She has $400 in a savings account and a $40,000 college loan. She has never missed a rent or loan payment. Unemployment won't be enough for her rent, so she moves into her Honda Element, a car that looks boxy enough to be a shipping container or a small house. Networking to find another job would be a good thing to do, but she doesn't have a network. Her Facebook page lacks friends. She looks at classified ads every day. No openings in her field. No openings for much of anything. She had thought that a social work diploma would guaranteed life employment, but apparently helping people, in addition to not paying much, is not such a big business.

She parks her car in a township parking lot down by the Bear River at night. She keeps looking for work. She misses having a shower—when she gets through this, she never wants to see a gas station bathroom again. Even though she doesn't have a job, she continues her volunteer job at the local food pantry, and at the end of her shift, selects a few things she can eat in her car. The warm November weather turns cold, and the first milky snows arrive. A silvery embroidery of ice forms on the river banks and on her windshield.

Liza continues her visits with Zitzelberger, two or three times a week. She visits in part to get warm. Mallard Pond set their thermostats at sixty-eight degrees. She feeds Pal kibbles from the food pantry. She has figured out that he will never attack a food source that keeps giving. An electric blanket could do no better than Pal in her lap. Hazel Hertz's refusal to help her niece confirms Zitzelberger's low opinion of her, a woman less sensitive to the needs of others than even him. Liza and Zitzelberger play an assortment of two-person vintage board games—Checkers, Monopoly, Chutes and Ladders, Candyland, and Uncle Wiggly—games of ups and downs for three-year-olds and higher.

"Isn't this a little bit like fun!" Zitzelberger says. He has never played board games, and every time they play, Zitzelberger has happy dreams when he sleeps. Dreams where things turn out fine, where he lands in the home space on the game board, a winner. Monopoly is his favorite. He loves to buy properties and houses, then raise the rent. He gets out of jail quickly, no matter what the price. He likes railroads better than utilities, he makes lots of trades between turns, and shows no mercy. "This is kind a not terrible," he says, "not unpleasant."

Frieda Weatherby enjoys watching Leo and Liza having fun. A teacher of language arts, a breeder of bird dogs and alpacas, a sporting clays instructor, captain of the ski patrol, and former owner of a lavender farm, Frieda Weatherby has lived and breathed resilience. She has found ways to make ends meet in northern Michigan from deep summer to deep winter. One afternoon, she overhears Liza talking to Zitzelberger about classified ads, and comes over to talk.

"Dearie, you lost your job?"

"Yes, after five years. I'm feeling pretty low about the whole thing."

"A bit tractored over?"

"Uh-huh. Kind of sozzled."

## The Lawnmower Club

"Did you love that job?"

"No, but I supported myself."

"I didn't think you sounded very upset by the loss of your job. Well, your next job should be better, the overflow of some hope, something you really care about...a dream, a vision, or a good hunch. If you care about your work, then your work is easier."

"I always took the next job that paid more money," Zitzelberger says. He bends down to pull up his tube socks, a sign of progress in his daily efforts to regain mobility.

"I do have a hope," says Liza, "but I think my hope's too big."

"Nothing's too big, honey! Young girls should have grand dreams. Tell us about your big hope."

"I would like to build some kind of heaven on earth," Liza says. The strong woman's voice inside her is speaking again. She can't believe herself. She feels the heat of a small flame inside her.

"That's way too big," says Zitzelberger, "and, besides, people have already tried it. You can get you jailed or killed for that kind of thing. Look what happened to Joan of Arc? And the idea sounds too Californian. When's lunch?"

"You should have your big hope," Frieda says kindly. "There are a million ways to bring Heaven on earth."

"Didn't you try to do that that with The Lawnmower Club, Mr. Z? Wasn't that your big dream, to create your own version of paradise on earth, and live your life in your own way?" says Liza.

"I think my highest aim in life has been to be halfway happy. You're talking about some kind of utopian nonsense. I had a little money when I sold my business, and I wanted a way to be left alone."

*"MONEY YOU MADE TAKING AWAY CARS FROM FOLKS!"* Mrs. Gnatkozski offers her two cents. Zitzelberger slouches down in his wheelchair, until his head rests below the level of his empty Manhattan tumbler.

"But did you feel happy at your club?" says Frieda.

"Where?" says Zitzelberger.

"The Lawnmower Club."

"I have no idea what you mean," he says.

"I feel happy every day right here at Mallard Pond," says Frieda.

"Yeah, you told me."

Zitzelberger knows she must be right, but he hates to see the peaceful smile on Frieda's face every day, and how she always dressed as if she had a future and somewhere to go. Sometimes he thinks he despises Frieda Weatherby more than Nurse Hertz. Mean and nasty, he knows well, but peace and goodness, are unfathomable. If you let down your defenses, who knows what might happen? He has never experienced anything close to peace and goodness—neither to the background music of cellos and violins, the deft brushstrokes of an artist, or the beauty of a ruby-colored sunset. He's never heard the voice of God or angels in the middle of the night calling him to higher pursuits. He's kept his head down and his feet placed firmly on the ground. He loved Mona in his own way, but she died on him out of the blue. He settles for the muted colors of small comforts, not the audacious primary colors of happiness.

Joy, love, goodness, peace and happiness are for other people. Any lumps of reside inside Zitzelberger like a brown stone castle grown over with thorns. He thinks of himself as a bad man in a bad story. Occasionally, he comes across someone that he judges to be a good person like Frieda, but he doesn't see that goodness in himself. *Good people like Frieda give people like me a bad name,* he thinks.

"Sure you're all right, honey?" Frieda says to Liza.

"Yep. Thank you." She goes on her way.

All this abstract talk is more than Zitzelberger can bare. He falls asleep and snores loudly, hoping not to wake before dinnertime.

On this particular day, Pembrook decides to visit Zitzelberger. He hopes that Zitzelberger has given up on returning to The Lawnmower Club. He has a blank real estate sales agreement stuffed in his coat pocket. He stumbles into the sitting room, and runs into a chair. The commotion wakes Zitzelberger. Pembrook stands before him wearing white-and-black flecked goose hunting camo. Because of the news headline, he's too embarrassed to be seen around town. He hopes that his mostly white camo will serve as an invisibility cloak against the wintry landscape.

"Pembrook—that you?" says Zitzelberger.

## Randy Evans

"Hello, ladies. Leo, I love your pajamas. Are those Ralph Lauren? You know, I have a pair like those—flannels with a pattern of playful hunting dogs. Boy did I have trouble finding this place—a dog and cat day care facility last I looked. I did see the sign the first time I drove by—but thought the sign read MALLARD POUND not MALLARD POND. How do you like my outfit? When did you first notice I had entered the room?"

"You got the sign right the first time," says Zitzelberger. "This place is like a pound. And we have a dog here that you should get to know. He pretty much owns the place. He's tearing down the hall after a nurse right now, but he'll be back soon."

"I would be happy to meet Pal. I have never been on a first-name basis with a dog, not like Joan of Ark, the woman in the Bible, who saved all the animals from the big flood."

## 13

# INSIDE AND OUTSIDE

THE COUGAR SEES no movement around the clubhouse. The unlatched front door knocks in the wind. Trees sway and limbs clack against each other in the background. He approaches in stalk mode. The clubhouse is an anomaly in the wide swaths of pristine landscape, the forest primeval except for this man-made structure. The clubhouse also serves as a symbol to the cougar—the part of the cougar that cannot live alone in solitude. He is exiled from the animal world by his unusual mind, and exiled from the world of humans, because he is an animal. He places one paw inside the door. Over the threshold that divides the human not animal, and the animal not human. The interior is darker than outside, where a half moon illumines the countryside.

The moonlight streams in through the cracked clubhouse windows to light up the inside like a movie screen. He looks around at the strange details of the interior. It looks like Plato's Cave with relaxed housekeeping—torn magazines, a computer screen sleeping, an uncapped whiskey bottle, crushed fast food bags, a can of ravioli, a jar of peanut butter, an overturned salt shaker, stained coffee cups, cigar butts on the edge of ash trays, scratched furniture, sagging overstuffed chairs, a potbellied propane tank, a bag of gold fish crackers, and boxes of lawnmower parts, everywhere. Every object casts shadows. Mice race here and there, adjusting to new circumstances presented by the large cat. They move stoically into hiding places, but one alpha-male mouse glowers at the cougar from behind a stainless-steel beer keg. He knows a killer has entered their squatter's homestead.

The cougar does not feel trapped or closed in by the clubhouse, but rather as if he has escaped from the great outside, in. He likes the feeling of living indoors, out of the weather. He feels like he might belong inside (*people over-glorify the outdoors*). What good fortune—like finding a bird's nest on the ground, with birds inside, or in this case, mice! He yawns, but his mind buzzes with thoughts. He worries that his ancestral genes may be closer to a house cat than to a lion—why else would he have these indoor inclinations? He really does like to be comfortable, but he also has a sense of his short lifespan—five years gone by so fast. So different for him, from birth, to feel like an oddity, not like others of his species, at least on the inside, something of a circus freak.

He thinks about the ephemerality of existence. He wants to live fully before he dies, but at a slow, reasonable pace. He yawns again, then lays down on the wood-planked floor and falls into an animal sleep. He dreams of humans. In his dreams, he rambles through the slender columns of ancient Roman ruins on the Lycian coast of Turkey. He walks unnoticed by the tourists through the ancient rubble. When he wakes in the morning, he has no remembrance of dreams.

Liza returns to her car home under the highway bridge by the river. She climbs into her sleeping bag. She pulls a hoodie over her head. Her windows frost over, and the car looks like a coffin cover. She's begins to feel a bit sorry for herself when tears freeze her eyes shut and the snot in her nose turns into little pebbles. It's very cold and dark down by the Bear River. She can hear the rush of water over the dam, the channels narrowed by shore ice. She's too cold to sleep, but after a time, the wind rocking the car lulls her, and she falls into a deep slumber with fits of dreams about all sorts of odd-looking mythical animals going down the river and over the dam, too strange to remember or tell.

Liza wakes in the morning, icicle stiff. When she cracks open her eyelids, something has changed in how she feels, as if fear of the future has been frozen out of her, like when a body says, "Don't worry about tomorrow, because you're going to die soon." She faces her calamities of joblessness and homelessness with unnatural calm. She has no idea how it's happened, but she accepts the gift, and decides not to think what she's going to do next.

Liza turns on the ignition and heats up the car—she has a quarter of a tank left. As she drives along 31 North past lakes dotted with ice shanties, she decides to treat herself to a warm breakfast at the Brutus Camp Deli. She pulls into an empty parking lot, trips up the steps, and enters a large, bright dining room, heated by a gas fireplace, the walls filled with dozens of fish and game mounts, animal skins, and antique rifles. She sits at the table closest to the fireplace, and orders coffee, orange juice, blueberry pancakes, and pan sausage, thinking about nothing but the food in front of her and the fragrance of steaming hot coffee. She talks with the waitress about the weather. The waitress says she loves days when the restaurant is nearly empty.

Pembrook ambles over to the clubhouse the next morning to look in the windows. He still wants to be unobtrusive, so he wears his full-length coyote fur coat over earth-toned tactical outdoor clothing. After his visit to see Zitzelberger at Mallard Pond, he feels assured of Zitzelberger's demise. When he manages to take over control of The Lawnmower Club from Zitzelberger, he plans to redecorate, give it the ambience of an English country house. He wants to get some ideas for a color board of paint and fabric swatches. He wants to redo everything

## The Lawnmower Club

in good taste, but with a musky motif of manliness, like one or two full body jungle mounts, game fish, muzzle-loaded rifles, and a small museum's worth of antique golf clubs.

Pembrook believes Zitzelberger is more than low class, someone who earned a living through rough and tumble commerce (he forgets that his grandfather did the same). He believes that people like Zitzelberger are born inferior. (At some college in the South, a hotbed of Confederate thinking, his father had funded a chair in eugenics, the science of improving the human population by controlled breeding.) Even though eugenics has fallen out of favor since the Nazis, Pembrook still sends contributions each year to support the school's emerging pop neuroscience program.

Pembrook slouches through life trying to fulfill some notion of family tradition, to be admitted to an inner circle that no longer exists, to do something noble and notable. It's his own self-fashioned trap. For Pembrook, the halls of highest human happiness lead to a clubby room by a roaring fireplace inside an exclusive club filled with cigar smoke and the chumminess of men like him. Perhaps he can restore The Lawnmower Club to fulfill this fantasy. Pembrook rises on his heels to peek inside the clubhouse where the cougar has spent the night.

The cougar rouses. The clubhouse has now become part of his territory. The sun rises a sailor-take-warning red, the cougar's least favorite color. He jumps up at the window to growl at the sun, at the same moment Pembrook peers in. The cougar cocks his head sideways in disbelief, screaming a cougar scream at what he sees as a coyote with a human head.

Pembrook releases a high-pitched, far-from-human scream, then scrambles away towards his house with the cougar following close behind, kicking up turf, not running Pembrook down, because unlike Pembrook, he pauses to look both ways before crossing the road. Pembrook has a death look in his eyes as he opens the side door to the garage. He doesn't even scrape the mud off his Wellingtons. The cougar enters the garage before Pembrook can shut the door.

This is Pembrook's big moment, his chance to lay his life on the line and perform a soul-stirring act for others to admire, his immortal badge of bravery *(maybe I'll get an honorable mention in the Gerald R. Ford Profiles in Courage Award?)*. Hand-to-paw combat. He visualizes a flattering headline on the front page of the local paper and begins to construct a statement for the press: *With the mountain lion's eyes blazing and fangs bared, I lurched against his massive body, grabbed his thick tail, and with all my might, launched him into space.*

Pembrook, foolhardy to a fault, goes *mano a mano* with the cougar. The eyes of the dangerous beast look like two burning coals. Daring serious injury or a gruesome death, Pembrook inflates his chest, and clenches his saggy pectorals, weak from a lifetime of inactivity.

Mimicking a boxer, he raises his fists above his shoulders. He hears his heart beat THUD, THUD, THUD, like he's connected his ears and chest to a stethoscope.

Pembrook says what could be his last words with fake bravado, *"I'VE ALWAYS WANTED TO SAVE A LIFE. IT MIGHT AS WELL BE MY OWN!"*

Pembrook looks at the cougar's large green-streaked alabaster eyes, his long finely formed body. He sees the cougar on a larger scale than his natural size, a stylized bronze sculpture towering over him. The cougar lunges at him. The big cat's roar travels up his long body like a vortex and comes out his open maw with the thrust of a jet engine, his teeth flashing like turbine blades. Pembrook lurches backward, hunches down on all fours, pushes off with his arms, and leaps backwards into the snare trap. A move in the wrong direction. He catches the trip string with the collar of his fur coat. Caged again! He tries to make himself look large as Angler had suggested, but it's very difficult when you're hunched up in a cage. At least, as Officer Angler had recommended, he has moved to a secure area,

The cougar paces around the outside of the trap, then pauses. He looks at Pembrook like child gazing at a clownish-faced creature in a zoo. He pauses to roll his eyes at Pembrook, then leaves and returns to a protective circle of large boulders in the woods. His best laid plans to keep out of sight fails again. He drops down in a furry heap, then stretches out for a nap, like the sprawled-out body of a derailed freight car.

This time, Pembrook has his cell phone. He calls the Skunk Whisperer, who arrives within fifteen minutes to find Pembrook tortoised inside his coyote coat, his heart beating like a trapped animal. The Whisperer says nothing. He pulls Pembrook out of the trap like a doctor dragging a newborn out of a birth canal. Pembrook knows he needs to save face. He speaks first.

"I'm so glad that you could drop by. I needed to talk with someone who knows more than me. You may think you know why I'm again trapped in this cage, and I would like to hear your ideas."

"Sorry, but I have no idea what has *befallen you*."

"*Befallen?* Where did you pick up such a word?"

"I happened to be reading Chaucer in the Middle English when you called. I love grandiose manners of speaking. I majored in English, but unfortunately, could never find a use for it."

"I use English all the time, but I know what you mean, no one wants to pay for it. How did you find work?"

"I founded a Laundromat business, bought used washing machines and dryers. To save money on repairs, I named the business OUT OF ORDER."

"Very clever."

"I shut the business down when the last machine broke down. Then one day, I decided to catch the robust and rising market for pest control, an area of expertise that I picked up while serving in Iraq. Starting another business put a strain on my marriage. My wife and I bugged each other most of the time...until she ran away with an actuary."

Pembrook's mouth drops open. *"DOGGONE IT!"* says Pembrook, "my wife absconded with an actuary, too. How likely is that?"

## The Lawnmower Club

"May have been the same one," says Whisperer. "How many actuaries do you think there *are* in northern Michigan? Both of us *cuckolded* by an actuary."

"Cuckolded?"

"Yes—*cuckolded by an actuary.*"

Pembrook wants to change the subject back to his immediate concerns. "Well, take a guess about what befell me, go ahead!"

Pembrook looks to Angler with the hope of a sailor sinking in a stormy sea. He needs someone to come up with an explanation of what happened, no matter how far-fetched, something less outrageous than what really happened. How can he ever explain how he has been snared twice in the same trap he had intended to use on the cougar? Whisperer thinks.

"Okay, you were forced into the cage by an intruder who was surprised when you *drew near* while he was *burgling* your house."

"Drew near? Burgling?"

"Yes, he was going to rob and kill you with his lance. But you said, 'No, young man, you will ruin the rest of your life if you kill me—take what you want, take my stash of cash and my coyote fur coat, and then place me in the trap in my garage."

"What miraculous insight!" (To Pembrook, the tale had the ring of truth.). "I'll be buggered, I've never been *burgled* before—or I should say *burglarized*, which is more standard."

"Let's call the police," says the Whisperer. (He's taunting Pembrook, because he knows Pembrook is such a noodle he has somehow entrapped himself again.) "Or maybe not, I suppose you want to give the young man a second chance."

"Yes, I could see remorse in his *visage* when he chanced upon me in the house," Pembrook lies. (Pembrook is such a blank slate, he starts picking up Whisperer's stilted English like a *bon sauvage*.)

"Well, I should not linger longer. I must to home. Of course, I *vouchsafe* you my trust, I'll reveal this to no man, mark my words...oh, by the way, I would like to *bestow* you with a three-year varmint control contract. Would you do me the honor to *adorn* this contract with your signature before I part? There is nothing *untoward* therein. Mere words with the force of law.

"*Vouchsafe? Bestow? Adorn? Untoward?*"

"Please sign at the bottom." As if on cue, across the moss green carpeting like gray dust balls in a hurry, three mice skitter. Pembrook looks to see if Whisperer is alarmed, but only sees a catlike grin.

"By the way, could you use my trap? I'd be happy for you to take it off my hands. I'm sure a man with varmint control endeavors could use a new trap."

"Thank you," Whisperer says, "I'm unable to contain my joy. Oh, and by the way, you need to lose the coat, otherwise, your story, *perforce,* might be fathomed as a fable. I would be most happy to relieve you of the coat."

Whisperer loads the trap into the back of his old blue pickup and drives off searching for the nearest place to stop, because he's laughing too hard to stay on the road. He plans to give the coyote fur coat to his girlfriend for Christmas. The interest of Pembrook's father did not result in breeding a genius. Pembrook watches Whisperer drive away from CLINGSTONE with the cage bouncing in the bed of his truck. He stumbles into his house and falls into a tweedy tailored heap on his chaise lounge, his ego shredded like wet grass cut with a dull blade.

Pembrook sniffles in the dark for the loss of a better life he has no clue how to live. "I've done nothing wrong, but nothing right," he says out loud. His mind goes white, and he passes out. He regains consciousness, then falls asleep like a troubled guest in his own house.

When he wakes, he changes into his dark-blue silk dressing gown, and in his monogrammed black slippers, wanders slowly from room to room of his house, still heavy with fatigue, a pursuit that belongs neither to the day nor to the night, halfway between a world of action and a world of rest, like his entire life. The house lays out before him like a body of memories with its ribs, knees, arms, and shoulders, a series of rooms in each of which he had one time napped or played as a child. He takes vague comfort from its solid structure, his one assured abode in the world. In each successive room, gusts of memories sweep his mind—better memories of his childhood when he played in earshot of his parents, could hear the chatter of squirrels and the twitter of birds in the yard, and see the qualities of daylight through the window change as the day progressed.

"I have everything I need, but I'm not as happy as when I was as a child. Life is so short, and forgetting so long."

Each room a dark cavity, lit only by the sky glow. He's feeling too low to play the piano or practice his accordion. He ponders if somehow his existence is someone else's cosmic doodle, rather than his own cloudy fiction of the way he animates himself. In his mid-forties, there is no arena where he presides over his own destiny.

*If I were my father, I would disown me. My whole life has been a personal assault on the free enterprise system. I must be a couple of DNA off from my illustrious ancestors.* Time after time, life has the upper hand, and things don't turn out as he expects. He keeps setting traps for himself. His house has no clues for his future, only hints of the past.

In his dressing gown and slippers, Pembrook walks out to his porch, no friend in sight, and looks west beyond the mold-covered nymph statues in his yard, to watch the November sun sink into Lake Michigan. The sun drops fast, like a red rock falling into a black crater, a sacrifice so a new day can begin. Twilight erases the statues. As Pembrook recedes into his house, a late-season black fly is tapping, faintly tapping, at his screen door. Before the door shuts, the fly buzzes inside to keep Pembrook company, along with the mice and pigeons that Whisperer has embedded throughout the premises, who if Whisperer can manage it, will live there happily, forevermore.

# *14*

# MAKING MUSIC TOGETHER

*L*IZA NEEDS SHELTER. Early December alternates between freezing rain or snow, and occasional cold sunny days when the absence of clouds bare the landscape to a bone-chilling cold. Liza survives from day to day on ramen noodles, still living in her car. She plods through the snow along the Bear River on a bright sunny day trying to stay warm. A bluebird falls dead to the ground in front of her, like a fragment fallen from the sky. She feels sorry for the fallen bird, picks it up and gently places it in her coat pocket. If she finds a patch of unfrozen ground somewhere, she can give the poor bird a proper burial,

*It's hard to live outside. I'm running out of cash. My feet are cold ALL THE TIME. I'm hungry ALL THE TIME. I WANT TO BE INDOORS WITH A FURNACE OR A FIREPLACE OR BOTH! I wish spring would come, an early warm spring. I feel like I'm shrinking inside these layers of clothes. I wish I could bring back my old job. I've forgotten how to think. Even my brain feels numb. If my parents were alive, I would go home. Aunt Hertz might offer to take me in, but I know she doesn't want me*

*So um I need to do something for Mr. Z—something to cheer him up. Something to cheer me up, and to make us both smile. Mr. Z. He's my only salvation! What if I get The Lawnmower Club members together? Maybe we can think of something?*

Liza calls Custer, Finnegan, and Pembrook to arrange a meeting at the Roast 'n Toast in downtown Petoskey. She explains her relationship to Zitzelberger as someone he tried to kill, but now sort of likes. Everyone but Liza orders coffee and bagels.

"Here's what I'm thinking, boys," she says. "Zitzelberger misses The Lawnmower Club. He feels trapped in Mallard Pond."

"What does he miss about the club, *whateveryournameis?*" Custer asks.

"My name is Liza, Liza Fitting, and he says he misses the sounds of the engines, the smell of cut grass, engine oil and gasoline," says Liza. "He doesn't say much about missing you guys, but I'm sure he does."

"I know what, oh my yes, this is a good idea, even if I think so myself," says Pembrook. "We need to create an audio recording from the cart shed, and give him something to hold over his nose while he's listening—like an oily shop rag that smells of gas fumes and grass clippings. If he succumbs from the fumes, at least he'll die happy, *ha, ha, ha.*"

"We could get together, and run our engines, one at a time, maybe on a harmonic scale—something symphonic

*The Lawnmower Club*

with razzle-dazzle rolled in," says Finnegan. "There could be a bunch of fun in that!"

"I see this coming together like a classical repertoire," says Pembrook. "Not one engine at a time, except in the beginning, but like 'Bolero' by Ravel, the revving of the engines could be orchestrated to build pace and intensity, and celebrate the mechanical nature of a Spanish folk dance. We could include the shouts and cheers of The Lawnmower Club members in the background, like peasants in a field."

"Are you mad?" says Custer.

"Yes, of course, I'm mad," says Pembrook, "and the idea's mad, so we'll have to play it fast like Toscanini did...fast...so it's over before it can be criticized."

"I know 'Bolero,'" says Liza. "I'm studying Spanish folk dance with Christine, my flamenco dance instructor. We need to match the lawnmower engines to piccolos, flutes, oboes, clarinets, saxophones, horns, and trumpets, then tubas, timpani, and snare drums. Nothing thin and tinny. We can do this—in a crescendo, no more than fifteen minutes."

"We'll need to match the lawnmower idle speeds to rhythm and pitch," says Pembrook. "I'm afraid I can't offer much technical assistance. I listen to music, but mostly by accident, like when I'm searching for pizza in the frozen food aisle."

"I can't help much with the music either," says Custer, "but I can find an old shop rag for him to smell while he listens. By the way, what's with the dead bird?" He looks at a bird foot sticking out of Liza's bulging coat pocket.

"Phew! It stinks," says Pembrook. "Did the bird forget to migrate?"

"The little bird toppled out of a tree, and I didn't want to leave it on the ground," says Liza. "I don't know what to do with a dead bird."

"Well, you can't eat a song bird," says Finnegan.

"Wild is wild," says Custer. "Creatures die and rot outdoors."

"I don't like to think of creatures dying alone in the wild," says Liza.

"This conversation tangles my brain," says Finnegan. "Your crazy idea about the singing lawnmowers seems normal in comparison." He moved his large right hand sideways hoping to make silence and knocks a mug of coffee into Pembrook's lap. Pembrook gets up and hops off to the dry cleaners, but not before a choral unison from the club members, *"LET'S DO IT!"*

Zitzelberger needs to get out of his wheelchair. He feels like a creature confined to a cage in a zoo. The sitting room is entirely too warm for his blood, he breaks out in a cold sweat sitting there, his snow-white flesh piling up like a stack of wet sponges. He's tired of feeling sorry for himself, weary of the endless chat in the sitting room (a front-row seat to a stage show of random memories). He feels thick-bodied and thick-headed from no activity, putrefied and petrified.

## The Lawnmower Club

The sparseness of the outside landscape, the absence of foliage, the naked sky and sun, makes the outside look even more spacious to him, a stark contrast to his interior confinement. He wants to break through the picture window in an act of auto defenestration like Chief Bromden did in the last scene of *One Who Flew Over the Cuckoo Nest*. He wants to see the lawnmowers trawling the fields of The Lawnmower Club again before he dies. He misses the duck pond outside the clubhouse deck, such a contrast to the frog-infested drainage pool outside Mallard Pond. Yes, and he has to admit, he misses the members as well as their machines. Bored, he counts Pal's stools sitting on islands of slush in the yard outside. Pal rummages through the barren exterior of Mallard Pond, sniffing and rolling in his own poo. He stares back at Zitzelberger, as if he has something to say, but can't find the words.

Zitzelberger needs to get moving again, get back to The Lawnmower Club to make everything orderly and shipshape. He's had more than a belly full of Mallard Pond, especially Nurse Hertz, who gleefully records any signs of senility and chronic pain. He looks out the window to see small airplanes hum overhead, trimming the clouds like flying lawnmowers. An eagle swoops in from the big lake with a large fish in its claws. The eagle's freedom of movement, how Zitzelberger longs for it. He's a large stone statue of an unhappy Buddha, with a large domed head, and tubes, like multiple arms, protruding from his tortured torso.

"I think I will die if I stay here much longer," he says to Willie Snowball, his eighty-five-year-old roommate.

"Hey, look on the bright side, you could already be dead," says Snowball. "Waiting to die...there's no harm in that." He places his hand on Zitzelberger's arm *(why do people always want to touch my arm?* he thinks).

"I have more things to do—got a late start. I was the last kid in my neighborhood to get a two-wheel bike, my parents didn't buy a TV before I was in the sixth grade, nothing more than a push mower until junior high school, didn't get laid until I was married, didn't get laid much after I got married."

Nurse Hertz walks into the sitting room and overhears Zitzelberger. "Why don't you write a memoir about your wretched life? You can document how you earned a one-way ticket to Hell!"

"Getting away from you is one big reason I keep clutching to life and returning to The Lawnmower Club."

"You'll need a miracle and lots of physical therapy to make it out of here," she says. Nurse Hertz does an about face, and walks away, flaunting her mobility. Her ass cheeks lag behind her like giant pompoms.

"Well, I don't think you're such a bad person," Snowball says, "and even though you're a bit feeble and flabby right now, you're an attractive man."

## The Lawnmower Club

"Do you happen to be gay?" says Zitzelberger.

"I get that a lot," said Snowball. "The truth is that everyone's born a bit of an invert. I've never come out...had wanted to wait until my parents died, and the rest of my family died...then coming out late didn't make sense."

"When did you know you were gay?" Zitzelberger says.

"Guys attracted me since I was eight. I pretended to be heterosexual. The burden of my name seemed enough to bare. But as I was saying my wedding vows at the altar, the preacher gave me a hard. I went through with the wedding, but from that moment, I knew...so, I hear you lost your wife."

"Yeah, forty-five years with Mona. She was both my wife and business partner. Together we made lots of money. I ran a LEO REPO, a car repo agency. She bought the cars and resold them for profit. MONA LEASE-A-CAR. We did all right, the two of us."

"My wife was an intellectual of sorts," says Snowball.

"Mona was, too, if you mean she read books."

"Well, I'll tell you what," says Snowball, "I'm going to die real soon, but I'd like you to be my friend until I fall through the trap door."

"Never been much for friendship—but I'll try."

# 15

# NOISE LIKE MUSIC

"LET HIM SAVOR SILENCE for the first few minutes," says Liza, "like the cart shed before anyone else arrives in the morning."

The Lawnmower Club members gather in the cart shed to create an audio recording for Zitzelberger. Alberto Albertine, an audio engineer in charge of noise abatement at a wood pallet plant, moonlights as sound master at the local NPR studio. He starts the digital multitrack recorder to the gentle murmurs of morning— birds chirping, drones of distant traffic, the sway of trees in the wind—then Custer coughs, and Finnegan farts. "Cut, cut," says Liza. "Let's back up to before the cough and fart."

"Yes, cut the gas," says Pembrook. "Are you quite done, Finnegan?"

"Not quite...one more, then I'll be good," Finnegan replies.

"No problem," says Alberto. "The farts help me check the acoustics. Sir, did you know you fart in both Middle C and E Flat?"

"I'm told my flatulence has quite a range," says Finnegan.

"You sound like a bad lawnmower muffler," says Custer. "If your furnace goes out, you'll never run out of gas."

"Well, you're laugh-out-loud funny," says Finnegan.

"Lawnmowerians, let's get back on task," says Liza. "Our objective is to stir the soul of Mr. Z, so he does what he needs to do to get out of Mallard Pond and return to this place he loves. We need to deliver the right sounds to the neural action potentials in his brain to motivate him to act." To make matters more difficult, Liza's grass allergy kicks in, and she has a long fit of sneezing. She recovers and restarts the production.

A dozen members, selected in advance for their lawnmower's particular sound qualities, begin to tune their engines. After listening to each machine, Alberto arranges the sequencing to build like "Bolero," and deliver the very best psychoacoustic effects possible from a chorus of lawnmowers. He concentrates his attention like an artist in the throes of creation.

"I need pure engine noise," he says, "no engine knocks. And be sure to check your moving parts clearances. Don't get any loose nuts and bolts into the mix, or any other forms of sympathetic vibration—it'll screw up the pitch, and please, no accidental creaking and clanking. Everyone detach your grass collection bags." He arranges the microphones for the first recording. "Now we want to begin at the lowest levels of audibility. How well does Zitzelberger hear?"

"*Whadidyajussay?*" Finnegan says.

"*I said, how well does Zitzelberger hear?*"

"No one knows, because half the time he doesn't listen to a thing we say," says Custer.

"We'll keep the high frequencies below 16 kilohertz. Let's start with your machine, Mr. Custer." Custer begins with his old six-bladed hand mower, going back and forward before the microphones. It makes a threshing sound like waves running up on the Lake Michigan shore, a perfect beginning. Without thinking, Custer starts singing his lawnmower song, and Liza cuts the action and asks him to stop.

Next, Finnegan presses the electric starter on his four-stroke Tecumseh engine (*kick, kick, sputter, sputter, sputter, sputtering, sputtering*), and then a soft *hmmmm* ensues. He runs the tractor around the interior of the cart shed, so the sound falls then rises as he makes a full turn, *HMMMMM*. Alberto keeps Custer threshing in the background, providing a backdrop to Finnegan's sound production.

Pembrook fires up his Briggs & Stratton: *Gor—illa, Gor—illa, Gor—rilla, rilla, rilla, rilla, rilla.*

The next member over chokes his Kawasaki, because his primer bulb is leaking. There is a fantastic, tympanic backfire: *KABOOM*. When the engine engages, it adds gravitas to the orchestration: *CRACKINABUT, CRACKINABUT, CRACKINABUT.*

The finale adds the big Scag Turf Tiger, the largest tractor in the shed, equipped with a 29 horsepower, fuel-injected Kohler engine: *snap, snap, snap, snap, Vonnegut, Vonnegut, Vonnegut,*

## Randy Evans

*VULVA, VULVA, VULVA, VULVA, BARROOM, BARROOM, BARROOM, BARROOM.*

The result resembles something better than noise, but far from music—a timbre of taps, a din of dings, gourd rattle, a sound like silverware clangs in kitchens, breaking glass, door knocks, knuckle cracks, head scratches, and kettledrum boom.

Before they leave, Custer places a red shop towel drenched in engine oil and gas into a bag along with old grass clippings.

Back in the woods, the nap-ready cougar hears the infernal noise of the lawnmower engines, but on this day, the noise sounds more like music. He relaxes, yawns, and falls asleep. He dreams of pecan-crusted rack of rabbit on a bed of puréed chipmunk, with a side of morels.

The next day, the club members join Liza at Mallard Pond. They gather around Zitzelberger in the sitting room, as Liza places large headphones on his head, and starts the MP3 player. Alberto's craftsmanship is outstanding. He stands with the rest, luminous with satisfaction. Custer hands Zitzelberger the red shop rag to place over his nose. After Zitzelberger hears the piece in full, Alberto plays it again out loud for all to hear. Everyone in the sitting room applauds, including Louise

## The Lawnmower Club

Gnatkozski and Frieda Weatherby. "Reminds me of *Bolero*," Louise Gnatkozski says. Alberto hugs her with gratitude.

Zitzelberger shakes and chokes with emotion. Large tears sally forth from his eyes. He locks the wheelchair wheels, places his firm hands on the chair arms, gets up a head of steam and with enormous effort reaches inertia. He stands for no more than a breath, then settles back into the wheelchair. "If I can do it once, I can do it again!" Zitzelberger says to applause. Nurse Hertz tries to break up the gathering, but no one wants to leave at the moment. Everyone looks for a way to stay, find a topic of conversation. They watch Pal outside the window curled over, taking his morning pretzel-shaped dump. When he sees he has an audience, he pogoes by the windowsills.

"What's a Pit Bull Terrier doing here?" says Pembrook. "Isn't having a *trouble breed* around a nursing home dangerous?"

"He's a good dog," says Liza, trying to be truthful as possible. "But when he's a bad dog, you don't want to be around. Overall, he's a good pooch...he's hardly ever in a foul mood." Pal ducks into the pond to chase two Mallards.

Nurse Hertz overhears, looks at Pembrook cross-eyed, and says, "We euphemistically call him a therapy dog." For no good reason, she turns around and bends way over like she's looking for her toes, flips up her lab coat and shows Pembrook the backside of her new rhinestone-studded blue jeans, as big as the night sky. *She flirted with me*, Pembrook thinks. *And the display of her rhinestone-clad hips was far from subtle, much more than a wink.*

"Will the dog hunt?" says Pembrook. "I've always wanted a hunting dog—not to hunt, but to match my hunting garb. A hunting dog goes very well with Orvis leathers, tweeds, and rugged lace-up boots."

Pembrook looks out through the window at Pal as if he's looking through the showcase in a shopping mall pet store. Pal is mostly white with a brown patch over each eye. He looks through the window *waggling* his tail at Pembrook. "I can see he is a very fine dog. I do hope he's for sale," says Pembrook. "I can give him a *good home*, better than here. I have goldfish, and I can't take *them* for a walk." Pal trots back inside, prances over to Pembrook, and greets him with two muddy paw prints on his chest. Pembrook ruffles Pal's scalp between the ears. Pal wags what he has of a tail—a fake wag like a fake smile.

Pal looks up batting his eyes and barks benignly, *"Arf, arf."*

"See there, he *likes* me. Like me, the dog is heavily muscled, with a barrel chest, rippling shoulders, and hearty haunches. I bet he could chase away robbers, and scare the creatures out of my attic with *one* bark, and perhaps track down wild animals like pumas. And I bet he's a rascally horn dog like me! I could breed him like a race horse."

Pal raises his head again to Pembrook pandering praise, *"Roof, roof."* In his doggy heart,

Pal's a con artist. He begins humping Louise Gnatkozski's leg.

"He must be feeling randy," Pembrook says.

# The Lawnmower Club

After the club members leave, Liza stays behind, and sits with Frieda Weatherby, Willie Snowball, and Zitzelberger. Willie plays his harmonica softly like a distant freight train whistle.

"You don't look too good, Liza," says Frieda. "You look scrawny most of the time, but now you look downright haggard, perilously frail—like a zombie. Where are you living? What are you eating? Have you considered cod liver oil or sipping birch sap?"

"Yes, you need more meat on your bones," says Zitzelberger. This reminds Liza of the same words her father used to say to her.

"We have more than enough to eat here at Mallard Pond," says Snowball. "You can tell by all the damned overflowed toilets. The food's not bad except the lasagna's over baked. It's like forking scabs."

"Since losing my job, I've zombied from one thing to the next. I'm living in my car under the bridge down by river. I've run out of money. I'm living a life so differently than the life I dreamed of living. I'm tired and cold and hungry."

Even though it's warm inside the sitting room, Liza clasps her hand and stomps her feet. She's more cold than hungry, and tired from fretful fitful sleep in her cold car. She looks crestfallen.

"Liza, you have been a boon to me in many ways," says Zitzelberger, "with the liquor and peanuts, the board games that I love to play, and the bazaar but beautiful recording of the lawnmowers. You've saved my life, after I tried to take yours. I want to offer you a job. Would you be my caretaker, not for me, but for The Lawnmower Club? You could move into one of the upstairs bedrooms, and live there. I can arrange to get the water, gas and electric turned back on. Would you do this for me?"

"*OH, MR. ZITZELBERGER, YES, YES, YES!*" Liza replies in a heartbeat. "Even though I almost died the last time I visited The Lawnmower Club, and was bitten by mosquitos the size of hummingbirds, I would be happy to go there and live indoors. *I AM SO GRATEFUL!* I have nearly frozen to death. I'm sure I could live there, and watch over your place...at least until you recover and return...but you should know, I'm not much of a mechanic."

"A woman can fix anything a man can," says Frieda. "But take Pal with you for a guard dog. A guard dog is what he was bred to do. He's not cut out to be a therapy dog."

As if his heart has been somehow softened by the divine intervention of an angel, Zitzelberger takes Liza's tattooed arm in his leathery, paw-like hands, thinking about the night when he tied her to a tree and left her to die from a cougar attack. He fights the shake of emotion moving from his hands to his entire body. He kisses her arm and says, "Forgive me, dear."

Frieda notices Zitzelberger's face soften. She's happy to see this change in her sitting room companion. No one likes to be around a grump! And she knows that all people want to love and be loved.

# The Lawnmower Club

The first big snow storm of the year arrives in mid-December. Large snowflakes blow sideways, and whiteout the land. Lake Michigan roars and howls like a wildcat. After a weather front passes through leaving a load of new snow, the drooping pine branches in the forest throw off snow clumps like white gloves. The forest and fields glow and glitter around the cougar in moon mist, and the constellations of stars shine through breaks in the clouds. The cougar breathes the pure air, then exhales a long sigh. *It's getting dark. Always does at night.*

The cougar treads through the snow in astonishing loneliness. His toe pads imprint teardrop shapes in the snow. Animals should not have to know what it is to be alone, but he knows what alone is. Wolves travel in packs, but mountain lions, even ordinary ones, are solitary creatures. Unlike other animals, he fears moving through the weary world unseen, living and dying without witnesses. The bright eyes of other creatures in the dark offer no solace. Melancholy rules. He feels ice building up like stones in his paws, and his fur cakes with snow.

The cougar hears bells ringing from the Sunday evening service of a distant church. Even though the sound moves from a hill beyond his range, he feels compelled to come closer. The bells keep ringing from the modest steeple. The white paint of the wooden church is peeling and turning gray, but the windows are yellow as butter. The evening service begins with the music of a pump organ. The congregation hymns, "All Creatures of

Our God and King." With a sound like muttering thunder, The Lord's Prayer follows.

Outside the white-framed building, the cougar looks at a small figure in the churchyard. As he moves closer, he sees a young girl dressed in ragged threadbare oversized clothes, and unlaced high-top scuffed brown leather shoes, much too big for her. Wings, too large for her small body, sprout from her sides and flutter like a friendly dog's tail. She's dusted with snow, and sparkles with ice crystals. The cougar is drawn to her, unafraid. He watches her, trying to get wind of her, not sure what manner of being she happens to be.

"Yoo-hoo how nice to see you," she says. She knows the cougar can fathom her words at some level of consciousness. "I'm an angel. In heaven, I'm called *Whatshername,* as I was called on earth. I lived in this area a hundred years ago, the youngest of thirteen children. My parents and older brother and sisters had difficulty remembering my given name, Grace, so they called me *Whatshername*, and it stuck. I died of tuberculosis at the age of three. I am the angel of the forgotten beings who live in this part of northern Michigan. You might wonder what the same God who created the seven bright stars of Orion has to do with counties, but Art, our father in heaven *(hallowbehisname)* uses man-made organizations when it suits his purposes. What Art always says, 'Sometimes you have to play their game.'

"Besides looking after people, my job description includes putting happiness and goodness back into people's lives. I use a white-powdered heart softener (won the God Housekeeping

## The Lawnmower Club

Award last year). I mix a bit with people's laundry detergent, and it works from the outside in, through their clothes and skin. We improvise in heaven. I'm standing outside this church, because I love to hear communion. It won't be for a while, because even though Art (*hallowbehisname*) gives the preacher 10 minutes of good material, he goes on for over 30 minutes." She turns her head towards the church, then back to the cougar.

"I watch over Liza Fitting, Hazzard Pembrook, Rory Finnegan, Harold Custer, Felix Angler, Zach Zuman, the Skunk Whisperer, Pal, the Pit Bull Terrier, Willie Snowball, Frieda Weatherby, Louise Gnatkozski, Hazel Hertz, and many others—and *you*. Very different folks, all of you. But Art in heaven (*hallowbehisname*) doesn't care much about sameness. I know you can't understand all of what I'm saying, but know this—you are loved, and when you die you will go to heaven like everyone else. You will not die alone in the woods and be forgotten forever. God's never forgets his creations."

The congregation engages in more off-key singing. To the cougar, it sounds like *upfromthegravyhearose*. He wants to speak to the angel, but he can only whimper. If he could speak words that the angel would understand, he would ask why he was born with the innards of a human, and the outsides of an animal. He would ask if God has created other half-human creatures like him, and to what purpose? He would ask where he could live in a greater state of peace.

"*Sh-h-h, sh-h-h, shush,* handsome big cat," *Whatshername Angel* says. "You don't need to talk." She continues. "I know your large brain is a burden, and as you become less natural, you are more prone to sin. Art (*hallowbehisname*) forgives you for attacking the dental hygienist in Wisconsin (she's doing fine by the way), and you are forgiven for snacking on defenseless chipmunks. Go and sin no more. You should know that even carrots hurt when they are bitten. Outside of Heaven, all life hurts. But know that you are a special creature. Nowadays, people hardly believe in angels, spirits, prophets, and saints, but even so, it is important for people to know that special beings inhabit the universe. Remember, you will never be abandoned. I'm going to stop now, because I talk too much...if you only knew what the world looks like to an angel."

Then she blesses him with a brush of her wings. To the cougar, her words sound like, "*In the gnome of the Gun, the Farther, and the Holly Host.*" The angel disappears into the moon mist with a kind smile on her face, as "How Great Thou Art," the closing hymn begins. For the first time, the cougar perceives that he has a soul, a weightless essence outside of his body and mind. He exhales promise and hope, like gentle wind in deep forest.

*REW, REW, REW, REW, REWWWWWWW.*

# 16

# WARMING UP

LIZA LEAVES Mallard Pond with light steps on a sparkling sunny day. She's buoyed by the prospects of having found a place to live and work to do. Driving ten miles north out of Petoskey, she sees the edge of The Lawnmower Club coming into view. The buildings are surrounded by enormous blue spruces and one ancient oak tree. Even without its leaves, the tall oak's massive crown, gnarly thick trunk, and heavy limbs cast a great shadow over the clubhouse. What had once been lush and green fairways in the summer appear waspy brown and ashy gray in the bare winter light. She stops the car in the empty parking lot to get her bearings.

The log clubhouse is to her left, and straight ahead, then a sharp turn to the right, a gravel drive leads to the cart shed. She uses the automatic garage door opener Zitzelberger gave her, and pulls her car into the shed. Even though Zitzelberger had to shut down the club in September, it's still full of lawn tractors. She unloads a large black plastic garbage bag of clothes and other personal items from her trunk, then closes the service door and heads for the clubhouse. Bare ground and upturned roots border the clubhouse—Zitzelberger has removed all the shrubs.

Now dark, she nudges the main door open, still ajar from when the cougar entered, and walks straight in and reaches for the lights. "Terrific!" she says, "The light switch works." A large overhead light fixture illuminates the inside entrance area. It's cave cold inside. She searches for the thermostat, and notices how cold permeates the premises. (Zitzelberger told her the location of three thermostats—one for the main dining room, one for the bar and kitchen, and one for the upstairs living area.) As she passes through the entrance hall, she notices old framed photographs from The Lawnmower Club's golf course glory days. In one, she sees what looks like Pembrook as a young boy standing next to his father, dressed in matching golf attire, their legs clad in knickers, each holding a club with the heads resting in the foreground. The restroom doors to the right and left are open and the water in the bowls look like the synthetic blue of antifreeze.

The two-story log house structure of the club house looks fresh-stained on the outside, but it's a terrible mess on the inside. Zitzelberger is not a great housekeeper. Liza sees the same trash the cougar had observed when he entered the clubhouse a few weeks earlier—she corks the whiskey bottle, stuffs assorted trash into plastic bags, piles up lawnmower parts boxes and empty beer cans, to take out to the cart shed. Because there's

## The Lawnmower Club

been no heat, everything looks dried up, even the mold has died back, and some of the wide-planked wooden floors have cracks. She finds the second thermostat in the bar/kitchen area, and hits ON—she hears the distant whirr of a fan. So far, all okay. She sees two mice skitter for cover. "I need a cat," she says. She scrubs the dirty dishes and glasses sitting around the kitchen.

Liza, wearing yoga pants, a sweater, and sneakers, walks around the rest of the interior of the first floor. To her left, a door encloses a modest golf shop. Golf caps with the club logos still hang on the wall, along with faded, mildewed golf shirts, and assorted bags of tees, divot tools, and small tubes of suntan lotion. A cash register sits on the counter with the empty cash drawer open and old score cards strewn across the dusty surface. On the wall by an exit door, there is an empty coin-operated pop machine. She hits the coin return, but it's empty. Other than some display racks, dusty plastic planters, and an untrimmed artificial Christmas tree, there is a locked wooden display cabinet with a set of old-fashioned golf clubs displayed inside, each resting in a marked slot. The slot for the two iron is open. At the base of the cabinet, a silver plate reads: SPAULDING EXECUTIVE SET WITH ALUMINUM SHAFTS, MILHOUSE HAZZARD PEMBROOK, FOUNDER, MASHIE MEADOWS, 1973.

Further in from the main entrance, an L-shaped bar sits in front of a dining area centered on a large stone fireplace. An American flag hangs from a soffit over the barstools and counter. A neon Bud Lite sign flickers against the back wall, and overhead, a single skylight casts a pool of winter sunshine on the floor. Wood is stacked to the side of the fireplace, so Liza decides to build a fire to draft some of the mustiness up the chimney. She crouches down with her head into the fireplace, and opens the flue. Twigs, dead leaves, and a bird's nest fall into her hair and the grate.

Liza carefully removes the remnants of the bird's nest, and starts a fire using bar napkins. She turns on the overhead TV, and the Golf Channel broadcasts from a green, warm country club in California: "What an awesome drive! He's gettin' her done this week. He's reaching greens in regulation better than anybody—if he can only get control of his putter." The clubhouse on the TV looks like a Spanish hacienda with white awnings, white stucco walls, and a poppy-red tiled roof. *Way too fancy for me,* she thinks.

Liza ascends the stairs with her bag of clothes, and finds two bedrooms (one with an unmade bed) on either side of a den, and a bathroom with a large tub and shower. She finds the third thermostat. The den is Zitzelberger's office, and a large oak desk stands centered by the slider facing the fairways and a duck pond. She notices glass rings and cigar burns on the sticky surface, and an old Panasonic Easa-Phone Answering Machine with the call light flashing red. Liza remembers all the messages she had left Zitzelberger during the time she had obsessed about putting him away.

Liza depresses the button for the message tape to hear the "Mission Impossible" theme song playing followed by

## The Lawnmower Club

Zitzelberger's message to callers, "Good morning, afternoon, or evening, caller. I'm either not here or I may be here and choose not to want to answer my phone. Your mission, should you choose to accept it, is to leave your name and number, and then I'll choose if I want to call you back. This message will self-destruct in two-seconds" (a recorded BOOM follows). Next, she presses the call button and listens: "Mr. Zitzelberger, this is Liza Fitting, the social worker—did you see the sticky note I placed on your door? Please call me." There are ten messages, all from her. Not a single message deleted. *Did he delete messages from other people, or were her calls the only ones?*

*The messages sound like I have an empty heart...a small, empty heart.* She plays on.

"Mr. Zitzelberger, I must talk to you about my assessment. One of your neighbors called Social Services to report you. He says you're having difficulties." How overreaching she had been, how disrespectful. "Mr. Zitzelberger, please call me—I have information for you about retirement homes and assisted living." Each recorded call results in an incremental wound, inflicted by her. Her lighthearted demeanor upon first entering the house has changed, and she stands there staring at the answering machine, feeling miserable. "No wonder he tied me to a tree," she says, "I sounded like a cold-hearted bureaucrat." After a drawn out self-accusatory silence, Liza looks for a place to sit down.

Behind the desk, a large, creaky brown leather-upholstered swivel chair rests on its side. The seat is torn open, and the mice have been using the stuffing for building material. Zitzelberger's second-floor outdoor deck, his command post, sits on the other side of the wall from the desk. Liza lifts the desk chair upright, and sinks in. She rewinds the cassette tape and hears her rapid uninflected tone of voice, hearing herself in reverse is worse, because she can listen to the condescension and judgmental tone in her voice. She erases all of her messages. "I wish forgiveness was this easy," she says to herself. "Poor thing...poor Mr. Z."

She feels the second-floor rooms beginning to warm as the furnace kicks in. The pleasing warmth causes her emotions to rise from misery to the lighter mood when she first entered the clubhouse. She has fresh thoughts of spring and summer, like lazing in a hammock sipping ice tea. She has never had time to lay in the sun, she muses, never had a tan line, has always lived on the razor edge of survival. The clubhouse is hardly a home (there are exit signs over the doors), but it's not a bad shelter, better than living in her car. She returns downstairs, and reclines on a corduroy sofa that leaves wrinkles on her face.

When she wakes, Liza senses a surge of energy, purpose, and optimism, like she has been plugged into some power. She stands up She flutters up on her toes, then stutter steps sideways away from the desk before dipping and lunging across the room, dodging furniture like an athlete. She theatricalizes her voice, and says, *"Oh woe is me! I'm such a strange creature—miserable one minute and happy the next. I swing from one extreme to the other, like a pendulum."*

## The Lawnmower Club

She rants and screams until perspiration runs down her face and arms and legs.

Since her passing, Liza has often thought about her mother, her injunctions to Liza from childhood. Elevated to saint status, she has refused to see her as she had been—an ordinary human being. "You mustn't ever make a scene," her mother used to say. Well, she's making a scene now, but a safe, private one, where she can't be embarrassed. She feels like an actor in a movie, exaggerating her voice and body movement. She goes on for a long time. Finally exhausted, she says to the room, "How did I do?" She reflects on her high need for praise and success. "What should I do now?" she says. "I know—take a bath!"

She draws a tubful of hot bathwater, scrounges in her plastic bag for bath bubbles to add, then sinks her food-starved body down into the sudsy, soothing water. Her body opens like a flower, and steam rises like fog around her face.

Liza runs a soapy washcloth over her skin, and observes how much better she looks without clothes. "My clothes never fit!" She has never been a great dresser. She wears loose-fitting consignment shop hand-me-downs, and doesn't know how to put outfits together. She has never had an older sister to help, and her mother dressed her in hippie clothes—tie-dyed tees, cutoff jeans, with flowers stitched over the holes, and flip flops. "I have a beautiful body!" she says. "Someday, I will show my body to a handsome boy like Zach, and he'll adore every inch of me, and say wow you are beautiful, Liza!"

*Randy Evans*

She listens to the wind whooshing through the fields outside, whistling through the giant oak tree, and thanks her lucky stars that she's inside under a sturdy metal roof, immersed in pleasingly warm water. After her bath, she finds one of Zitzelberger's Carhartt work shirts in the closet, and pulls it on for pajamas. Resting upright on a shelf inside the closet, she sees a framed photograph of Zitzelberger's deceased wife. The couple look happy, standing arm-in-arm by a tour boat like they're on vacation somewhere warm. Looking down at the closet floor, Zitzelberger's shotgun lays disassembled on the floor, the wood stock and blue steel barrel, along with a pile of shells. In two pieces, the shotgun doesn't look scary like it did the night he caught her behind the clubhouse. She wonders why the gun parts and ammunition are scattered on the floor.

Liza retreats to the bedroom. She reflects on all that's happened. She misses her chaotic, thankless job, but she has no choice in the matter. She begrudges her situation to no one, but feels uneasy, like she did when she was a little girl stretching her arms out between the rungs of the monkey bars, between holding on and letting go, when one arm reaches into the vacant air before grasping the next bar. She stares at a dried-up blueberry and the crumb of a muffin on the floor.

For now, she's happy to have found a place to sleep, and doesn't mind the mildewed pillows, wrinkled sheets, and rumpled old blankets. She layers the sheets and blankets, climbs into the center of the bed, and lets her head sink into the pathetic little pillow. She feels snug and warm and dry and safe.

## The Lawnmower Club

She likes the way her body smells from Zitzelberger's masculine bar soap. The bath and the weary weeks living in the car knock her into deep sleep almost immediately. She doesn't wake until midmorning the next day. She wakes assured that she's in a safe place.

In the morning, Liza finds a can of Chef Boyardee cheese ravioli in a cupboard, a can opener and silverware in the kitchen. She dumps the ravioli into a pot on the gas stove, and heats it up for breakfast. She's so hungry, nothing could have tasted better, but she makes a grocery list while she eats. She ponders taking the car and driving to the store, but she doesn't feel like leaving her new nest. She finds a tin of stale coffee and a stack of dusty filters. In a dented aluminum percolator, she makes a pot of strong coffee.

Liza returns upstairs and sinks into Zitzelberger's big easy chair. She sips the strong, black coffee from a chipped John Deere mug inscribed RUNS LIKE A DEER. The gratitude she felt the night before still remains, all the anxieties have been frozen out of her during her weeks living in her car. And for the first time in weeks, she feels rested. *I could live like this for a long time, at least until I think of what to do next. I could fritter some time away doing no more than taking care of what Mr. Z wants me to do.* She looks out through the large windows, and tries to imagine how the fairways would look in the spring and summer. She hears the reassuring click of the furnace cycling on.

Liza's curious about the drawers in the big desk, and after overcoming guilty thoughts, she opens the center drawer. Inside she finds a single-lined pad of yellowed paper with one spidery handwritten sentence: THE LOSS OF A LAWN, LODGES INSIDE A GRASS CUTTER FOREVER. She notices what look like tear stains on the paper.

*This must be Mr. Z's one simple statement to the world.*

She walks downstairs and feels a draft from the front door that doesn't want to close. She grabs one of the up-side-down chairs from a table in the dining room and lays it sideways against the door to stop the draft, and to keep it from clacking against the jamb. She adds cleaning supplies to her grocery list, but stays indoors the entire day, feeling pampered and secure.

She discovers detergent, and a working washer and dryer in a back alcove, so with the sound of water rattling in the pipes, she launders her clothes, and the sheets, pillow cases, and blankets from the bedroom. Liza reads a cozy mystery for the rest of the day, and takes another bath. She sleeps deeply for a second night, and wakes with no remembrance of dreams. Rubbing her eyes, she reminds herself how she got to this grand place.

The morning of the second day, Liza goes to the grocery store, and when she returns, starts cleaning the clubhouse from top to bottom, dusting first. "What a mess!" she says. She wants the floors clean enough to walk on in her bare feet. She pulls on the knee pads she bought in town, and gets down on all fours, and scrubs the floors until they glisten, moving like a woman with a purpose. As she works her way across the floors, she's surprised to discover large, muddy paw prints. "Wow, what big paws you have, creature! They look big as oven mitts!" She has no idea what sort of animal has visited the clubhouse, but she vows to fix the latch on the front door.

Liza walks out to the trash bin, and remembers how Zitzelberger held her there by gunpoint, and led her to the tree where he tied her and cut her arm and left her to die. Such a long time ago. She breathes in the cold northern forest air. She forgives him again, and forgives herself.

When Liza finishes her work for the day, she decides to visit Mallard Pond to report her progress to Mr. Z. She stops at the liquor store and picks up some more whiskey and peanuts. Zitzelberger wears street clothes rather than pajamas, and he's clean-shaven. He sips his Manhattan, and asks meticulous questions that Liza can't answer—the status of the buildings and equipment, service dates on his maintenance tags, meter readings, the temperature of the cart shed—not a single question about housekeeping. He appears undisturbed by her inability to answer his questions.

"Do you like the clubhouse?" Zitzelberger asks.

"Yes, it's warm and cozy. And I feel peaceful there, and I don't worry about anything at all."

"Why, of course. Most of the time, I felt the same way when I lived there. You look healthy today, bright and rosy like a flower. Before, you looked like you needed to see a doctor."

Liza changes the subject. "I listened to my messages on your answering machine, and I hated myself when I heard them," she says.

"I saved your messages, because your concern moved me, even though you were trying to do me wrong. But I replayed the messages over and over, because I didn't understand exactly what you were talking about...and once I almost called you one night."

A loud silence follows.

"Mr. Z were you thinking about doing something terrible?"

"What if I did? Let's talk about something else. If you press me, I'll tell you a good lie...but I don't want to lie today."

"But please, tell me what you were going to call me about."

"Have you ever tried to start a lawnmower with an old spark plug? You know, when you keep trying to turn over the engine and nothing happens? And so you give the engine a rest, and when you try again, the engine starts. That's what happened to me one night in the club house. I felt like giving up, put I hit the ignition one more time, and a spark jumped the gap to ignite the old combustion chamber. So since that night, that's what I've been doing. I keep crossing the gap, one day at a time."

"Like lightning?" Liza says.

"Like a slow bolt of lightning."

"I don't know much about spark plugs," says Liza, "but I understand what you mean."

"Talking about these things gives me a headache," says Zitzelberger.

"It's the same with me. It's hard to bring up difficult subjects."

"Let's walk down the hallway and back. We have to visit more often."

Before Liza leaves, she pecks Zitzelberger on the forehead, while a smiling Frieda Weatherby eavesdrops.

Liza returns to the clubhouse, and falls into another deep slumber. During the night, the *Whatshername Angel* enters the clubhouse, climbs the stairs, and tiptoes to the bed. She blesses Liza with a touch to her forehead, and murmurs unearthly words into her ears. Shortly afterwards, she disappears into the moonlit landscape.

The third day in the clubhouse, a cold front moves in. The temperature drops twenty degrees, and snow clouds dump a heavy blanket of snow over the fields. Even as wind and snow blow hard against the clubhouse, Liza continues to sleep deeply and well. Morning comes like a miracle. She decides to turn up the heat, and once again, swan around the clubhouse, but this time naked. She celebrates liberation from a lifetime of doing what she thinks people want her to do. She floats through the clean clubhouse barefooted like a spirit, ready for anything, ready to redirect her life. She's a capable and intelligent woman, amazed at what life can supply, and pleased to be in a private place so warm she can walk around all day with nothing on.

*Randy Evans*

The cougar wanders his solitary way through the dark night in the direction of The Lawnmower Club. The whirling snow sifts over the fields and forests. He remains enthralled by his encounter with *Whatshername Angel*. He sees a white light in the clubhouse, like a sentinel in the storm. He hasn't been inside the clubhouse since the day he looked outside through the window to see Pembrook, clad in his coyote fur coat, peering in. The cougar approaches slowly.

# 17

# THE BOOKCASE

ZITZELBERGER WANTS TO RETURN TO THE LAWNMOWER CLUB. With hard-earned new strength and mobility, he's feeling ready to get back the life he had created before the cougar attack. He works with two young physical therapists, Eustace Crutch and Sara Bellum. He doesn't care much for Eustace, but Sara's okay because she keeps encouraging him, one step at a time. The physical therapy begins to show limited results, and he wobbles around the sitting room at Mallard Pond, yanking his walker forward while shuffling his legs, and taking occasional steps.

He pretends his walker is a lawnmower, and the women are shrubs. "My legs are rubbery," he says. "But I get stronger every day. I know I can do this." He makes loops around the sitting room, while Willie Snowball and the women watch, and politely comment on his progress in soft voices, Willie reading quietly, the women inhabiting the room away from the windows, clumped together like hibernating bears.

*Randy Evans*

Louise Gnatkozski hears Zitzelberger sputtering to himself about his condition. "Eustace says it's useless to work on walking," she says, "and she should know. You don't need no legs if you have arms. Look at me. I can hardly walk myself, but I don't need no legs to play the piano. I never use the foot pedals." Zitzelberger imagines Mrs. Gnatkozski playing the piano with her legs.

"That's Eustace," he says. "Most things are useless to Eustace."

"Well, don't believe her," says Frieda Weatherby. "You need to have faith."

"Faith in what? I've spent my entire life keeping my feet on the ground, in touch with the real world. Do you really believe life is more than that?"

"Yes, I do, and I wish you did too." She places her hand on Zitzelberger's arm. "Mystery and magic and a belief in life beyond this one lightens the burdens of living."

"You mean belief in things like Harry Potter's magical creatures, and God's heavenly hosts? It's so hard to make sense of what you can't see."

"You have to begin by looking at the stars with wonder in your heart. For one who mows lawns, it must be hard to take your eyes off the ground."

"Well, you have to keep a straight line with the right amount of overlap."

"I don't think you're getting my point."

## The Lawnmower Club

"I have always trusted what's in front of me. I don't want to argue about this. I've never stood up for my lack of belief, but I don't believe in flying angels, mythical animals, or an afterlife that I can't be checked out in advance. I know I could be a better man, but I have no one to help me with that. I'm on my own, and I don't want to be bossed around about it. I don't want to be bossed around by God or anyone else. If believing in things you can't see helps you get through life, good for you. Not for me."

"I know you'll sort things out, Leo. You don't give yourself half the credit you deserve. But I hate to see you return to your club where you live alone. It can't that great without people around who love you."

They break off conversation, and look out the window. Frieda looks up at the blue sky above a ridge of swaying trees growing crookedly out of high rocks. Zitzelberger spots Pal roaming towards the dumpster, his nose pulsing like a beating heart. If Pal had the capacity, he might agree with Zitzelberger. *EAT, SLEEP, SHIT.* What more can life supply?

"These books are all trash," says Zitzelberger. He wobbles around the perimeter of the sitting room in the late afternoon, looking for books on the floor-to-ceiling shelves. He sees romances with neon dust covers. He pads around, curious to find something new in the sitting room. Regardless of what Mrs. Gnatkozski thinks, the physical therapy has helped. Every day, he exercises, and slowly begins to feel semi-normal, ready to leave Mallard Pond, so he can return to The Lawnmower Club before spring mowing.

After dinner, he returns to his room, hoping to have a good night's sleep after his exercise. Snowball's sitting in his chair like a limp pillow.

"I'm dying," Snowball says, looking out the window, speaking with a permanent sadness.

"Well, we're all going to die, aren't we? Why do you think you're dying now?"

"I have this feeling rising in my guts," says Snowball. He totters over to his bed, and lays down face up with his hands folded over his chest in a coffin pose.

"Do you need anything?" says Zitzelberger. "Something I can do?"

"No, but I'd like you to take this damned gold watch they gave me when I retired. Didn't get much of a pension after 40 years, but I got this damned watch. I have no family left, and I want to pass it on to someone...no one in particular, but since you're here, you might as well have it. If you don't want the watch, give it to Nurse Hertz, and tell her to stick it up her fat ass."

"Well, thank you for the watch, but I'm still puzzled—how do you know you're going to die?"

"Because I know." He lifts up a heavy album and opens it for Zitzelberger. "See this? Pictures of my relatives. Don't they all look healthy, even though they're all dead? No...tomorrow I

## *The Lawnmower Club*

will be gone beyond the stars and the old moon...you'll see. I've lived long enough. I'm pooped."

The conversation with Snowball disturbs Zitzelberger. He can't sleep, so he shuffles into the empty sitting room after midnight. The golden glow of one dim lamp gives the room an eeriness not present during the day when the light is emergency-room bright. In the background, he hears the beeps of monitoring machines. He decides to try again to find a suitable book to read.

At the end of wall of bookshelves, there is a row of worn hard bound books with bookmarked pages, and broken bindings covered in dust... The sun-faded books look unmoved, perhaps untouched for years. Zitzelberger remembers Frieda had told him about a rabbi from Chicago who lived at Mallard Pond a few years before his death. *Must be the rabbi's books.* He reads the titles: *The Torah: A Modern Commentary, The Gates of Prayer, Legends of the Jews, The Tanakh, The Collected Stories of Isaac Bashevis Singer, God in Search of Man: A Philosophy of Judaism, and Trends in Jewish Mysticism.*

On pickup duty for Snowball, *Whatshername Angel* stands nearby. She's wearing black jeans, ankle boots, and a red TIME'S UP tee. Unlike the cougar, Zitzelberger cannot see her—his consciousness is too narrow to see spiritual beings in the real world. She guides Zitzelberger's selection to one book from the collection. He steadies one hand on the walker, and pulls *God in Search of Man* from the shelf. He blows the heavy dust of the cover. He opens the book to page 315 under the guidance of the Angel, and reads a passage: *"The music in a score is open only to him who has music in his soul. It is not enough to play the notes, one must be what one plays...the holiness of the mitzvah is open to him who knows how to discover the holiness in his own soul...in order to partake we must learn how to bestow."*

He turns the page, and reads, *"Man cannot live without acts of exaltation, without moments of trembling and revering, without being transported by grandeur. When superimposed as a yoke, as a dogma, as a fear, religion tends to violate rather than nurture the spirit of man. Religion must be an altar upon which the fire of the soul may be kindled in holiness."* There is a handwritten note in the margin by the second passage: "Send Sara a birthday card, buy new dust bag for sweeper, dog needs her shots." (The rabbi used the margins of his philosophy book as a scratch pad.)

The passage makes sense to Zitzelberger, not on his own, but with the inspiration of the Angel, the words play on him like sunbeams on the surface of water. He has always been around religion, attending Lutheran Services with his parents on holidays, going to Baptist Vacation Bible School as a child, attending weddings and funerals, all entirely harmless, little wine cups, stale bread, word games, and bad music. Untouched by any form of transcendence. Governed by extreme skepticism. He reaches up to the shelf again, and pulls down *Major Trends in Jewish Mysticism* by Gershom Scholem. There is another handwritten note inside the front cover in the same handwriting as

## The Lawnmower Club

the other book: "This is one of the most difficult books I've ever read. I would not wish reading this book on my worst enemy. Reading this book was like having the flu."

Even so, Zitzelberger cracks open the book to page 280: *"...there is no sphere of existence including organic and inorganic nature, that is not full of holy sparks."* For Zitzelberger, the idea of a holy spark within him strikes a flicker of hope. Could he be a spark along with other sparks of souls, dispersed throughout the world—like sand like seeds like stars? Zitzelberger feels uplifted by the idea of sparks connecting one being to the next and all beings to the Divine across the universe. *Humans are sparks of divine light. So there is a part of me that belongs to others. The soul in me is one part of a larger undivided soul. Like spark plugs, Snowball and I can connect.*

Zitzelberger stays in the sitting room until the feeble light of dawn arrives. For the first time in his life, he counts his blessings all the way to 100. He resolves to no longer drag-ass his past around like a rear double-bagger lawn tractor with its front wheels in the air. Like a spark plug, he resolves to cross the spark gap to others by leading a better life, one filled with acts of kindness, lived in harmony with others. *Whatshername Angel* has heightened Zitzelberger's awareness. He wakes up from a life-long spiritual sleep,

When he returns to his room, he finds Willy Snowball's body stretched out like a plank. A morning shadow covers his body. Willie has packed most of his possessions in an old suitcase, but the suitcase is open. He's folded and stacked his pajamas and robe on a chair beside his bed like he had planned a long trip, but left everything behind. He notices how Snowball has removed the bookmark from the novel he had been reading all week. His head rests on his pillow. Zitzelberger closes Snowball's empty eyes, and untangles a twist in his hair. He places his hand on the top of Snowball's head, soft-hard, like a volleyball.

Zitzelberger feels a new kind of loneliness sitting in the room with a dead man.

At The Lawnmower Club, he had never quite learned how to live alone, but this feels different. The prospect of Snowball's vacant bed bothers him. It will need to be changed or removed or disposed of in some way, it no longer serves a purpose. Or will he get another roommate? Are there other men on the waiting list for Mallard Pond? What will happen to Snowball? Have his divine sparks, set adrift in the cosmos, been gathered by a divine presence, or has Snowball fallen through what he had called a trap door into nonexistence, into a long dark sleep of nothingness or into a fiery pit like a snowball in hell?

Zitzelberger looks out the single window of his room with a fixed stare. He opens the window for fresh, cold air, and hears the birch and popple trees creak and squeak on the ridge above Mallard Pond. The sky whitens into another day, like it usually does.

# 18

# THE WOLF MOON

*A*LONE WOLF HOWLS at the wolf moon. After a front moves in with branch-breaking winds, a January thaw turns the northern Michigan landscape to slush. Morning brings splotches of sunlight through thick humpy low clouds, and the loud cries of birds. A flow of fur and flesh, the cougar sifts slivers of sunlight through his fur as he climbs the clubhouse steps. He noses through the unlatched door, and smells the scent of Liza, her morning coffee, laundry detergent, and mouse nests. Liza on a bath towel in Zitzelberger's desk chair with nothing on nor on her mind. She looks out on the partly sunny morning landscape of The Lawnmower Club. Two gulls stretch out in flight, etching the gray clouds with brushstrokes of white.

The cougar ascends the staircase, and enters the room where Liza sits with her back to him. She hears the cougar's faint footsteps, and slowly swivels around. Liza recognizes the cougar from the night he approached her when she was tied to the tree by Zitzelberger, when he passed her by to follow Zitzelberger and break his neck. She's not afraid, but decides to pull on some clothes in case she has to make a run for it. *The cougar is my protector, my spirit animal sent by some mysterious force...or maybe not,* she thinks. The shiny wet coat of the cougar glistens in the mottled sunlight filtering in from the windows.

"Hi big kitty!" she says. Liza approaches the cougar. She rubs his ears. "Your ears are cold! It's a bit cold out there isn't it? Why don't I build a fire, and you can lay down and take a little nap while I find something for you to eat?" She notices the cougar has tracked in mud on her clean floors, so she goes into the kitchen, wets a towel with warm water, and carefully washes each of the cougar's paws, then dries them with her bath towel. The cougar lets Liza touch him without fear. Liza hasn't talked to anyone in days, so it's great having someone around. She gives him a shallow bowl of milk. The cougar sees a passing mouse, and snatches a snack. He crawls over to the hearth, drops down on the hard stone, and falls asleep, purring like a kitten.

Liza has never had a pet, but loves animals. She doesn't know what to do with a mountain lion. Will the wild thing turn on her out of some predatory instinct? Will he return to the woods after eating? While the cougar sleeps, she leans over close to examine the magnificent animal in detail. He opens his keen, intelligent eyes, his pupils restricted to a tiny circle—the iris of a wild beast not tamed to focus down to meet the human eye. For a moment, the cougar and Liza look at the other like each is a miracle of life.

The cougar places one of its front paws on her arm, and rests it there. Liza removes her arm and reaches for the cougar's head. She laughs as they wrestle on the floor like two animals. The cougar plays gently. After a time, Liza lays on her back by fire, and the cougar rests his head on her stomach. Over the coming days, they take long walks together ranging through the forests and streams. Liza sees the world through the eyes of the cougar, the cougar experiences the pleasing life of an indoor cat who knows the outdoors, put prefers the comforts of shelter.

Pembrook wakes up in the middle of the night to the howl of a wolf. Every noise startles him. Even though his heart is healthy, he lives in a state of perpetual heart failure. His feet are cold. His whole body is cold. He misses the warm body of his ex-wife, especially in a cold winter bed. Pembrook cannot fathom why, if she wanted a more exciting life, she ran away with a cold-blooded actuary. What more could they have in common other than simple arithmetic?

*Life is unpredictable*, he thinks, *in all probability, at this very moment, she now warms the cold-blooded body of that actuary? Perhaps I need a pet, for example, a dog—yes, a warm-blooded dog might do. Could I stand to have an animal sleep in my bed? Would a dog snag my high thread count sheets or expensive silk pajamas?*

## Randy Evans

*Give me pet allergies or some kind of dog flu? What breed would be best for a person of my stature and class? Perhaps one of those imperial lion-dogs who sat at the feet of the ancient Chinese emperors... were they called shitzies?*

The next morning, Pembrook returns to Mallard Pond, and talks with Nurse Hertz about buying Pal. "He's an attractive and feisty little beast," she says. In truth, Nurse Hertz would love to get rid of Pal, who is always creating havoc in the patient rooms by tearing down the shower curtains. And besides, the relatives of patients complain about having a pit bull as a therapy dog. They show her news clips of family bit bulls, with no history of violence, suddenly eating children without provocation.

"I would like to purchase the dog," says Pembrook. "I know he's not worth much without a good family background, but I'd be happy to pay *something* for him. You can look upon it as a donation to help with the marvelous work you do here." Pembrook holds the false belief that he's a shrewd negotiator, always self-assured that he has the upper hand in any negotiation.

"Oh, Pal, is a very special dog—a key to the morale of the place," says Nurse Hertz. "Well-bred, he comes from a long line of champion therapy dogs, you know. He won first place in the nursing home therapy dog competition at the Westminster Dog Show last year. However, we seem to have lost his pedigree papers. I'm sure he has a name longer than Pal, like Prince Pal, the Pooch of Prussia."

## The Lawnmower Club

"Well, I have quite a family history myself," says Pembrook. "I know something about good breeding, and I see a bit of myself in the dog's good manners, so he must have something going for him. Though I have never hunted, I bet I can train him to hunt."

"A hunting dog with good breeding comes with a price," Nurse Hertz says, looking at Pembrook with one eye half open, like she's sighting down the barrel of a gun.

"I have the financial resources to pay for a well-born dog. I'm sure you won't be asking anything unreasonable. And I must say, these negotiations attract me to you in ways I've never imagined. You are a persuasive woman, in a divine way, pleasant but shrewd, and forgive me for saying so, but your nursing uniform compliments your figure in ways beyond my ability to count...and oh do I love the purple and blue floral pattern." He wonders what he means by these bold words, looks for any effect he may be having on her, but she looks far from friendly.

Nurse Hertz sells Pal to Pembrook for $1,000, along with his dog dish, a water bowl, his favorite shower curtain, and a half sack of kibble. The residents say their good-byes, but no one complains much, because they don't complain about much of anything. Zitzelberger seems to be the only one to care. He will miss Pal's entertaining antics. He makes sure that Pembrook takes Pal's favorite toys to his new home—a stuffed pheasant with a squeaker, and a chewable wine bottle labeled SLOBBERNAY.

"Now you be good to that dog," Zitzelberger says. "And remember, dogs are not people. You need to take care of them like you take care of a lawnmower—have a maintenance schedule, check all their parts once a week, and give them running time, lots of running time."

Pembrook fastens a heavy leash to Pal's collar. "Stop it, Pal. Stop," he says. A louche pooch, Pal licks his balls with the gusto of a tourist sucking an ice cream cone on a hot summer day. He wags his stumpy tail as if he's been praised.

Pembrook pisses Pal off by taking him to the vet for shots. Then he takes Pal to a pet groomer to have a bath and his nails clipped. Pal can't stand the way he smells. Pembrook selects the shampoo, a Melon Ball scent. When Pembrook takes him home and lets him out in the yard, Pal rolls around in a pile of deer poop. Pembrook watches from his porch while reading a pamphlet from the vet titled "Your Guide to Gonadectomy." He reads, "Your dog probably won't even notice his testicles are missing." Pembrook feels happy that he's not a dog, because he would very much miss his own testicles, if they were removed. The very thought of castration gives him a queasy feeling. He reaches down to gently and reassuringly fondle his balls.

Feeling a bit guilty about what he intends to do, Pembrook has a heart-to-heart chat with Pal. "Balls are over-rated, Pal. Ask any woman. Do you know what a mess you could get yourself into with unwanted litters? And it says in this brochure, that you will be less likely to roam without balls. You can get lost when you roam. It happens to me all the time. And another

## The Lawnmower Club

plus, if you don't have testicles, there is no way you will ever have testicular cancer...at least I don't think so." At some level of animal consciousness, Pal knows that Pembrook must be an idiot.

The next day Pembrook has Pal neutered. Pal misses licking his balls. Pembrook pets Pal while reading another brochure titled "Neutering Aftercare." Then to add more insult to injury, Pembrook takes Pal to a pet store and buys Pal a herringbone dog coat to match Pembrook's Harris Tweeds. "Oh, Pal, you look positively *woofy!*" Pembrook says. Pal rolls on his back, nipping at the coat, but he can't tear it off. Pembrook reads that desexed dogs need fewer calories, so he cuts back on Pal's food. Pal thinks that for the rest of his life he will feel hungry, and that never again, will he get laid.

When Pembrook marches him around town, Pal feels shy around female dogs, and humiliated around male dogs, all razzing him about his missing parts. Food-deprived, chronically depressed, and forever desexed, he decides to focus on non-testosterone-fueled activities like killing Pembrook in his sleep, and planning the perfect escape. He wants his wobbly balls back. He wants to preserve his innate instincts to drive, herd, hunt, guard, and procreate. He hopes that he may someday feel his old attractions. At night, he looks at the moon through Pembrook's window, and longs for Mallard Pond where he ruled over the old people like a Russian oligarch. He misses kind, sweet Liza. Jolted from his reveries by a tug on his collar, Pal sees a woman leading a bitch down the street, walking towards Pembrook and him—a glamorous, leggy Standard

Poodle. The poodle gives Pal that "look away thing" he sees all the time these days.

Zitzelberger presses the red emergency button to alert the nurse's station to Snowball's passing. Nurse Hertz arrives and flips on the light switch, exposing Snowball's melting body to the naked florescent light. She speaks to the other nurses in matter-of-fact language, like this happens every day, as Zitzelberger knows it often does. A doctor arrives to pronounce him dead. Zitzelberger walks his walker down to the sitting room where everyone talks somberly about the news. Mrs. Weatherby does not wear her bright and peaceful demeanor. Zitzelberger approaches her chair and touches her arm, the first time, he has acknowledged her in any human way. Frieda takes his large hand and places it around her small hand. She bends her head, places a handkerchief over her eyes, and becomes a one-woman waterfall. After a few minutes, she looks up to Zitzelberger.

"We will miss Snowball," she says, trying to regain her composure, places her handkerchief back in her pocket. A bible rests face down on her knee. "He was part of our congregation."

"Yes, he was part of this little world we all belong to," says Zitzelberger. His tears never reach the surface.

"Did I hear you right? Leo, you have always acted like a big silo. Are you saying that you feel ties to other people?"

## The Lawnmower Club

"This whole odd living experience has forced me to look inward," he says.

"And what do you see when you look inward?"

"Sparks," he says. "We're all sparks."

Frieda Weatherby takes hold of Zitzelberger's arm, and he doesn't mind anymore. She touches his arm as if her eyes have become her hands, and she runs them over his rough skin like a blind woman who finds a face. "Sometimes you look quite beautiful," she says. "I want you to be here."

"And you, too," he says. "You look beautiful, and I'm happy you're here...it's pleasant to have someone to bicker with." Except for her bright eyes, Frieda's face reminds him of a garden statue he saw once, worked smooth by the sun and wind and rain.

"I promise to bicker with you as much as you like," Frieda says. A quiet joy radiates from her eyes.

A man from the funeral home walks into the sitting room. "Anyone want to see Mr. Snowball before we roll him away?"

"We've *seen him*," *Mrs. Gnatkozski says.*

But almost everyone manages to shuffle out of their rooms and line the hallway as Snowball rolls out to the parking lot. He has a frozen smile on his face.

# 19

# THAT DOG WON'T HUNT

"WHISPERER," THIS IS HAZ PEMBROOK. Saying the word prompts him to whisper as he speaks. "I heard you do dog training as well as pest control."

"Yeah, I also do snowboarding instruction in the winter—we all have to work more than one job around here to make a living. I train bird dogs—start 'em out on pigeons with shock collars. I get the pigeons from the varmint control side of my endeavors."

"You told me once that to get a cougar you need a dog. Well, I have a dog, and this cougar can no longer be protected. He's a known threat. He tried to kill me twice, as you well know. Felix Angler, the Conservation Officer, is aware of the cougar's presence hereabouts. He told me that he saw the cougar up close a few weeks ago, not far from my house. Angler said he would have stayed longer to stalk and capture the animal, but his wife called and told him to pick up dinner...why am I whispering?"

"I can't train a dog to hunt, if he's not bred to hunt...but you say you have a pit bull mix?"

"Yeah, I mean, he looks like a hunter to me. He has a daunting demeanor, if you know what I mean—a strong body and aggressive personality. Maybe he has some coon hound blood in him? They say he was a champion therapy dog, as well."

"I don't know who told you about champion therapy dogs, but that's pure fiction. There's no such thing as therapy dog championships. Did you think to ask if the dog's registered?

"No, but it's for the best," says Pembrook. "The training might have harmed his killer instincts."

"Well, I've heard of pit bulls tracking deer, coon, rabbits, and fox. Never heard of a pit bull cat tracker, but I'll be happy to give it a go...for $45/hour. You'll have to have him stay at my place, so I can train him 24/7. I'll only bill you for the time I'm awake."

"It's a deal!" says Pembrook. "In the meantime, I'll sign up to retake the Hunters Safety Course. I flunked the first time. Can you believe it? I shot the game warden in the foot. You have no idea how painful that looked. Believe me, it was a hard lesson, but I learned what a gun safety's for. You have to keep the safety on until right before you pull the trigger, and while you're doing all that, you also have to aim."

The Whisperer works Pal first on ground game like squirrels and possum, but depressed Pal shows little interest in hunting, and doesn't follow instructions from anyone—not for food or praise or the thrill of the hunt. Not to avoid pinching choke chains, or jolting shock collars. One day, Whisperer gives up when a pigeon attacks Pal, and Pall hunches down in terror. He decides to call Pembrook, because he has run up a $7,500 bill.

"Your dog's a big pussy. Sad to say, he won't ever be a hunting dog. He doesn't bark on the trail, doesn't climb trees, doesn't like to kill. He ran away from a turkey and let a pigeon attack him, and he's gun shy. When I pull the trigger, he heads for the next county. I tried my best, but it's no use. I'll bring him back over to your place along with my invoice. It cost you a lot for no good, but at least you have the satisfaction of knowing the dog won't hunt. Hope you didn't pay too much for the him. Sometimes people take advantage of good-natured people like you."

"Do you think having no balls is a factor?"

"I said you're good-natured, nothing about you balls."

"I mean no balls on the dog. Do you think having a dog missing balls affects his hunting ability?"

"He has no basic hunting instincts. Neutered dogs can be excellent hunters—you can't blame the missing balls. I don't know about the dog's background, but he's a lover not a hater, and as far as running's concerned, he's no greyhound."

"Yes, he must have a seedy background. That would explain a lot. Once your bloodline's *corrupted*, there's no going back."

"Don't feel bad. It's not your fault. And say, when I bring your dog back, I'll check the bait traps in your attic—no charge. There's a great deal of infestation this time of year."

## Randy Evans

Pal is miserable. He's capable of hunting, but doesn't want to—not for Pembrook or the Whisperer or any man. He decides to run away from Pembrook, and take his chances in the wild. He was a local celebrity at Mallard Pond, and never had to do a thing. The old people liked having him around for comfort, companionship, and general entertainment. He was spoiled, but never knew how well he had it, until Pembrook took him away, and tried to make him a clothing accessory and hunting predator. He leaves after dinner one evening—he simply walks through the open cast iron gate surrounding Pembrook's yard, upon which he profusely pees. He runs into a hollow full of dense brush, and succeeds in ripping off his herringbone tweed coat. He hopes to never see Pembrook again. In the dark, he can see Pembrook inside the house practicing his accordion. Pembrook doesn't even know Pal's missing.

Pal picks up Liza's scent and follows his nose to the clubhouse, careful to look both ways before crossing the road. After a rough start, Pal and Liza had left on good terms. Liza was upset when she heard her Aunt Hertz had sold Pal to Pembrook. She had intended to visit Pembrook to check up on Pal, before the cougar arrived. As Pal nears the clubhouse, he picks up the scent of a wild animal. Now he has an approach/avoidance conflict—should he find Liza or flee for his life? He slowly climbs the porch stairs, careful not to scrape the wound where his balls used to hang like badges of courage. He pokes open the front

## The Lawnmower Club

door. He walks in far enough to see a nine-foot long, 200-pound cougar laying in front of the fireplace. The cougar's eyes roll sideways towards Pal, gives him a toothy warning snarl, and tenses his body for action.

Like a giant chipmunk, Pal falls over paralyzed with fear, all four of his stubby legs pointing up in the air, exposing his wound. His heart stops beating for a moment. When he comes back to consciousness, he looks up from Liza's lap. She's stroking his forehead, and talking to him in soft tones. He rolls his head dolefully sideways to see the cougar. He faints again. After a few hours, Liza introduces Pal to the cougar, and by the next morning, it looks as if they might all settle down to a tranquil domestic life in the clubhouse. Unknown to Liza, the cougar takes Pal to the woods the next afternoon, and teaches him to hunt like a wild animal. The cougar demonstrates by pouncing on a chipmunk. *Wiggle, wriggle, chomp, chomp.* Hunting with the cougar enhances Pal's self-esteem, and he misses his balls less. Pal teaches the cougar how to whimper when begging Liza for treats.

Pembrook can't believe his dog has left him. Not even a dog wants to live with him. He calls Officer Angler the next morning to report his missing dog. He says Pal may be a victim, perhaps the cougar has carried him away in the night.

"Am I getting this right?" says Angler. "You're saying that you own a Pit Bull Terrier therapy dog that has been carried away by a cougar?"

"Yes, Officer. I do believe the cougar still roams in this neighborhood, and has perhaps done my dog harm. I would search for the dog myself, but I'm a bit afraid to go outdoors at the moment. Not that I'm a coward, but I must to tell you, I have recurrent nightmares about my body being ripped apart by a gross, green, grinning monster. Mr. Putzkin, my therapist, gets pissed when I bring the subject up. He tells me to cut back on caffeine, schedule massage appointments with his girlfriend, learn to do the tango, and take a fly fishing trip with his guide service. But nothing works...I can tell by my goose bumping skin. Did I say the dog was wearing a herringbone tweed coat?"

Angler has learned to ignore about everything Pembrook says.

"Now as I recall, you have a high privacy fence around your yard. So the cougar leaps over the six-foot high fence, and corners your pit bull terrier. Without a bark, the dog lets the cougar carry it away, leaping back over the fence with the dog in its jaws."

"Do you think that's *possible?*" says Pembrook.

*"You are asking me if that's possible?" says Angler.*

"Well, I do think my gate was open, so the cougar didn't have to leap in and leap out with the dog attached. You see, I was practicing my accordion, so I may not have heard the dog's feeble barks for help. The cougar could have dragged him away

## The Lawnmower Club

by the scruff of his neck, or his herringbone coat, and shook him to death or worse. If he survives, we'll need professional care."

"Professional care?"

"For the dog. Mr. Putzkin, the psychologist, says he does animal therapy on the side."

"Mr. Pembrook, I am so happy that you called the DNR. I intend to file a report immediately. Anyone who sees a mountain lion carrying around a pit bull in a herringbone coat will be urged to call the DNR Office without delay. In the meantime, you should be cautious when going outdoors. And if a wild animal ever happens to get inside your house, lock yourself in the bathroom and let the animal have its way. You don't need to be a hero. Now for my report, does the dog have any distinctive markings?"

"He's mostly white with a brown patch over each eye, he has a scar where his balls used to be, and he's wearing a designer herringbone coat. And he still limps from his operation."

"So you had him neutered, dressed him like a dandy, and he lit out while you were playing the accordion? I can't imagine why I dog would be upset with those conditions."

"I sincerely doubt if the accordion music played a role in his departure. My music has a soothing effect on both people and animals. Back in the day, I used to play the drums, the harmonica, and the accordion all at once...a one-man band."

"Very impressive. What happened to the band, Mr. Pembrook?"

"We broke up...so sad. I developed drummer's leg."

Felix Angler manages to hang up the phone milliseconds before he falls out of his swivel chair, laughing all the way to his lunch hour.

Liza calls Pembrook after several days. "Hello, Mr. Pembrook. Pal is with me at the clubhouse. Guess he ran away from home. Do you want him back? He's doing fine here."

"Oh, oh, I'm so relieved. I'm thrilled he's okay. I was afraid he might be cougar scat by now. Do I want him back? Well, of course, I do...or maybe not. At the end of the day, I don't think Pal liked me. He didn't like me at the beginning or middle of the day either. He never loved me like a best friend, if you know what I mean. Do you have something in mind? Would you like to buy him?"

"Oh, I couldn't afford to buy him, but why don't you let him stay with me over here. Mr. Zitzelberger has hired me to be his caretaker for The Lawnmower Club while he remains at Mallard Pond. I think Pal was meant to be a guard dog more than a therapy dog—he could help me out, and you could visit him whenever you want."

"But I paid your Aunt Hertz $1,000 for that dog."

"Well, maybe Aunt Hertz will give you a refund, but I wouldn't count on it. You can board him here for free, since you're a club member. What do you think?"

## The Lawnmower Club

"Okay, it's a deal! I'll be over to visit...but not soon. I 'm about to leave the country for my annual ski vacation. This is the time of year I begin to feel trapped in between seasons—too many restaurants shut down, and there are so few cars to follow that I get lost. I'll contact you a when I get back in a month. Do you want me to bring over his water and food dish and kibbles?"

"No, you would be surprised at what you might find here. The place is like a three-ring circus. A real zoo. I have to get things better organized."

Pembrook looks in his hallway mirror, and says out loud, "I'm relieved, because I can see it in my face. That dog might have shortened my life from stress alone. I'll have to find other ways to get my exercise."

# 20

# A MOMENTARY HERO

*P*EMBROOK PACKS HIS BAGS for the great ski resorts of the Alps to follow the seasonal travel patterns of his fine-feathered forefathers. He's happy to leave town. Not much has been going well lately. For one thing, he trapped himself twice in his garage in a snare intended for the cougar. Next, the local newspaper featured him as a buffoon for these unfortunate incidents. His foray into pet ownership failed. And worst of all, the cougar remains at large.

Pembrook thought Pal would be a good hunting dog, a dog who would track down the cougar. Now the dog lives with Liza, not him. He still plans to wrest control of The Lawnmower Club from Zitzelberger, and return the club to its former glory as a bastion of upper class civility. But living as he does in a state of perpetual accidents, one unpredictable ambush after another, he finds planning difficult. Perhaps a break will help? He further hopes his house and attic will be free of mice and pigeons when he returns, an extremely dim hope, since the Skunk Whisperer keeps his attic well-stocked with varmints.

For a reasonable weekly caretaker's fee, the Skunk Whisperer offers to watch Pembrook's house in his absence. Pembrook plans to meet him for breakfast to hand over the keys.

He invites Officer Felix Angler to join them, to make sure Angler stays on alert for the cougar in his absence. How wonderful it would be to return from his ski vacation to find the cougar captured or killed!

Across the road from a boat ramp on Crooked Lake, Angler, Pembrook, and the Whisperer meet at a breakfast and lunch place loved by locals. The cooking and eating take place in one kitchen/dining room, filled with men and women hunched over coffee, and talking through a haze and sizzle of eggs, bacon, sausage, and fried potatoes, hissing and steaming on the grill. Large windows open to the lake, a panorama of boating activity in the summer, and ice fishing in the winter.

The January thaw ends, and the bitter weather crawls on. Outside the restaurant, the sky and lake look icy and austere, gray and white, under a high dome of clouds. The trees overhanging the lake edges stand brittle, threatening to break in the lightest of winds. The air smells like ice. Lake Michigan's Little Traverse Bay hasn't frozen over yet, but the inland lakes have two to four inches of ice. The newscasts warn people to stay off the lakes. Even with the marginal conditions and warnings, ice shanties dot the lake like hunting blinds in November fields.

"Oh there you are, Officer Angler! So good to see you! I do hope all is well with your many endeavors. *So-o-o*, been tracking the cougar?"

"Actually, he tracked *me* down, *ha, ha, ha*. I thought he was going to eat me, but he spared my life," Angler says. "I lived to tell about it."

"You're a funny guy, and you look so serious in that uniform. I have to tell you, I was also tracked down by the cougar, and accidently trapped myself for the second time. *Yes, can you believe it? Twice. Ha, ha, ha.* We are both very funny, don't you think? By the way, do you know the Skunk Whisperer?" says Pembrook. "I'm sorry, I don't remember your proper name."

"Zach Zuman," the Skunk Whisperer says.

"Oh yes, you have quite a reputation in the county," says Angler. "Do you know the Better Business Bureau registered some complaints about you a few years ago?" Angler stares at the Skunk Whisperer, expects him to squirm and stammer. Instead, the Whisperer replies placidly, like a saint interrupted in the middle of prayers.

"Oh that, yes. A vast misunderstanding. I went to their offices to clear my good name, and found their offices infested with mice, so many I lost count. I removed the little varmints free of charge. Now the BBB's mouse free, and I'm free of complaints." The Whisperer pauses to wipe a drop of coffee from his chin, and he leans closer to Angler and says quietly, "Let me know if you ever want the DNR offices inspected, Officer Angler. To concentrate on catching those little pests, you need to be focused. No one needs little creepers running up their pant legs."

The tiny restaurant radiates warmth and good will, a shelter from the outside, where it's cold as a witch's elbow (okay, witch's tit). Pembrook faces the back wall, and the other two face the road, with the lake beyond visible through two large picture windows. They look at the daily specials scrawled on a white board. Pembrook thinks he may splurge and order corned beef hash with two soft-poached eggs on home-made rye toast. He looks around for catsup. Whisperer eyes the thick blueberry pancakes, wide as a hubcap, and pan sausage that has just been served to the neighboring table. He looks for the maple syrup—he wants pure Michigan syrup. Angler browses the menu like a deer looking for the acorns. He already knows he wants, in his case, biscuits and gravy with a side of crisp bacon. He grabs a bottle of hot sauce, and relocates it to his side of the table.

Even with his focus on food, whether by nature or training, Angler's eyes scan over the top of his menu. He's always aware of his surroundings, looking for anyone or anything that's out of place, possibly about to cause trouble. He sees who is sitting at the tables and on the counter bar stools in the restaurant, mentally checking for people not from around the area, people possibly on the loose. He looks beyond the inside of the dining room, through the partially steamed-up windows, to the cars and trucks passing by on the road, and beyond the road, to the lake flecked with ice shanties strung out from a distant point of land.

As a reward for his diligence, Angler lays his eyes on trouble.

*"TWO PEOPLE THROUGH THE ICE!"* he shouts, and before he finishes the last word of the sentence, he's out the door, Pembrook and Whisperer trailing behind. Pembrook's amazed at Angler's eyesight. He squints to make out two distant stick figures twitching way out on the lake. He notices how his feet keep slipping on the ice. Why did he not wear boots to breakfast? Why did he leave his gloves and hat in the car? His leather-soled python penny loafers will never be the same. He tries to mimic Angler's lumbering gait, but he only manages to stumble and slide like a child with a new pair of skates. He can't keep up. He keeps belly-flopping on the ice like a fresh-caught perch. He keeps moving forward with mixed thoughts stitching through his excitable brain.

Should I go back to supervise the rescue efforts from the safety of shore, or keep moving on to what could be my demise, a possible drowning by entrapment under the ice and burial at sea?

Whisperer runs to his truck for a safety rope, and follows Angler in the direction of the two figures, at least five hundred yards out in the lake. The victims thrash around in a water hole the size of a backyard inflatable swimming pool. A woman screams.

Angler's a big man, and the first to go in. Even though he's only up to his waist in water, he's having a hard time getting out. Whisperer has given Angler a wide berth, and carries on with the rope, but about one hundred yards farther out, he also goes through the ice, this time over his head. By now two volunteer firefighters arrive, and Pembrook sees them pulling an orange plastic sled out on the ice. Pembrook passes Whisperer and Angler, and grabs the rope like a battle flag, and carries it onward towards the dark silhouettes in water. He keeps looking over his should to see who might be watching.

Pembrook moves closer, sucking in the frigid air, his legs rubbery from fatigue. He had intended to be a bystander or a witness or a spokesperson, but now he's the main character, the last man standing, a reluctant hero. He can see a woman and a small boy. The mother is active, but the son looks blue-faced and quiet, like he's faking death. Pembrook stops walking, crouches down carefully, and lays his belly flat on the ice surface. He begins to crawl towards the open water, careful to keep the rope grasped in his one numb hand.

The ragged surface of the ice scratches and rips at his skin, and he can feel hot blood warm his face. Pembrook no longer thinks Pembrook thoughts at this moment—how he looks to photographers or what he will say if he survives. He struggles in the present moment, his fifteen minutes of fame. He fixes his beady eyes on the two heads in the water. He realizes that no one will come to take over for him— he's the action figure—*I'm carrying on in the great tradition of those intrepid souls who dared all for glory: G.I. Joe, Captain America, the Lone Ranger, Superman,*

## The Lawnmower Club

*Batman, Hulk Hogan, Luke Skywalker, Mr. Rogers, Three Amigos! and others I can't remember.*

Pembrook gets close enough to throw the safety rope. The woman screams at Pembrook like he has caused the whole disaster. He calls for her to secure the loop under her arms and then secure the rope around the boy. She looks exhausted. She says that she plans to sue the lake. Pembrook reaches them, but he hasn't enough strength to do more than hold on. He hears ice cracking and heaving all around him. The woman pulls him towards the open hole. Now the boy looks unconscious for sure.

*"KEEP YOUR HEADS ABOVE THE WATER!"* he shouts. *"TAKE DEEP, SLOW BREATHS!" "GRIP THE EDGE OF THE ICE!" "KICK YOUR LEGS!"* He had watched an ice rescue the other night on TV, so he keeps repeating what he can remember. (The strong, masculine sound of his own voice impresses the hell out of him.)

The mother and boy try to elbow their way up onto the ice, but the solid ice keeps falling away. The woman gets more hysterical. Pembrook edges closer, calling out reassurances: *"FIRE IS WORSE! PEOPLE ARE WATCHING! YOU WON'T DIE ALONE! SHOUT OUT YOUR NEXT OF KIN! GO AHEAD AND SWEAR! IT'S OKAY TO PEE IN THE WATER!"*

*SWOOOMP!* Pembrook caves through. The shock is fantastic. His body tells him *you will die very soon*. It's a good thing, he thinks, that he had prepared his obituary upon high school graduation. He needs to keep a positive attitude, pay attention to his breathing, and focus on survival. He visualizes himself saving himself in order to brainstorm rescue ideas. He forgets to include saving the mother and child, important witnesses to his acts of heroism.

He pulls his monogramed Mont Blanc fountain pen out of his pants pocket, removes the cap after a few tries *(righty tight, lefty loose?)*, and uses the point with both hands, like an awl, to pull himself back up onto the ice. He isn't all that strong, but adrenaline does the job. Back on top, his face feels raw, and what in his body does not ache is numb. Pembrook grabs the rope again, but nothing happens. He sees the Whisperer flailing in the icy water behind him. He feels apathetic, unconcerned about his condition, a sure sign of a condition that he knows begins with "hypo."

Ice fishermen approach the large opening in the ice from the opposite direction of the shanties across the lake. Apparently, the woman is related, and had been on her way out with a thermos of hot coffee, when she and her son went through. The ice fishermen are running way too fast towards them, and several fishermen crack through the ice at once. Now close to a dozen people are in the water, with a growing crowd around the firm edges of the ice near the road. Time passes in fits and starts. Everyone hears the *thock-thock-thock* of heavy helicopter blades. The Coast Guard has arrived, but there are too many people to rescue, spread over acres of ice. Everyone looks up at the useless helicopter like they're watching a flyover at the beginning of a football game.

## The Lawnmower Club

Moving enough not to be frozen in place, Pembrook begins to feel a tug coming from behind him. The safety rope had been woefully too short, so people have tied pieces of their clothing to the end of the line (coats, scarfs, long underwear), along with more ropes and blankets. While the rescue rope is constructed, people link hands and feet in a human chain. Then the two volunteer firefighters attach the end of the makeshift rope to a tow truck, and the rope begins to drag people ashore. The iced-over people are picked up when they reach firm footing and carried to safety, some hoisted over the shoulders of others in a firefighter's carry, some grasped by their stiff arms and legs, some dragged onto the orange sled and hauled off the ice.

Performing what he can remember of CPR on the boy before the EMS and police arrive, Pembrook saves the day. He does compressions to the rhythm of Bee Gees lyrics: *Well. you can tell by the way I use my walk, I'm a woman's man: no time to talk. Music loud and women warm, I've been kicked around since I was born.* The boy gasps back to consciousness, either jolted awake from the CPR or from Pembrook's awful singing. The boy's mother gives Pembrook a frigid bear hug, her breasts hard as frozen milk cartons. More excitement follows.

The Whisperer goes into cardiac arrest. Pembrook renders CPR on the Whisperer, and saves his life. They look like two dogs kissing, but all agree if it had not been for Pembrook, Zach Zuman never would have arrived at the hospital alive. Gratitude and guilt overcome Zach. He's been saved by a man whom he has cheated in many different ways. EMS and police finally arrive, and load the iced people into one vehicle or another, transporting them, like trays of ice cubes, to the regional hospital.

When the victims arrive in the Emergency Room, attendants remove their wet clothes, and wrap them in heated blankets. Pembrook has a mild case of hypothermia, but he's released the next day in time to see his picture on the front page of the *News and Review*, along with Angler and the Whisperer. The three of them are now local heroes, but Pembrook is the biggest hero of all. He decides to cancel his European ski vacation to remain in town, to bask in his celebrity hero status. Back at CLINGSTONE, he looks in his hall mirror. He is surprise to see how much like himself he looks, considering all that has happened. Maybe his face has always been the face of a hero?

*But I need to have a more heroic-looking body. I must go back to working out. I'm a shadow of my former self, compared to when I had a gym membership. I need to get rid of my ab flab. Maybe I'll enter a triathlon or two this year to prep for the Iron Man? I can already swim and ride a bike. What's hard about that?*

The next day, he visits Zach in the hospital. Zach thanks Pembrook for saving his life, and he confesses his many Pembrook-related sins. He tells how he planted the mice and pigeons in the Clingstone attic, and grossly overcharged him for Pal's training. He asks for forgiveness, and promises to give Pembrook a lifetime varmint control contract, and help him to find a companionable hunting dog. His confession omits giving any of Pembrook's money back, or returning the coyote fur coat.

"Sir, you have wronged me," Pembrook says, "but I'm a forgiving man, since I'm not at all perfect. I suggest you memorize the Seven Commandments as a guide to your future conduct, at least the ones people can understand, and the do unto you rule." After visiting Zach, he decides to stroll downtown to make appearances in the coffee shops and retail stores. He hopes people will see him and say, "*Wow, you're the man on the front page! The man who saved the boy!*" Unnoticed, he decides to visit Mallard Pond.

News of the Crooked Lake ice folly precedes Pembrook's visit to Mallard Pond. Zitzelberger sees Pembrook's picture on the front page of the paper, holding a blue-faced boy smiling in his arms while the mother stands to the side with a frozen smile. The headline reads: HEROES ON THIN ICE. As Zitzelberger slowly mouths the article, Pembrook arrives in the Mallard Pond sitting room.

"Hello, Leo! How's your physical therapy coming along? I see you're using a walker now. Did you see my picture in the paper? Not my best look. The cameras caught my normally soft warm eyes in an icy stare, because my eyeballs were frozen like gelato. But sometimes a man must step-up, like the pioneers did in ancient America against the native warlords."

"Pembrook, there you go playing the hero while I'm stuck here at Mallard Pond," says Zitzelberger. "Woooooooo! Why don't you go tell Hazel Hertz all about your adventure? She said that even though you had to be rescued, she was proud of you."

"Proud?" He changed to a hushed, confidential way of talking. "She must be impressed with my heroic actions. I will seek the full advantage of my momentary glory...my day of splendor in the ice. I'm still freezing, thinking about that cold day in hell. I can see her taking me in her arms, and warming me with her ample body...you know, the emergency room doctors said that I might have succumbed to permafrost."

# 21

# LAWN'S EARLY LIGHT

PAL AND THE COUGAR FROLIC through the frosty fairways of The Lawnmower Club on a cold February morning. The sky turns from reddish-orange to clear steel blue. The cougar teaches Pal how to stalk prey, how to run full-tilt, and how to pounce. Pal introduces the cougar to the pleasures of taking a roll in dead seagulls, and demonstrates numerous angles of repose for effective napping. They nap together. The cougar never ceases to amaze Pal—the way he can go from totally asleep to totally awake in an instant. Pal laughs when, like a house cat, the cougar gacks up a hairball. While ramming through the clubhouse, they knock over Zitzelberger's Old Spice, breaking the bottle. For days, they both smell bad enough to choke a skunk. The two animals develop a two-way language that sounds like *bluh, ruh, ruh, ruh, bluh, ruh*.

Liza sleeps late, nestled under a down comforter in the upstairs bedroom. A local carpenter has installed an oversized magnetic dog door in one of the porch sliders so both animals can come and go at will. Liza has never been happier in her life. She loves her two animals. She knows that Zitzelberger will be coming home soon, but she has no concerns about the future. She lives in the present, her body and soul filled with peace and optimism. She feels safe and still and warm under the clubhouse roof beneath the huge oak tree. The old tree covers the clubhouse like a protective embrace.

The winter has alternated between arctic temperatures and temporary thaws. This day, the turf loosens from a warm-up—enough for an animal to dig in. The cougar unearths a thirteen-thousand-year-old mastodon bone. He gnaws away on what should be preserved in a museum. Pal wants the cougar to share the bone, but he's rebuffed. The big cat and big dog are buddies, but sharing the mastodon bone with Pal would be like pouring a twelve-year Single Malt Scotch for someone who only drinks Bud Lite. Pal shoots up a hill to search for his own bone.

On the highest hilltop in The Lawnmower Club, the freezing and thawing earth has yawned open to reveal a terrible sight. Pal's eyes pop out. He dog screams, as he runs away. Returning in ten minutes, he digs and sniffs in the half-frozen soil at the remnants of a human hand sticking out of the mud. The bony, skeletal hand grips a forged two iron, the missing club of Hazzard Milhouse Pembrook.

Pembrook's father had disappeared during a magnificent thunderstorm after complaining in the clubhouse bar that he had picked up a bad slice with his two iron. He left the clubhouse a bit tipsy, climbed to the top of the highest hill on the

## The Lawnmower Club

course, and raised his two iron like an extension of his arm to the heavens—a perfect lightning rod. Lightening sent down its white spider legs and struck him dead. A bolt drove him into the ground, and interred him ramrod straight like a fence post. He remained there as a hidden monument to human folly. He was driven so far into the ground that the iron he held high over his head was buried where Pal found it thirty years later.

Pal has fun unearthing the skeleton, and drags Pembrook's father's upper arm bone, the one that held the two iron, into the clubhouse. Liza is aghast. She calls Officer Angler, because he's the only local enforcement person she knows. With his family background in taxidermy, she figures he can identify the bones. Angler delivers the bone to the local morgue, and then calls Pembrook.

"Mr. Pembrook, this is Officer Angler. I found your father's humerus."

"Ha, ha, ha...wait a minute, why am I laughing. What's humorous?"

"Nothing. This is serious."

"What's serious?"

"I found what we believe to be your father's humerus."

"Funny, never impressed me as comical. And how did you know him? He's been dead many years."

"No, no. That dog, Pal, found one of your father's bones half-buried on a hill above The Lawnmower Club, his upper arm bone, the humerus. When we went up there, we also found the the upper leg bone, the femur, and a two iron."

"That's not funny," says Pembrook. "My poor father found in a shallow grave after all this time. What about the rest of his bones? You know, the head bone connected to the neck bone, the neck bone connected to the back bone, the back bone connected to the thigh bone (did you find the other one?), the thigh bone connected to the knee bone, the knee bone connected to the foot bone, the foot bone connected to the heel bone? I learned that in high school biology."

"Only those two limbs," says Angler. "The county coroner says he was struck by lightning. The golf club looked like it had been melted by intense heat. So the bolt probably traveled straight through the club into your father's brain. The coroner made a joke about not even God can hit a two iron, but I thought that was insensitive. Are you okay?"

"This terrible calamity hits me like a bolt out of the blue," Pembrook says. "My father was killed by an act of God, like in the Bible, when God-awful vengeance was rendered upon the Brobdingnagian giants, or was that the Babblelongians? I don't know. Poor Daddy, he never knew what hit him. He never liked electricity."

The long-lived mystery has been solved. Pembrook's celebration of his fame and his attempts to hold on to his new-found manhood are cut short when he receives a confirming call from the county morgue. His father's DNA has been matched to thumb prints on old savings bonds.

Pembrook visits the county morgue to examine the stony bones. "My father has become a fossil!" he says. He has no idea what to do. There's no one to call. Returning home, he sits alone on a love seat in the parlor, disconsolate. He stares at his polished winged-tip shoes, then looks at his father's portrait, hanging in a gilded frame on the wall. He had been so enlivened by his grand heroic moment out on the Crooked Lake, but now everything good seems in the past. Through a turn of fate, he reaches another low. He sinks into a tufted cushion and despair. Like a character in a novel, he needs a plot twist to move his life in a happier direction.

Pembrook begins to shake, and no matter how hard he tries, he cannot get breath into his lungs. He thinks he must still have shivers from his lifesaving activity, or the effects of powerful emotions generated by his unaccustomed courage. Out of nowhere, *Whatshername Angel* appears. Physically spent and emotionally numb, he doesn't mind that an angel is flying down from his ceiling. Nearly disinterested, he watches her approach.

"*You-hoo how nice to see you.* I happened to be in the neighborhood, and saw you sitting here in the dark."

"You look like an angel," Pembrook hazards a guess, "like a soul taking a body along for a ride."

"Yes, I *am* an angel. I'm sorry you found the remains of your father, but he's been with Art in heaven (*hallowbehisname*) for a long time."

"Uh-huh," Pembrook says, still shaky. "Well, I want to believe you. You have an air of truthiness."

"Yes, heaven is a very fine place, much like the earth...but I sometimes say too much—don't want to give away secrets."

"Well, I wish my father were still around to help me know what to do next," says Pembrook. "I'm at a crossroads. The life I intended to lead hasn't happened, and the life ahead of me...well I'm a bit puzzled, you see. I confess that I've been too attached to material wealth, eat runs in the family. I can tell I'm upset... by the sound of my voice."

"Your spirit's exhausted, but you need to have hope," *Whatshername* Angel says. "Things will get better soon. You mustn't be upset. I'll check in on you once in a while. Now receive this heavenly declaration from on high: *GO TO WORK, HAZZARD!*" She disappears.

Pembrook gets up and climbs the stairs to his bedroom. He lays down in his clothes, and falls into a deep sleep. The next morning, he wants to work. He's never worked. He has no idea what work he wants to do. But he wants to work. Not because he should work, but because he can.

She told me to go to work, her last words, 'Go to work, Hazzard.' Yeah, I probably should go to work...and learn how to live more simply, but at the same time, well-dressed. I must move on and not look back like that woman who turned into a tall malt.

## The Lawnmower Club

The next morning, in the midst of a wild windstorm accompanied by sleety snow, Pembrook pulls an earflap down on his red Stormy Kromer cap, and trudges from CLINGSTONE over to the clubhouse to return his father's two iron to the wooden display case. The sky is black as night. The last of the fall leaves descend, and spangle the ground. He walks in unannounced, while Liza plays with her pets and a rubber ball by a warm fire. Pembrook no longer sees the cougar as a threat, because the *Whatshername Angel* has changed his heart. He's happy to see Pal, and gives him a pat on the head. By now Pal has forgotten who had his balls removed.

As Pembrook eyes the cougar, he amazes himself by his calm. *I could see myself fainting right now. I could see myself succumbing to the cougar as I almost did twice before. I could see myself jerking and twitching and spilling my blood. But no...the cougar looks no more dangerous to me than a domesticated pet. Gee, am I braver now after I saved the people at the lake? I should check my demeanor in a mirror.*

The cougar sees Pembrook as the familiar goofball who lives next door. He ignores him and continues his ball play with Pal. There's something about Pembrook that Pal doesn't like, but he can't put his paws on it.

The inside of the clubhouse has become a free space where reality and imagination intermingle in pleasing ways. The clubhouse is now more than a building, because it houses human and animal creatures who have suffered, each in deep and separate ways, and creatures who are growing in love. In such a place imagination flourishes.

The wind blows so hard that the windows shudder, but inside, the clubhouse provides a safe and cozy shelter.

Pembrook knows what a dump the clubhouse used to be, and how dark the place had been. Zitzelberger had not replaced the light bulbs as they ghosted out one by one. Liza has created a clean, well-lighted place, like the café in Hemingway's short story. Two lamps emit a golden glow. Pembrook smells oatmeal cooking on the stove, and a slice of bread has just popped out of the toaster. The fire roars in the fireplace, and the pleasing aromas of oats, cinnamon, and coffee fill the air.

"Liza, you have transformed this place—nothing at all like my empty house. I don't know how you managed to do it...especially living with a wild cougar and a crazy dog. You seem so calm, like Jesus when he slept in the lion den."

"That was Daniel, but yes, I love this place."

"Sorry, I often mix my Testaments."

"Would you like breakfast?"

"Well, yes, thank you. I happen to love oatmeal, and the coffee smells marvelous. By the way, you may wonder why I'm carrying around this two iron. I wish I could say it's whimsical, but it sadly happens to be my father's two iron. The one Pal found the other day...the two iron my father held into the sky the day lightning struck and killed him. Daddy must not have been thinking clearly that day. It runs in the family, I'm told."

## The Lawnmower Club

Pembrook walks into the golf shop, unlocks the wooden case, and places the iron into the missing slot.

"There, Daddy, your clubs are all back together again!" He returns to the kitchen where Liza has placed two bowls on a table. They both sit down over coffee and oatmeal. *How nice it would be to sit down each morning with coffee, oatmeal, and a good woman...of course, someone older than Liza*, Pembrook thinks. He conjures a fantasy about Nurse Hertz in nighties, serving him quiche and grapefruit. Liza sees his attention drifting, so she changes the subject.

"Mr. Pembrook, I think it's time we brought Mr. Zitzelberger back to The Lawnmower Club, don't you?"

"Are you out of your mind? Have you talked to your aunt about this? I thought she wanted to imprison and torment him at Mallard Pond for what he did to you that awful night. But what a wonderful thing to have someone who wants to forgive you and help you like you want to help Zitzelberger. I must confess, my thoughts about Zitzelberger and the club have been far from altruistic. You're a better person than me. I'm a genetic knockoff of my avaricious ancestors."

"Aunt Hertz has spent a lot of time with Mr. Zitzelberger. She admires how he keeps working to walk. I don't think she's forgiven him for what he did, but she doesn't hate him any longer. And Frieda Weatherby keeps telling her not to be so hard on him. My aunt also has troubles of her own. Her boyfriend dumped her after five years—he said she was difficult and mean. She's been so grouchy that last week she told Mrs.

Gnatkozski to stop stumping her fingers on the piano. Mrs. Gnatkozski cried and went on a four-hour hunger strike. I told Aunt Hertz that she should see Mr. Putzkin, my therapist. After only six sessions, she's decided to be more kind to people. She gave me a hug the other day, and told me she loved me without reservation. Can you believe it?"

"What a wonderful change! You know, I have always thought your aunt was oddly attractive. She is a *big woman* in many ways and directions. I don't know why I'm telling you this, but I have always been something of a curiousitarian about plus-sized women. There's something in the way your aunt moves that's like no other woman—I think that's a song."

"No, I'm sorry but I don't know what you mean, Mr. Pembrook. You talk like your words walk on stilts. Tell me straight—do you like my auntie?"

"Afraid I do...well not afraid in the fear sense, but she does excite me. I lost my wife a few years ago, or rather I should say, she left me—for an actuary. So, let me hear me say it, I'm divorced I'm divorced, and I'm okay! I never thought it would happen to me...with my family background. The Pembrook's have always slogged through unhappy marriages—a family tradition. Who knows? Maybe that's why my father held up the two iron on the hill out there in the middle of a thunderstorm. Oh, by the way, I don't even know your aunt's first name"

"Hazel."

"Hazel Hertz. I like that alliterative sound. Hazel Hertz, Hazel Hertz."

## The Lawnmower Club

"Can you believe that her maiden name was Rivet, and then she goes and marries a Hertz."

"Did you say your wife left you for an actuary?" Liza says.

"Actuarially, yes."

"Hmmm. I think his name is Humbert Number," says Liza. He's the only actuary in northern Michigan, and I know he ran off with at least two married women and one married man. He tried to pick me up on a Saturday night at Don's Bar. He told me he liked flat-chested women, because they looked like teenagers. Then he opened his coat, and tried to show me his actuarial tables. I thought he was real creepy. Imagine an old guy like him interested in a 25-year-old girl, and thinking I would be interested."

"And as for older men and young girls, I would never look at a young girl like you with lust in my heart...for more than a long moment."

"Well, thank you—I feel perfectly safe around you. Aunt Hazel says you have sweet Teddy Bear eyes, and wouldn't harm a flea."

"She is so right. Although the need to take bold and decisive action occasionally lurks and flickers in my consciousness. I don't suppose you heard that I'm a bit of a local hero these days?" He gives a self-deprecating smirk.

"Why, yes. I admire someone who has the presence of mind to take charge in a crisis."

"I took a CPR course in case I ever needed to help someone help me. I never thought I would use it—so unsanitary. But I did what I had to do. The whole experience of heroic action sort of helped me. I've always been a bit timid. Now, I want to live in a new way. I want to find some worthwhile to do, like work... maybe as a clothing consultant to poorly-dressed men who have the means to dress better. I will atone for my life without purpose. I will become an entrepreneur like my grandfather, who was led by the invisible hand of Ansel Adams...no that's not right...Allen Smith."

"Mr. Pembrook, *HOW INTERESTING!* You and I seem to be in the same place. I've always felt awkward and uncertain about what to do with my life as well. I've been laid off from social work, so now I want to do something different for a change. I want to follow a new path, better use my talents, stop being a —"

"—a lay about. I get it. I want to leave more than vacant space when I die. I have a new mantra: *GO TO WORK!*" Pembrook says.

"*YES, THAT'S IT! GO TO WORK!* I need to work again. I believe my life work has something to do with the art of loving... loving animals, along with doing big and small things to bring heaven on earth."

"My skills are neither divinely inspired nor related to animals," says Pembrook. "My kernel of power lies in my well-honed interpersonal skills. I am thinking about using them on your Aunt Hazel Hertz. Ah, but I need to be careful—I can overwhelm women when I switch on my charm. But I must admit I'm a keeper. Sometimes I imagine me to be the lone male

*The Lawnmower Club*

survivor of global warming— required to repopulate the earth and sprawl my family tree far and wide across what remains of a post-epileptic earth."

"Oh, no way!" says Liza. "I had no idea you had such imagination!"

"Yes, I have imagined having a large offspring. Alas, at present, I have no living relatives..."

Pal and the cougar are rolling around in front of the happy-making light of the fireplace while Liza and Pembrook talk. The two animals take turns jawing at each other—faking each other out with ferocious gestures. The cougar gives Pal a lesson on how to exaggerate his size by making his hairs stand on end. They take turns trying to scare each other—the cougar always wins. Liza pulls a tray of chicken bits out of a microwave. "The cougar likes his food at mouse temperature," she says.

"The cougar has such a beautiful coat—I wish I had a fur coat like his," says Pembrook. "Too bad fur-bearing animals can't be relieved of their coats once a year, you know, like sheep—but I could never be a fur trapper. I know firsthand what it feels like to have your heart pounding out of your skin when you're trapped."

"Oh, Mr. Pembrook, you are so cute. Sometimes your humor mystifies me. Would you like some more oatmeal or coffee?"

"Please, I enjoy being here with you and the animals. This place seems to have a magical feel about it," says Pembrook. "Maybe it's because a mountain lion and a pit bull are cavorting about in such good humor—like they're tame. I have to say, that cougar is like an SUV among cats—a cat under normal circumstances that would make the average person run for shelter like I did twice before. If only their claws were retractable."

"More brown sugar and raisins?" says Liza.

"Yes, thank you." Pembrook pulls a red handkerchief from his back pocket to wipe his face. The cougar raises his head and begins to hunch his back.

"Gentle, gentle...you be good boys...you don't get to play if you're going to be rough!" says Liza.

Pembrook ignores the cougar and continues talking. "I have to say there is something powerful and scary about having a wild animal in your house...something that brings back memories of Africa, if you've been there...an animal that could cut you to ribbons in less than a minute. Even so, there is something human-like about this large cat...I can't tell for sure."

"I feel safe here," says Liza. "This clubhouse has gone through so many ups and downs, there is no longer any fear of disaster in the air, like the worst things have already happened."

"Yes, like lightning not striking the same place more than once or twice," says Pembrook.

The wind blows fiercely outside the clubhouse, and rattles the rafters. Liza looks out the window.

"We should all stay inside until the storm passes," says Liza.

"I dare say, the wind is roaring out there like a jungle cat!"

# The Lawnmower Club

**BOOM—WHOOSH.** A sonic boom sound rocks the clubhouse and shakes the frozen ground. A fatal bolt of lightning blasts the black oak that has stood over the clubhouse for over one hundred and fifty years. The tree's crown bends way over, and two thirds from the top, the trunk cracks freakishly. The tree topples over and crashes down on the clubhouse, the upper branches spread over the roof like a broom, the heavier limbs and a twenty-foot section of trunk sever the clubhouse in two. The gnarled old tree trunk destroys all below it in a crushing embrace, as if the clubhouse had been constructed with papier mache. The roof of the clubhouse opens like two large jaws to the open sky.

The tree has stood almost forever close by the clubhouse, its canopy shading the starter shack in sweet familiarity, and before the club days, spreading its calming limbs over generations of native people, farmers, children of farmers, domestic and wild animals, and all manner of birds. Always bending its head away from the stiff winds coming in off Lake Michigan, this particular day, the weather is brutal enough to change its fortune. Nothing remains but hissing ruins and a thin layer of brownish dust over all. The wooden display case housing Hazzard Milhouse Pembrook's golf clubs has been smashed, and the two iron bent in half.

The tree no longer shelters the clubhouse, and the owl who lives inside it. The destroyed clubhouse no longer shelters its unusual occupants, no longer stands across from Pembrook's house to be coveted by him, and no longer provides Zitzelberger with the hope of a return to what he regards as an asylum from the madhouse world, a grass-cutting sanctuary for himself and his lawnmowerians.

Pembrook and Liza are all over each other on the floor, and end up in an embarrassing Kamasutra position, with her scissor legs around his delicate neck. When Pembrook opens his eyes, he sees Liza's panties and crotch an inch from his face, her knees in the vicinity of his ears, and her jeans ripped off, dangling from one leg like a tattered battle flag.

*I will never forget this moment. It will reside in my brain forever,* Pembrook thinks.

Liza opens her closed eyes and untangles herself from Pembrook. They sit dazed in the wreckage. Pal and the cougar have hightailed on a full run for the woods. An Alpha mouse directs the exit of the other critters. Chipmunks chip high-pitched alarms, and lament their fallen comrades, strewn about the clubhouse floor like fallen soldiers.

The inside of the clubhouse has become outside. Everyone is covered with ice, water, snow, dust, white powder, and insulation. Water pipes are bursting and gas lines hissing. They all sit in a big heap of glass shards, shingles, pipes and wires. Pembrook's face is covered with oatmeal. Manifold little somethings skitter around among the rubble. Everyone's eyes look startled and saucerish.

"Are you okay?" Liza says.

"Eh, okay," says Pembrook. "Do I look all right? I hope I don't have any brain damage. We might have been totally

## The Lawnmower Club

pancaked. Should we call 7-1-1?" He begins taking selfies for insurance purposes. His shirt has been ripped off his torso, and he modestly covers himself with his arms. "I don't tan below the neck," he says.

"Your eyes look like pinwheels," Liza says. Snow begins falling through the gaped open roof. It lands and melts on Liza's face. She looks up through the tree-ripped roof to see sky-ripped clouds. It feels strange to be outside, when moments before, she was inside—having coffee and oatmeal with Pembrook. Not a wall is left standing, but nearby, the cart shed stands untouched.

"Do you hear that?" says Liza. Over the wind and settling rubble of the clubhouse, she hears the slow, luffing wing beats of the *Whatshername Angel.* Liza turns her head to Pembrook, and says, "*It's a miracle we weren't harmed!*"

"*YOU ARE SO RIGHT!*" says Pembrook. "We had no more than a mothball's chance in hell of coming out of this unscathed...I do see the need for a new shirt and some dry cleaning—I better take my pulse—I hope this doesn't make the news—I have so many accidents for a stay-at-home person—this is like a nightmare, but I can't wake up—I better cancel my appointments for the rest of the day...oh, that's right, I have no appointments." In fact, Pembrook has no more idea what he will be doing from one day to the next than a baby. He continues to walk as he talks—in fast-moving circles, goose-stepping over all the random obstacles about him.

## Randy Evans

The storm passes quickly, and the world turns still and starkly silent. After the weather clears, Pal returns from the deep woods—alone. He romps in the grass, playing with the red rubber ball he uncovered in the clubhouse debris. Every few minutes, Pal twists his neck in the direction of the woods. The cougar has vanished.

# 22

# ZITZELBERGER'S IN PARADISE

WILLIE SNOWBALL HAS NO FAMILY to attend his brief memorial service in the Mallard Pond cafeteria. A local preacher has agreed to do the service with a fill-in-the-blanks eulogy that hammers away on the promises of an afterlife. Zitzelberger sits in his wheel chair in a row of folding chairs along with Louise Gnatkozski, Hazel Hertz, and Frieda Weatherby. Hazel wears Snowball's gold wrist watch with pride—Zitzelberger has conveyed the watch without conveying Snowball's wish. Frieda places her hand on Zitzelberger's arm, now a familiar resting place, her touch like rose petals, more intimate than a kiss.

The preacher walks in briskly and glad hands everyone like he knows them, and begins to read the familiar scriptures, and because Louise is too upset to play the piano, they sing "Amazing Grace" *a cappella*. The women continue to converse in whispers while the preacher drones about being saved and how the seal of salvation is like the seal on a Ball Mason Jar of pickled vegetables, and how the seal lasts *FOREVER!*

*"You expect people to die in a nursing home,"* Louise says.

*"Yes, but we went for over a year with the same silly group,"* Frieda says.

"Well, eventually, we all poop out," adds Louise.

The preacher closes the memorial service with an offering. He happens to carry collection plates wherever he travels. As the benediction ends, Liza and Pembrook walk in.

"Oh look, Mr. Pembrook has come to pay his respects to Mr. Snowball," says Hazel, "and Liza, there's Liza!" Everyone stares at their beat-up looks.

*"WHAT IN HELL'S NAME!"* says Zitzelberger. *"WHAT HAPPENED?"*

Thanks to the intervention of the *Whatshername Angel*, Liza and Pembrook survive the tree crashing through the clubhouse roof without serious injury to themselves or to the dog and the cougar—but they are bloody, bruised, and dazed, tangled up in debris, and frightened. Liza and Pembrook limp across the road to CLINGSTONE. Pembrook changes into dry, warm clothes, and loans Liza a pair of his denims and a flannel shirt.

Liza and Pembrook decide to inform Zitzelberger of the bad news. After dropping off his soiled clothes at the dry cleaners, Pembrook drives Liza over to Mallard Pond. Liza worries about

## *The Lawnmower Club*

how Zitzelberger will react to the destruction of the clubhouse, his dream. On the drive to Mallard Pond, she says, "What will we tell him? I mean, I was supposed to be the caretaker, and the place is plain gone. And the cougar. How do you explain the cougar?"

"I have to agree he's a rare cat," says Pembrook. "Let's talk this out. I prefer to chat while I drive. It takes my mind off my poor driving. WHOOPS!" He sideswipes a parked car. "I've always regarded side mirrors as unnecessary accessories."

Gloria continues as if nothing has happened. "And how do we explain the two of us in the clubhouse?" She looks down on the shirt she borrowed from Pembrook's closet. "This was not a good choice," she says, "what will the old ladies think about me wearing a man's shirt...your shirt? It's all so awkward." She buttons the top buttons.

"Not as awkward as finding us all dead," says Pembrook. "Think what people would say if they found us both dead in a sweaty pile with my face buried...forgive me, I don't want to be crude...in your genitalia, or your vagina, or your privates, or your hoohah? I've never been educated in the anatomy of a woman's nether regions."

"Mr. Pembrook, you don't need to explain everything to everyone all the time—why don't you skip talking about this altogether?"

"Yes, it will be our little secret...and yes, everything has been awkward and weird for some time, like a grim fairy tale— Pal digging up my father who was struck by lightning, the cougar coming indoors like a house cat, and us eating oatmeal and drinking coffee as a tree falls through the roof of the clubhouse...and then, I almost forgot, my visitation."

"Visitation?"

"Yes, I don't know what else to call it, and I'm usually so good with words. Yesterday an angel appeared in my house. Not exactly a Bible-type angel, because she wore hand-me-down clothes and scuffed-up high top shoes. But an angel nonetheless. She didn't scare me at all. It seemed like you and me now looking at each other and talking, like nothing super-un-natural was going on. Now that I think about it, perhaps the angel saved us from the falling tree *by divine intervention!* Excuse me ... this chat about the super-un-natural is awkward. I can tell by my words, I feel weirdish," says Pembrook.

"Well, angels are good things. I've heard angels can be helpful," says Liza. Maybe the angel saved us, but I'm very about the tree...a fine old tree and for all the creatures who lived in the tree or on the tree...the nests, you know, and the holes in the trunk. I guess it's not in the natural order of the universe for God to prevent old trees from falling. I hope the fall wasn't too painful for everyone involved."

"The big oak tree fell on the clubhouse, and we were almost killed," Liza says to Zitzelberger. She turns to Pembrook, and expects he will say something, because he usually does.

## *The Lawnmower Club*

"I didn't see it coming. After the tree fell, I think it made a THUNK, and I was struck by the thought I was still alive," Pembrook says. "But there I was—tangled up with Liza! I'll never forget opening my eyes to see...Liza and I were alive. (Pembrook gives Liza a knowing wink.) When you almost get killed, it makes you think about dying, you know...like what's next? Oh dear, my mind is having erratic thoughts. I'd hate to think my brain's been damaged."

Nurse Hertz jumps to her feet and heads towards Pembrook, "You poor dear, you've scratched your handsome face. Let me clean you up." Pembrook gives her his practiced self-deprecating smile. Hazel ignores Liza, her own niece, who also has bruises and scratches. Pembrook grimaces from his injuries, even though he has no pain. He likes to be nursed.

Zitzelberger stands up with great effort, and reaches out to Liza. "My dear girl, you look like you've been in a tornado—you often look like you've been in a tornado, but today...well, you're a real mess. Are you sure you're okay?"

"I'm okay, but I'm afraid the clubhouse has been destroyed. It's been leveled to the ground by the old oak tree."

"Well, we should get someone out there and board up the place," says Zitzelberger. "I imagine we can find a good contractor to make the repairs. I'm feeling so well these days, walking on my own now, I can probably make it over there to take a look for myself...maybe supervise the repair work." He looks at her with hopeful eyes.

"You don't understand," says Liza. "There is no *there* there any longer...only debris. I did salvage a few things." She shows Zitzelberger the neat triangle of his father's veteran memorial flag, and the small framed photograph of Mona. He looks at the picture while the news sinks in. His face drops like a mudslide. The temple of his ingenuity, the headquarters of his kingdom, has been destroyed by the random falling of a tree. He has lost his paradise.

*"I DON'T KNOW THAT. I DON'T KNOW THAT..."*

Silence follows Zitzelberger's unfinished sentence, and the unspoken words hang in the air like a big tree before it falls. Whether Zitzelberger stands up too fast and loses his breath, or the heart-stopping bad news about the destruction of his beloved Lawnmower Club does him in, he falls like the mighty oak tree. He keels over backwards on Frieda Weatherby and breaks her arm. Liza bends over Zitzelberger and lays her head on his chest. "His heart has stopped beating," she says, "I heard it beating...then it stopped...oh, there it goes again."

Zitzelberger wakes up inside a beaver lodge, and the beaver begins to nibble on his leg. He looks at the beaver who looks back at him with a black look in his black eyes.

"You know, this is my home, and I have not invited you into my lodge. You're here by mistake, on your way somewhere else. *Don't look me in the eyes.* This has happened before—a comic

## The Lawnmower Club

cosmic screw up. You'll be on your way in an eye blink. *When you leave, don't look back!*"

Zitzelberger's eyes lose focus, and his hearing fades as the beaver says, "*Nice gnawing you! Ha, ha, ha.*" Then he hears the playing of a harmonica—Snowball's harmonica.

"Sorry, old boy," Willie Snowball says. "You were misdirected at first. It happens all the time. You're in heaven right now to have a look around. You may think you're dead, but you're not. By the way, thanks for attending my little memorial service, and giving Hazel the gold watch without my insult. One less thing to regret."

Snowball's holds his harmonica. He's surrounded by all the dogs he ever owned.

"You look amazed to see me. I have quite a following here. Seems people like my harmonica a lot better than harps, especially the way I play it—loud, jazzy, and hornlike." He looks around at his dogs. "I'd like you to meet Belle, Buster, Chili, DeeDee, Maddie, Pepper, Spot, and Target—all my dogs lived long lives—longer than two-term Presidents. They're old dogs, so their faces look like mine."

"I never developed any kind of faith growing up," says Zitzelberger, "so I don't know why I'm here. I mean, my whole life, everyone told me I was going to Hell—my mother and father, Mona, my wife, and the people who yelled go to hell when I hauled their cars away—I made a respectable living, but nobody respected me."

"Well, you're here for a short look. I bet you're hungry. We're having baked chicken and green beans for dinner, a favorite of the senior center types.

Zitzelberger looks around him, and sees nothing but earth in heaven. There are hills and trees and lakes, and people walking around and talking. Snowball sees Zitzelberger's surprise. "Art (*hallowbehisname*) made heaven to feel like home. So what did you think, people would be be sitting on bean bag clouds and doing craft projects?"

"No, I didn't know what to think, since I never expected to be here. But I did think it would be a place where people worked on hobbies, or prayed all day and read the paper before cocktails."

"It's less divided in heaven, so people find they have more in common."

"Not a great place for privacy," says Zitzelberger, "but looks like there's an abundance of room—and I don't see any shrubs. I have always thought there was something wrong with shrubs. Everyone looks happy around here."

"Art in heaven (*hallowbehisname*) loves all creatures, and gives them the best right from the beginning," says Snowball. "And I'm happy to be here in one piece. As for me, I had thought of heaven as a bunch of disembodied souls hanging around in crystal balls praising God."

"Well, for most of my life, I've thought there would be no afterlife...just a long sleep."

"But did you hope there might be something more?"

# The Lawnmower Club

"Yes, I guess I did."

"Well, there you have it! Art (*hallowbehisname*) wouldn't design people with a built-in hope for eternal life, and then disappoint them with death—he's a people person!"

"Have you seen him, you know, Art?"

"Not yet...some dim-sighted people like me have to improve their vision for all that heaven has to offer—like restoration work on an old lawnmower, but for the soul rather than the body. Most people aren't anywhere near perfect, I know I'm not, so we need more time. In good time, everyone becomes the original work of Art (*hallowbehisname*) he made them to be. People enlarge themselves from living in harmony and peace with their fellow creatures. Over time, everyone loses the restraints of selfishness, and enlarge their spirits. And when people stop feeling so damned individual, they blend into the raw material of the universe...like heavenly sparks!"

"Unbelievable! You know the night you died, I felt a certain presence in the sitting room. I haven't been the same since. I read from an old rabbi's book about divine sparks, like you said. It seemed like I was getting over a lifelong sickness without knowing what was wrong with me. I healed into something more than a big pile of bones and fat."

"Don't get too set on losing the fat when you die. The bones stay on earth, but the fat goes to heaven. The ladies, in particular, don't like to learn that cellulite travels to the afterlife... but I'm talking too much. I wanted you to have an eye blink of heaven, so you know it's not a fantasy. That's all for now, unless you want to stay for dinner."

"Wait—I need to know—can people mow lawns up here?"

"You bet—can't you smell the cut grass? As you can see, heaven and earth are much the same."

Zitzelberger's face lights up. "*Why yes, I do smell cut grass!*"

"There's something soul-affirming about grass odors," says Snowball, "but I always had my yard done by a service...bad back."

"If heaven's like earth...what about suffering? Do people suffer in heaven?"

"Yep, people suffer in heaven. What do you think you do with a perfectly good soul? It's one of the things souls do best. Troubles flicker like little lights all over the place around here, but as on earth, love swarms and overwhelms everything—love beats suffering to the finish line every time. You see, we're all knotted together—"

In a swirl of radiant light, Zitzelberger returns to his position on the sitting room floor at Mallard Pond. He looks at the colors on the back of his eyelids. The buzzing florescent ceiling lights shine down on him, so he sees a pink dull fire like the end of a lit cigar. When he opens his eyes, he looks windblown, like a man who has been somewhere fast, even though he's been sprawled out on the floor. He cannot remember much about

## The Lawnmower Club

where he's been, but he breathes like an athlete. He feels like new, like he's been refitted with a new carburetor and plugs, like he's mowed his way from earth to heaven and back.

# 23

# SO SILENT

"OOOH, MR. Z," Liza says, "we were SO worried. We thought you had died...your heart stopped...then restarted." She drips large tears as she leans down to where he rests on the sitting room floor, kisses his paper-white face, and lays her head on his chest.

"Wha—what? Where am I? Oh, it's you, Liza. I've had a weird experience!"

"Oh, no way...did you have one of those out-of-body things?"

"Huh?"

"You know, when you go out of yourself, and float around the ceiling in altered form, and look down at your body...and see white light everywhere around you."

"Oh...nothing like that...I traveled to heaven completely awake, and had a little chat with Willie Snowball...I can't remember much, but...they allow you to cut grass in heaven, and sometimes you have baked chicken and green beans for dinner, and even screw-ups like me have a chance to be there."

*"WOW!" says Liza. "You're amazing, Mr. Zitzelberger. To heaven and back!!*

"Well, you looked dead to me," says Mrs. Gnatkozski. "I started selecting sheet music for your memorial, and I found 'There is a Green Hill Far Away. I thought you might like to have a song that includes the color green, because you're so obsessed with grass. Wanna have me play it for ya now?"

"Not now, please," Zitzelberger says.

"Well, dang it, if you say so," Mrs. Gnatkozski responds with hurt in her voice.

Zitzelberger speaks in low tones to Liza. "Um, you know when you told me you wanted to bring heaven on earth?"

"Yeah...still do."

"Okay, uh, when I was there, it looked pretty much like here. I always thought the worlds beyond this world were different. I see things differently now. I'm not so desperate about getting back to The Lawnmower Club. Losing a building in the whole universe of things isn't a big deal. I've lived under the illusion that I'm separate from everyone else, and what's mine is mine...but it's not true if you see the big picture, you know. And now, I can see, that at least for me, The Lawnmower Club was a lonely place."

Liza looks confused. "Alright, Mr. Zitzelberger. I'm going to need some time to get used to you this way, but it sounds like you had some kind of awesome dream trip. That's really cool!"

"Ahhhh, but what about lawn mowing?" says Hazel Hertz. "What about that? I thought you lived to mow, along with all

## The Lawnmower Club

those other crazy people out there riding their lawnmowers for no good reason? Did you hit your head when you fell?"

"Yes, I don't understand either," Liza says. She sees Zitzelberger turn his eyes in Frieda Weatherby's direction.

"Mowing's important, but not the most important thing now," says Zitzelberger. "I hope when I die, I can keep on mowing, but I have other ways to be happy. I thought I had what I wanted, and look what happened!" He glances over at Frieda Weatherby with soft eyes. "The world's bigger than The Lawnmower Club. I'm bigger than The Lawnmower Club. You were right all along, Liza. I don't want to live alone anymore. Not when there's people like Frieda around...especially Frieda." He gives Frieda a wild and happy look, and the kind of vigorous smile that he must have kept to himself for a long time.

"This will take some getting used to," says Frieda. "The big tough guy has a heart. I suspected so all along. You remind me of the big teddy bear someone lost at the Emmet County Fair one year. I dusted him off, and took him home with me. He sleeps with me every night, right beside me on my pillow. All people need their comforts."

"But what about The Lawnmower Club?" says Liza, altogether missing what Zitzelberger has said. She has not been to heaven and back. She thinks he's gone off his rocker, and two old people making eyes at each other seems bizarre, even disgusting.

"Pembrook always wanted to take charge. His father used to own the property. Maybe it should be his legacy," says Zitzelberger. "You think differently about things when you learn that what you thought was a bunch of crap actually exists." Liza turns her gaze to Pembrook, expecting an enthusiastic response, because Zitzelberger has just given him the opening that he had longed for.

"Oh, I daresay I'm not so ambitious as in my younger days," says Pembrook. "I can tell I'm getting older, because the dates keep changing." Pembrook sighs at Hazel, and fails to register what Zitzelberger has said—the words he has so longed to hear—The Lawnmower Club might be available to him. He looks into a wall mirror beside where he's sitting and says, "I'm mesmerized by Hazel. When I look into Hazel's eyes, I experience a nameless emotion... and when I look in the mirror, I can see the same look in my own visage—a fine-looking chap in love. *YES, LOVE!*"

"*I'm fond of you, too, Hazzard,*" Hazel says with an unfazed smile. "*Don't ask me why.*"

Then Pembrook turns to her and says, "I'm so happy to hear you like me, because women are not attracted to me in large numbers. I intimidate them due to my polished, self-assured exterior and effortless grace. I must confess, Hazel, I have had creepy and lustful thoughts in your direction. I have wanted to touch the skin underneath your nursing uniform since the first day I met you. But now I feel something more elevated, like you and me together every day for the rest of our lives. *THINK ABOUT THAT!!*"

## *The Lawnmower Club*

"Why, Hazzard, you are so full of shit, but I mean...in a nice way," says Hazel. "People think you're crazy, but you are so much more than crazy. I understand you. You don't know what you think until you see what you do."

"Yes! No one has ever captured me so clearly," says Pembrook. "I'm very happy to know that someone understands me. Do I look happy to you? We need to have some sort of refreshment to celebrate—hot cocoa, no that's too heavy, how about some kind of juice, or maybe Ginger Ale? No. Tea. What about tea?"

"Hazzard, I would love some tea," Hazel says. "I'll check the kitchen for cookies, sweetie pie."

Frieda bends over Zitzelberger with her arm in a temporary sling and gives him a kiss, then places her arm on his arm. She says with sparkling eyes, "I've tried to tell you about heaven on earth for a long time. There is no separation, you see. This world is a place in heaven."

In the background, Mrs. Gnatkozski plays the piano and sings: "*...when through woods and forest glades I wander, and hear the birds sing sweetly in the trees ... how great thou Art, how great thou Art.*"

Over the music, Hazel Hertz leans close to Haz Pembrook with sweet whispers—very strange for everyone to see, since Hazel is rarely sweet and seldom whispers. Frieda sees this going on, and says to Zitzelberger, "There's a lid for every pot!"

This mushy talk flummoxes Liza, almost sickens her. Everyone's pairing up, with a notable exception, her. She's the youngest by far. She feels her composure cracking.

Pembrook's waning ambition to take over the club, Zitzelberger's lack of concern about returning to The Lawnmower Club, Aunt Hertz's absurd interest in Pembrook overwhelm Liza—all too much for her in such a short time. It's like a story ending with all the loose strings tied into neat little knots, but without any personal satisfaction. Unlike Zitzelberger, she feels the loss of The Lawnmower Club. Rather than sleeping in a bed and sitting by the cozy fireplace, she'll have to go back to living in her car.

Liza creates a scene in the sitting room. She shrills—

*EVERYONE STOP! STOP, STOP, STOP IT, ALL OF YOU!"*

All the people look at her like with similar expressions, like they are carved wooden figurines with permanent painted-on looks of surprise on their faces. Gritting her teeth, Liza takes a phone book from a table, raises it high above her head, and slams it to the floor. THWACK!

Liza runs out of Mallard Pond, and stomps down a steep, worn path to Lake Michigan. The high wind blows against her, and sand stings her face. The lake looks bigger and more dangerous this time of year.

*It looks like people are pairing off, like everything's been prearranged. I always feel like the outsider. I don't belong to anyone or*

## The Lawnmower Club

*anything—not to a club, not to a person, I live life in the first person singular, alone...solo...like the cougar. We don't fit in. And I can't find my cougar! I need my cougar!*

Near the shore, she stands below a crooked basswood tree that groans against the offshore wind whooshing in from the frozen bay. Swollen clouds sit heavy in the dreary sky burdened with something dark like bad memories. The wind swirls the tree limbs and Liza's stringy hair. Liza picks up one stone after another, and hurls the stones out on the ice piled up against the shore. She throws and throws until she can't throw any longer. She wants to shout or scream like the gulls above her piercing the wind, but she can't. The stones shatter bits of ice, but the seascape remains unchanged. The stones sit on top of the ice, and seem to look back at her—the stone faces mocking her. If the ice were water, she could break up the image, but nothing she does changes anything.

The jagged ice appears stationary, even though the shifting block fields boom like thunder. A body of lack frozen water stands like one dark giant slab of stone beyond the ragged surface of ice fields. Above the shore behind her, big trees bend their wind-warped heads. The sky looks crazy chaotic with clouds of different shapes moving in different directions, wispy white phantoms before an ice-age dark sky. She has never felt more stuck. She begins to wail and finally gives way to fury.

*What about me? What's going to become of me? Where does Liza Fitting fit? I don't want to live by looking around me for one thing or another, and no one special around to miss me, and nothing worthwhile accomplished. I want to add up to something...be someone to someone. I've been a good girl my whole life...I've done nothing wrong, but nothing right. I've found a thousand small ways to murder myself. I work for the betterment of people, but I don't believe in betterment...not for me. I let everything tear me apart.*

*FUCK!* "*FUCK, FUCK, FUCK, FUCK, FUCK, FUCK, FUCK, FUCK!*"

Liza looks up to the crown of the single basswood tree swaying over her. A single gnarled and tangled leaf clings to the tree against a mono-gray sky.

Exhausted, empty, unafraid, Liza arrives at a neutral place where her vast defenses have let themselves down for a rest. Suddenly and silently, the whole black and white windy world dies into stillness, like someone has turned a switch off. The stormy weather front has passed. She smells a hint of something in the air, she can't make it out at first, but it's the promising aroma of spring. She hears the sound of creek water sliding under clear ice from the surrounding hills. She looks for a melodramatic epiphany, a slow rising orchestral chorus to build around her and fill her with a sense of belonging, beauty, and love, but nothing happens. The insensitive seascape of the lake stretches out before her like an ocean. No joy and wonder fills the still air, no savior arrives on the scene with comforting words—there is only Liza looking out on the ice.

She stands there for a long time like a statue. Then she sees the figure of a small girl out on the lake, looking bird-boned, like a feathery, weightless bird. From the distance, Liza sees what looks like a silver hubcap over her pale head. Liza's mouth opens in wonder as *Whatshername* Angel approaches. Liza hears a voice calling to her:

"Hello, how nice to see you! Poor thing. People around you are learning to love each other, and you feel like you don't belong."

Liza turns her back on the angel, then turns around to see if she's disappeared. The angel's still there wearing wrinkled old clothes. Liza feels trapped in a dream, unable to move.

"You scare me," Liza says.

"I'm as real as anything," says *Whatshername Angel.* "You will find your way to love, Liza. When you decided to help Mr. Zitzelberger after he broke his neck, your heart changed. When your love of animals overcame your fear, your heart expanded. You are ready for what you most want. We're all outcasts of one sort or another—little sparks free floating in the universe, but we end up together sooner or later. You'll be all right. Oh, and in case you have doubts, it's okay to be a good girl. And you will find someone special to love you. There's a lid for every pot!"

"Thank you," Liza says.

The single leaf separates from the basswood tree.

Liza feels a cold sweat inside her clothes like meltwater trickling into the lake. Her anger has vanished. Her fear has fallen away. The look in her eyes isn't relief or gratitude or forgiveness, but the uncivilized look of an astounded animal. As the *Whatshername Angel* evaporates in the mist, Liza begins to hum a little made-up tune that sounds like hope. She begins to feel more like a red-blooded, throbbing member of the human race—with a whole universe in need of her pity and love, and a world willing to give back to her in return. Her face lights up with joy. She reaches down to the beach, and picks up a small chunk of ice, placing it on her forehead like a blessing. Liza has found a fine traveling companion for the rest of her life—her best self, hushed and waiting to emerge.

With a rosy flush on her cheeks, Liza moves away from the frozen lake, ready for decisions and action. She must find her missing cougar. She returns to her car in the Mallard Pond parking lot, and drives to CLINGSTONE, where she finds Pal, but no cougar. He hasn't showed up. Liza and Pal cross the street to continue their search. They pass the ruins of the clubhouse and the large root ball of the toppled oak tree, laying there like a huge heart ripped out of the earth's body. *I guess it was the tree's time to fall*, Liza thinks, *but how snug we were in the clubhouse before the tree fell.*

Liza and Pal walk slowly through the golf course. There are deer tracks, rabbit tracks, and turkey tracks everywhere, but no cougar tracks.

## *The Lawnmower Club*

Officer Angler returns to the brushy margins of The Lawnmower Club, this time without his tree stand. He carries a single-barreled shotgun. He walks around the swamp to the landfill where the cougar keeps its lair. Skulls and bones of prey scatter the ground, victims of the cougar's crushing jaws. He sees a half-eaten deer carcass, a fresh kill. Angler picks up tracks in the mud and snow leading west, away from The Lawnmower Club. He follows the tracks through the woods for over five miles. The tracks keep going on, but Angler has walked his limit. Passing by long, blue, spiky shadows of pine, Felix returns to his truck, and drives a roasted chicken home to Margaret Jo. "The cougar's moving on," he says to himself. "Maybe the tree falling on the clubhouse frightened him away. Who knows what an animal will do?"

For the cougar, living in the clubhouse with Liza and Pal was too good to last, certain to end someday by the uncertain forces of man or nature. Separation from Liza stresses the cougar, but his survival instincts stir him to action. A year after he attacked the dental hygienist, he thinks that things may have cooled down in Wisconsin. Besides, it's time to seek a mate. Masses of older neurons cross synaptic gaps like sparks arcing to the ignition coils of a million spark plugs.

## Randy Evans

The cougar feels a deep limbic impulse to flee, a subcortical electrical charge to preserve the self, surfaces from his brain stem, and maps his return home—*ZZZZZT!*

The cougar travels west through the rolling hills and stubble pastures towards Lake Michigan, then heads north following the shoreline. His body gears itself to a narrower range of life, centered on rapid movement. His wordless knowledge of a higher order of existence, and the memory of his unusual life, fade in the face of the immediate challenges of his journey. He appears and disappears as he moves through the fields and forests like the in and out of a breath. He sees a bright, clear object, ten feet ahead, sticking up from the snow. It's a glass shard from a broken bottle. He almost overruns it, but catches his right forepaw. The glass cuts a cleft on his pad. He stops to lick the blood, then moves on with a slight limp.

After running for several hours, he reaches the shore where Lake Michigan and Lake Huron join like the slender branches of neighboring trees. As the sun turns to darkness and the rising moon to blood, the cougar spends the night by the blocks of blue ice and torrents of dark water. Before sleep, his higher consciousness returns, and he thinks of Liza and Pal sleeping beside him in clubhouse, all happy and warm by a crackling fireplace. He sheds a sad tear for the life he would never know again. The roar of flushing water brings him sleep.

At first light, a redheaded woodpecker alights on the top of a white oak tree about fifty feet high. The cougar sits beneath the tree, well-hidden in pure and unfamiliar silence. He looks

## The Lawnmower Club

out on the South Channel of the Straits of Mackinac. It's a day short of March. In the frozen air, the sun, having melted the darkness, looks like a child's sketch with all its rays, no cloud in the sky. The cold winter has closed the shipping lanes, all humps and crevices, except for the blue trampled course opened by an icebreaker. The narrow passage curves through the frozen face of the Straits like the sneer of a smile with ice edges turned against the water like broken teeth. The cougar creeps out to the ice. Wanting to go home to Wisconsin encourages him. He reaches the reamed out open water gap and plunges in without hesitation. The frigid water shocks the cougar, but he swims free and hopeful.

Even though the watery passage is the hull width of a freighter, a current carries the cougar away from the ice ridges on the other side. He keeps moving his legs with his head up—his lungs heaving like bellows. When he reaches the other side, he's exhausted. With one mighty upward thrust against the downward drag, the cougar crawls out of the water, then slides back into the freezing current, feeling both human-like horror and the hypothermia common to warm-blooded animals. His coat glistens with frozen water. The ice clinging to his head, flank, legs, and paws weighs him down as he drags the heavy water like a shroud. His front paws keep slipping back into the water. His eyes freeze shut. The undertow sucks at his haunches. He holds on to life with his last working muscles. He's swallowed by the icy water's jagged teeth. A mighty wind rushes over the water, like the wind that carries souls out of this world. Like when He lost his boy, not even God can watch. He waits on the other side.

Now a dead wild creature, the cougar's body floats east like a cloud shadow towards Boblo Island. His magnificent tail of muscle that had steadied the cougar throughout his life, trails behind him like the streamer of a fallen kite. He floats off the edge of his wordless world, as the undertow sucks at his haunches. The day the cougar dies is beautiful in every way but one. The sun streaks slanting light, the wind-split clouds hurry across the silver sky, the white gulls chatter, the bright waves chop, and the air carries the fragrances of spring.

Divine sparks sparkle on the water. The once land-bound animal slips below the surface, heart, spine, bone, skin, blood, and vein, into the mystery of the unseen real world, as real as invisible wind and transparent stars. He's smacked down by circumstance. He will never return to Wisconsin. Nothing more can happen to him. He belongs to heaven.

## 24

# AFTER THE TREE FALLS

THREE DAYS AFTER THE FALL of the great oak tree and the destruction of the clubhouse, Leo Zitzelberger, who had momentarily given up on his dream of returning to The Lawnmower Club, has lunch with a local architect in downtown Petoskey. He no longer needs a walker, and when he goes to town, Frieda Weatherby accompanies him. People regard them as a couple, and walking alongside amiable Frieda, Zitzelberger doesn't look as formidable as he once did. People no longer pick up their children or heel their dogs.

Leo's back is straighter when he walks, not like the slumpy posture of his former days. When he smiles, Frieda tells him that he looks handsome, so he keeps smiling all the time to everyone. She has exchanged her faded dresses for new bright-colored ones. "Old ladies need to wear bright colors" she says, looking down at her yellow dress. Leo wears the first new clothes he has bought in years: a button-down blue shirt beneath a navy suede vest, tailored khaki slacks, and what he calls his going-out shoes. He looks neat and clean, and his shirts smell like ironed cotton.

This morning, Hazzard and Hazel are about to meet Leo and Frieda at the local coffee shop.

"I thought those two despised each other, Haz," Hazel says. "When they were at Mallard Pond, they argued all the time!"

"Argument is often an expression of love," says Pembrook. "Not for me, mind you. I don't like conflict, and I hate to lose arguments, which most of the time, I do. In our case, I do what you say, and we're both happy. You might say you're smarter than me, so you solve our problems, and I compliment your solutions. I'm much more peaceful now that we're together... I can tell in the morning when I shave and don't cut myself. I think it would be nifty if we could be married someday. It would be so fantastic to break my family tradition of unhappy marriages, and even think about having children."

"Marriage maybe, but little Hazzards—oh, oh, oh—we'll have to discuss babies, sweetie," Hazel says. "Can you imagine a combination of us? If it turns out to be a little asshole, you can't get rid of baby mistake in a yard sale. It would have to live in our house."

"With your brains and my good looks, what could go wrong?" says Pembrook. "No matter, I'm so happy to be Velcroed to you for the rest of my life. You have saved me from my nightmarish past, which no longer creeps into the present. *YIPPEE!* You make me want to mount a white horse and say *'HI-YO, SILVER, AWAY!'*"

## *The Lawnmower Club*

"Hazzard, keep talking like that and I'm the one you'll see galloping off."

Leo and Frieda arrive, and the two couples sit down for coffee and tea. The architect has arrived with plans for building a cottage at The Lawnmower Club site where the clubhouse used to be, a place for Leo and Frieda to live for the rest of their days.

Liza walks in carrying Pal in her arms like a monster lap dog. She joins them at their table. She orders black coffee, eggs, and toast. She's tired, cold, and hungry. She and Pal have hunted for the cougar for a week all over Emmet and Charlevoix Counties. They should have placed a tracking collar on the cougar a long time ago.

"We've lost him, but we'll find him," Liza says. "I know he's alive. Nothing can happen to a cougar around here."

"Did Angler track him?" Zitzelberger asks.

"Yes, but he gave up after dark. He told me that the cougar tracks were leading west."

"Well, I imagine he had enough of us," says Zitzelberger, "you know, the lawnmower noise, the trespassing golfers, the guns and traps, and most of all, the tree falling on him."

"Yes, he's long gone," says Pembrook.

"I'm not giving up," says Liza. "He's all I've got. I came in town to get some backpacking equipment. I'm going to pick up where Angler left off. You can all live to be happy, but I must find him to be happy. Oh God, let him live. Bring him home to us!"

"I can tell by your determination, you intend to do this," says Pembrook," but take the Skunk Whisperer with you. He knows this area well, and he'll keep you safe, although he's not trustworthy. I'll ask him myself, he owes me a million trillion thanks for saving his life."

"Months ago, I met him in a bar," says Liza. "He seemed nice."

"Where are you living dear?" says Frieda.

"Aunt Hazel has taken me in."

"Lucky dog," says Pembrook. "I wish your Aunt Hazel would take *me* in."

"Maybe I will," says Hazel.

*"ME? ARE YOU REFERRING TO ME?"* says Pembrook.

*"YES, YOU HANDSOME DEVIL!"*

"Hazel, I am unable to contain my bursting brain. WILL YOU MARRY ME? I cannot imagine our future together, minus me."

"Yes, Hazzard. That would be nice, I think."

"Oh, Hazel...you make me so happy...how authentic I sound. I'm certain we can jostle through any tensions that may develop during the course of our marriage."

At first light the next morning, Whisperer and Liza head out, and pick up the cougar's tracks first followed by Angler. They recognize each other at once.

## The Lawnmower Club

"I never thought I'd see you again," he says.

"Did you try?"

"No, I should have asked for your number."

"I sort of liked you," Liza says with a smile.

"I sort of like you, too."

A pair of tall, gray Sandhill Cranes return from the South to nest in a field before them, rattling like throaty trumpets. The weather breaks above freezing, but the woods are still full of snow, and at least for the moment, the cougar's tracks are well-defined, glazed over with ice. They wear snow shoes when needed, and remove them when the footing improves. About ten miles to the west, the tracks turn north and follow the Native American footpaths along the North Country Trail. Pal shuffles along with his nose in the air. Liza notices how easy it is to walk with Whisperer. They match strides.

As they crunch snow through the pine boughs, Whisperer says, "Hey, uhhh...Liza...if the cougar has decided to take off, maybe for Wisconsin or farther, how do you think you're going to find him?—and if you don't mind the question—why do you *want* him back? He seems like a lot more than a pet to you."

"O-M -Gosh, I'm sorry...I've been freaking out, and never explained the cougar to you. I love the cougar, because he gave back the little girl magic in my life, because he made my little world bigger. He's like a friend who lights up your eyes when you see him. He made me feel protected. To me, he is more than an animal—though all animals are awesome. He's almost human, but more than human. And now he's gone wandering off—*WITHOUT ME!*"

"No way. I've always liked animals, even though I make a living killing them. I spend most of my days filling traps with poison."

"The cougar kills, too," says Liza. "He loves to eat mice and chipmunks. I wish he didn't have to kill to survive. Guess I wish you didn't have to either."

"Awww...killing isn't fun, but the money's good." The Whisperer's long legs and big feet trip over a fallen tree trunk and he goes nose down in front of Liza. She drops to her knees to help him, grabbing his arm at the elbow. She looks into his deep blue eyes, and wipes away some dirt and a scrape of blood from his forehead.

"Hey, are you okay?" she whispers.

"Yep, I was too busy talking. I don't say much, but I like talking to you. When I first met you at the bar, I liked you right away."

"What did you like about me?"

"You looked like one of the smart girls in my high school class...very serious, but someone I could make laugh. I liked your eyes, and the funny way you dressed. And you said you liked animals."

"I wanted you to call me."

"I didn't call you, because I was unstrung...getting out of a bad marriage."

"Remind me, what's your name?"

## The Lawnmower Club

"Zach Zuman. After my divorce, I wanted to shrink away from people. And I was still messed up from Iraq when my marriage fell apart. I kept waking up at night and diving under the bed, and didn't know how I got there. But I thought about calling you more than once. I found your number. Still, I knew I wasn't ready to see anyone, because I kept playing and replaying my marriage, like reruns of old TV shows. I didn't see any hope for salvaging my miserable life. Gradually, things got better. Then I fell through the ice the other day, and ... something happened to me. Maybe it was the shock of the cold water or knowing I wasn't going to die. All I know is that I didn't want to keep going on in the same way. Since then, I've known there's something better in my future. And then you called."

He looks away from her to get some distance from the conversation.

"Well, Mr. Zach Zuman, we have a lot in common. I don't want to keep going on in the same way either. I like taking care of unusual animals. I live with a pit bull therapy dog, and until a few days ago, with the cougar. Where we lived was destroyed by a falling tree, and the cougar ran away. He was probably frightened to death. Mr. Pembrook suggested that you might help me find him. I must find him. Would you help me? The cougar makes me happy, and I love him. It's difficult to explain."

"He sounds awesome!" says Zach. "Living with a mountain lion—what a hoot! Bet it cuts way down on the door-to-door people."

"He's my perfect pet!"

"Yeah, okay I get it. Not so weird. Hazzard Pembrook lives across the street from the clubhouse. He asked me to help him trap the cougar. What a fiasco! He wanted to take over the clubhouse from Zitzelberger, but the cougar was scaring everyone away. Smart animal, for sure. Pembrook trapped himself twice in his own traps, but the cougar got away both times. Pembrook's the one who saved my life the day everyone fell through the ice out on Crooked Lake.

Liza lifts his arm, and helps him to his feet. She hadn't seen him since their conversation in the bar months earlier. He's over six feet tall with a lean body, a good head of curly brown hair, and a full beard. He has good-looking hands, and long arms like hers. His wire-rimmed glasses give him more the appearance of an English major than an exterminator, like someone you might meet in a book store or library—dorky, goofy, a bit self-conscious—like her.

*Zach Zuman. Looking at Zach is like looking deep into a mirror. I can see my reflection.*

"I'll help you find the cougar, and then maybe you can help me find something else to do. I've done about everything that I didn't want to do already. I'm open to about anything but the doing the tango. Pal, this way." They continue following the cougar's trail. On the crest of a hill, Liza notices something different in the foot prints.

"Look, the tracks have changed," Liza says. She sees the familiar tear-shaped toe pads of the cougar, but a dark line slants the right forepaw print.

## *The Lawnmower Club*

"Must've cracked his paw on something," Zach wrinkles his brow. "It's larger than the other paws, like it's swollen. Look! A blood trail."

Liza and Zach follow the injured cougars tracks until dark, then backtrack to the highway. Liza's car is too far away, so Zach calls Pembrook. He picks them up, and drives them all the way back to his place to sleep for the night. Pembrook has no idea what the two of them are doing. Zach and Liza sleep in separate bedrooms. Pal sleeps with Liza. The next morning, Pembrook goes into town and comes back with donuts and coffee. When he comes into the kitchen, Liza notices an I LIKE IKE button on his lapel. "What's that button you're wearing?" says Liza.

"This little button is from the presidential campaign before Dwight D. Eisenhower ruled our land in the fifties. I was a young lad at the time, and my parents pinned it on me to wear to school. I was a member of the Late Childhood Republicans Club. That was the first presidential election I can remember... and the last. I don't stay up with current events, because there is too much to know. It's like the whole world is a showroom for my ignorance. Better to build a wall between yourself and the world to avoid feeling dumb. Even quiz shows can make people feel stupid."

"What a great pin," says Zach without a beat, "we all have our favorite little childhood artifacts. I can't imagine living without my baseball card collection." Zach's acceptance of Pembrook's eccentricities pleases Liza. *If he can put up and be nice to a flake like him, there's hope for me.*

After breakfast, Pembrook drives them back to the trail in his 1959 Continental Mark IV. The car needs a major realignment—it wobbles along the narrow, tree-tunneled road like a drunk. Much to his chagrin, Pal gets left behind at CLINGSTONE. Pal had hoped for a walk in town, because he's now on a first-name basis with the long-legged poodle named Lola, who doesn't mind that he has no balls, and no longer gives Pal that look away look.

By noon, Zach and Liza arrive at the Straits west of Mackinaw City. The Mackinaw Bridge looms to their right, and across the Straits the small houses of St. Ignace backdrop the white ice and hurrying black water. They walk out as far as possible on the ice, then Liza follows the paw tracks with her binoculars. The tracks go straight across the ice, and then disappear at the edge of the shipping channel. Neither Liza nor Zach can pick up a hint of tracks leading away from the other side. They stand there for a long time, silent as two herons looking out on the ice and water.

"Do you think he made it across?" says Liza.

"I don't know. He could be on his way to the to the Dakotas where cougars live in large numbers...maybe he came from there, and he's going home."

"*OHHHH*...I don't want my world without him in it," Liza says. "I hope he's all right...I want him to live forever." They

## *The Lawnmower Club*

return to the shore, and sit down on a log, huddling together against the blasting wind, looking out on the cold Straits, watching the cars and trucks move like toys over the steel grid surface of the mighty bridge. Liza leans against Zach' body, and feels sheltered and warmed. They sit there for a long time, and watch the water of the newly-opened channel passage silk under the bridge like a shining river.

Zach cradles his arms around Liza. "Okay, I want to believe he made it across," he says. "Let's walk into Mackinaw City and find coffee and something to eat."

*"I HOPE HE'S ALIVE?!"* she says, "because I don't like my pets to die...none of my pets, ever." As the two walk into town, she cries the cry of all those who have lost their animals, and mumbles as she cries: *"Na-uh, he can't be gone...can't be gone... can't be gone."*

"Are you okay?" says Zach. After spending most of her life dealing with things on her own, Liza feels comforted. She reaches for his handsome hand.

# 25

# THE KEYHOLE BAR

LIZA AND ZACH pass McGulpin Point Lighthouse, and after a few miles, arrive on Central Avenue in Mackinaw City. They are looking for a late breakfast or early lunch. They bend into the wind and rain. Dead leaves swirl all around, and wood smoke fills the air.

"I hate leaving the trail," says Liza. "Do you think it's hopeless?"

"He's gone, Liza. I'll keep looking if you want, but I think he's gone. He could be in Wisconsin by now."

"Then he'll come back. I can't let him go like nothing's happened. I refuse to believe that he's died."

"We should go home for a few days, and get more supplies and dry clothes."

## Randy Evans

Mackinaw City loses tourists after the fall leaf season. The main street looks wide and empty. Fudge shops, tee shirt stores, and restaurants stand behind the vacant sidewalk. Almost everything closes except the Post Office. Near the end of the street not far from the deserted ferry docks, a gaunt man in an apron crooks an unlit cigarette between his lips as he opens the door to a local diner—the Key Hole Bar.

Tired, cold, and hungry, Liza and Zach enter the Key Hole. They pass a long whiskey-colored bar, and take a high table across from the kitchen serving window. They feel warmth from the stove radiating into the dining area along with aromas of the day's specials. Stacks of small and large white plates sit on the window shelf. Behind the window, the thin cook wears a baseball hat and one large earring. He leans over the grill, and begins to fry potatoes in bacon fat. The walls are covered with barn wood, and thousands of keys are embedded in the countertops with countless more hanging on nails. A sign over the bar reads: "Mackinaw City is too small to have a town drunk, so we all take turns." A framed hockey jersey and Detroit Red Wings "Wing-Nut" souvenirs decorate the walls next to mirrored ads for Bud, Miller, LaBatts, and Leinenkugel.

Near the street by a window, two men sit at a square table. They order without looking at menus. Not used to seeing strangers in the off season, they raise their eyebrows at the two strangers. The eavesdropping works two ways. Liza and Zach listen when one of the men starts talking about how to make chili out of bear meat. The other changes the subject to local politics and then to the latest foreclosures. They order brandy shots and coffee, and converse with the waitress for a long time. She leaves Liza and Zach unattended.

Towards the back of the bar, a pool table stands alongside a single video game with blinking lights. A jukebox belts out Bob Seger's "Like a Rock": *Like a rock, the sun upon my skin, Like a rock, hard against the wind, Like a rock, I see myself again, Like a rock*. The Redwings are smoking the Blackhawks on the TV by the bar.

"Do you follow hockey?" Zach asks Liza.

"Stanley Cup," she answers.

"What about it?" he asks.

"That's all I know about hockey."

The menu offers a history of the bar, a header reads "unlock your appetite," and "anything but breakfast." The waitress comes over and apologizes for the delay. They order steaming bowls of clam chowder and perch sandwiches along with black coffee. Zach had grabbed a tourist brochure at the door. He unfolds the colorful newspaper to show the local attractions: Agawa Canyon, Beaver Island, Drummond Island, Mackinac Island, Pictured Rocks, Tahquamenon Falls, the Soo Locks, Les Cheneaux, White Fish Point.

"Liza, have you been to any of these places? Have you seen northern Michigan?"

"No, I've never explored the area, and I haven't been much of anywhere, not even Detroit or Chicago. When I worked, I didn't have much time off. Never had travel money."

"Doesn't matter to me. I haven't traveled much myself. What do you like?"

"I like animals…better than people. I grew up in this area, and I had lots of pets—cats, dogs, birds, fish, rabbits, turtles, hamsters, a ferret and a guinea pig—not at the same time. My parents were killed in a car crash when I was seventeen. I was their only child. Every year my memory of them fades a bit more, but I remember fighting a lot with my mother right before the crash, and afterwards, I was angry that they had to die and leave me on my own."

"Very tough. What did your parents do for a living?"

"My father was a butcher like my grandfather, but he wanted to move up in the world. He applied to medical school. He wanted to be a surgeon—he was always good with knives. He never got into medical school, but he took up wood carving. My mom wove rugs, so they set up a shop and both made a living by selling their crafts. In the summers, my dad mowed lawns, and in the winter, he plowed snow with his truck. My mother cleaned houses. They saved up enough money to send me to college. After they died, I went downstate to MSU, and returned up here after graduation. In some ways, I'm glad they laid me off from my social work job. You burn out quickly in that type of work. What about you?"

"My parents live over by Indian River. My dad retired from the phone company, and my mom still works as a nurse. My brother and I grew up fishing and hunting. I had always liked reading, so when I got to college, I majored in English

## The Lawnmower Club

Literature. I liked 17th Century poets like John Donne, George Herbert, and Andrew Marvell. But there's not much money in English. So I joined the Army—served two tours in Iraq. When I came home, I interviewed for jobs, anything I could find that paid enough money to get by."

"So you were married?"

"Well, that's a question out of the blue. Yes, I married a girl I knew in high school, but she wanted more out of life than I did. She kept pushing me to better myself, but at the time, I had no idea what I wanted. How about you?"

"Single, one of the most single girls you'll ever meet. I can count my dates on one hand. There's nothing about me that's cute or dainty or polished. I'm a little ragged around the edges." Liza fishes for a compliment.

"You look pretty nice to me. Your face has a healthy glow, you have beautiful eyes, and I like your dark brown hair."

"What exactly are we talking about right now, Mr. Zach Zuman?"

"You and me."

"We'll have to see," Liza says. "I don't know how to talk sports and I've never been anywhere. I bet you want a girl who knows the difference between a Redwing and a Blackhawk, and can talk about river cruises, and her last shopping trip to Chicago." She tries to be flirtatious, give him a coy smile, but it's all new to her, delightful but new.

"Those things aren't important to me," Zach says.

"Uh-huh, well let's see—"

## Randy Evans

The waitress appears with the check.

They both search their pockets and backpacks to scrape up cash for the tab, and walk out of the dark bar into gray daylight. The clouds scud by fast. Without cars, campers, and trucks to hold it down, the wide boulevard looks like it might lift off in the wind like a long roof. The ferry lot is desolately empty. The seasonal ferries sit cradled on blocks. Liza feels lighter than air, like the sea gulls wheeling around and squawking above her. Zach reaches out for her hand, as they turn at the lake, and walk up North Huron Street towards the Mackinac Bridge.

When they arrive at a series of small parks along the shore, a filthy dog with ragged fur stumbles towards them, sniffing at the ground. Her ribs stick out and her tongue hangs down. Her floppy ears are full of small sticks and burrs. She has no collar. *Must be a stray*, Liza thinks.

"Liza, the dog looks like somebody's hunting dog—look at her black and liver-colored patches. An English Setter. Who would let such a fine dog loose?"

Looking for a midday meal on the shore, the dog chases a seagull, but the gull rushes to the sky. The dog sniffs and paws a discarded beer can to see if it offers food or drink. So emaciated, she looks weightless as a bird. She stops and looks skyward with open jaws like she's trying to drink the watery

## The Lawnmower Club

air. Then she collapses to the ground in the middle of a pile of old snow.

"Puppy! Puppy! Come here, Puppy!" Liza calls in a playful voice. The dog hunches back on her hind legs and doesn't move. "She looks frightened," Liza says.

"She looks like all the stray dogs in the world," says Zach. "She's too tired to move, too weak to bark. You can see her ribcage."

Liza moves closer to the dog, then scoops the dirty, stinky dog into her arms. The dog lets Liza hold her. "Find some food and water for her, Zach. We'll wait here on this park bench."

While Zach searches the town, Liza sits with the dog looking out on the Straits. She looks for the cougar, hoping that he will magically appear. She rubs her fingers over the dog's spongy paws, thinking of the cougar, while she hums a little tune. She gently combs her hands through the dog's stringy coat.

A few yards in front of Liza, the great volume of water moving through the ice-broken channel looks like cold blue blood flowing out of an artery. She watches a freighter edge through the Straits, and then disappear in the distance. The wind shifts, and turns colder.

Fifteen minutes later, Zach returns with cooked chicken and rice from a restaurant kitchen. "This should work for now," he says. He feeds the dog out of wax wrapping paper, then pours bottled water into a small paper bowl. A light wet snow has fallen on and off all day, but now storm winds surge snow in cascades from low clouds. Zach takes the dog from Liza, and they run for the nearest shelter, a red brick building with a barely-visible sign in front of a large open porch.

Bounding up the steps to the porch, they're greeted by a retired auto worker who owns the Deer Head Inn. "My name's Ian. I own this place." Ian's a large man, and wears a UAW baseball hat, a wool plaid shirt and jeans. He's holding a cup of coffee in a white ceramic mug. They're all standing on the front porch of Ian's bed and breakfast, not knowing what to say next. "Stay here. I'll get some blankets for you and towels for the dog," Ian says.

When Ian returns, Zach says, "Ever seen this dog before? We found him down by the lake. As you can see, he's in bad shape."

"Nope. We seem to get tons of strays in this town for some reason—both animals and people. It's what you get when you're on one end of a five-mile bridge. You folks have a car?"

"No, a friend will pick us up in the morning. We've been backpacking the North Country Trail," Zach says.

"Not for the faint-hearted this time of year," Ian says. "Well, you folks aren't exactly my typical guests, but if you need a place to stay, I have a room...the place is empty. I don't normally take dogs, but I'll make an exception since she looks like an orphan. I have a dog myself, and if the two of 'em get along, they can sleep in the kitchen." An old Black Lab limps out to the porch and sniffs the stray with interest.

Liza and Zach wrap themselves in wool blankets, and dry the dog. They move into the sitting room, and Ian takes the dogs into the kitchen.

## The Lawnmower Club

"Okay, are we going to sleep here tonight?" Liza says. "I mean...in the same room? I don't want you to assume...about sleeping together. We should talk—"

"Well, he said the place was empty. I suppose we could get separate rooms," Zach says. "If you're more comfortable—"

"We can sleep together, but we should keep our clothes on, don't you think?"

"We're soaked to the skin, Liza!" says Zach. "See...even my lips are wet." He pulls Liza gently out of her chair, and gives her a wet hug then moves his head towards hers. She lets their lips touch, then she gives him a kiss back.

"Wow! Excuse me, I—." Liza kisses him a second time.

"—let's go upstairs and see if we can dry out our clothes," Zach says.

The world-wise proprietor feeds the dogs, and sits in a kitchen rocking chair by a woodstove while the dogs sleep. Upstairs, Liza takes a hot shower, then Zach. Liza lights a candle, and lays on the bed, uncovered and vulnerable. She lets her hair fall down around her shoulders. Zach comes over to the bed, and says, "Wow, you are beautiful, Liza!" The two make slow love, as the candle swallows itself. They wake up surprised to see each other's arms and legs, naked as morning. Liza says, "If I were Queen of the Universe and could pick one day a year to repeat, it would be yesterday and last night."

"May I ask you something?" Zach says.

"Yes."

"Do you want to—"

"What?"

"Do you want to find out if we have a future...together, like—"

"Sure."

"Did I mention that you were beautiful."

"Yes."

"Inside and out."

Their clothes not quite dry, they lie curled up in bed. They feel grand and hungry. An hour later, they walk downstairs to the kitchen. Ian prepares cheese scrambled eggs, slabs of bacon, and hot blueberry muffins, while they sip coffee with the dogs sitting at their feet. Ian gives them an old collar and leash for the stray. He takes their information, and promises to contact the humane society and the sheriff's office, and call if someone's missing an English Setter.

"If you decide not to keep the dog, bring her back to me," Ian says.

"I doubt if I'll give her up unless I have to," Liza says.

Liza calls Pembrook for a ride home. She has not got over her sorrow about the cougar. She has not figured out her new relationship with Zach. She resides in a middle place, but even so, feels content to be sad and happy at the same time.

Late morning, Pembrook rocks and rolls down Central Avenue in his big car. It looks like an aircraft carrier moving slowly through heavy seas. The engine mumbles under the long hood.

## The Lawnmower Club

The car has a red exterior, and white leather seats inside. Pembrook has it detailed once a month, and yesterday had been the day. The car's right front fender and headlight are smashed. He sees Liza and Zach. Liza holds a mangy dog in her arms like a small sack of potatoes. *I hope they don't want to take that dog into my clean car.* He's not sure what to do. He opens his mouth wide like he's airing out his brain.

"Haz, thanks for picking us up," says Zach. "That's some car. Moves like a crippled moose."

Liza sees a look of horror on Pembrook's face, as he fixes a stare on the dog. "We have a new addition" she says.

"Well, what a surprise!" Pembrook says. "I go through life surprised, so this is nothing new. But do you have a dog with you? You found a dog? I thought you were looking for the cougar."

The stray snarls at Pembrook. *Dogs know people.* Pembrook responds with mad laughter, then his face turns white like he might have a fainting spell.

"I bet you have an old blanket in that big car of yours," Liza says, anticipating his concerns.

"I do, I do. I keep the blanket in case I'm ever stranded in the wild. So, I take it you want to bring the pooch home?"

"Yes, she needs someone to take care of her right away," Liza replies. "God only knows what might be wrong with the poor thing."

"Well, hop in...all of you. Does the dog look like it has rabies? Oh well, you two are quite kind to rescue the dog, and quite the troopers going off into the woods. I've had an adventure of my own on the drive up here. Things could have turned out worse if it hadn't been daylight. Picking you up the other night in the dark was very frightening. I don't go out in the dark hardly ever. As a matter of fact, I know little of the night, although I know it's been going on for a long time. By the way, where did you two spend the night?" He receives no answer. Zach changes the subject, which is easy to do with Pembrook. He talks to Pembrook about a subject he knows zero about, hockey.

As Pembrook roars out of town trailing a settling cloud of blue exhaust, Pembrook says, "You have no idea how narrow the roads are up here where Michigan squeezes together at the tip of the mitten! Even an expert driver like me has close calls. On the way here, I narrowly missed hitting a deer, two turkeys, and a cow. Then *OOPS!* I missed a woman standing out in the road in a pink bathrobe reading her mail—but her mailbox wasn't so lucky. I must admit, I'm a bit of a road hog, and this car is far from a compact."

Zach and Liza sit in the back seat with the dog. The two new lovers hold hands in as much silence as Pembrook will allow. They see his eyeballs bouncing in the rearview mirror, so not even a chaste kiss is possible. They ride safely back to Petoskey, a small miracle.

# 26

# SPRING MOWING

LEO ZITZELBERGER AND FRIEDA WEATHERBY move into their new cottage the following summer. The cottage looks like something in a children's storybook—made all from local stone with white wood trim and a green metal roof. The cottage stands on the former site of the clubhouse, which Leo had been wise enough to cover with insurance. Frieda surrounds the house with flower gardens, and to Leo's dismay, a variety of shrubs. They plant a new oak tree where the old one once stood. Tuning their machines with great enthusiasm, the original lawnmowerians begin to trickle back to the club. They don't miss the clubhouse, because they had never been invited inside. All the mowers require is the cart shed, which had been unscathed by the tree disaster.

That same summer, Hazel Hertz and Haz Pembrook are married by Benjamin Putzkin, the therapist and magician, who also happens to have a preacher's license. Pembrook schedules the wedding the day after Hazel accepts his proposal. He's afraid she might change her mind.

At a rambunctious Moose Jaw Junction reception, Pembrook plays the accordion to the extent of his limited repertoire: "You Can't Always Get What You Want," "The First Time Ever I Saw Your Face," "Killing Me Softly With His Song," "Take Me Out to the Ballgame," "Old MacDonald Had a Farm," "If You're Happy and You Know It," "Don't Fence Me In," and a medley of Lawrence Welk polkas. For his grand finale, he plays a piece of his own creation, "Soy Candle in the Wind."

After the music, Pembrook steps up to the microphone to propose a toast, since he's decided to be his own best man. Everyone takes a glass of champagne, except Pembrook, who swirls, sniffs, and then swigs tap water from his crystal champagne glass.

"I gave up drinking alcoholic beverages a long time ago, because it fogs my mind. However, people still ask me if I'm inebriated, but I say, 'No, I'm like this all the time!'" Not a hint of laughter. "Well, ha, ha, so much for my humorous introduction. Can you believe I rehearsed this?"

"Oh, oh, I want to take this opportunity to give a shout out to all the Mallard Pondians who have so generously departed from their busy schedules to appear at our celebration. My heart filled with joy when I saw the van pull up and unload you all. I can still see a few stragglers shuffling to their seats with those cute little yellow tennis balls on the legs of their walkers. Don't trip on floor mats! And a shout out to my fellow

*The Lawnmower Club*

lawnmowerians. I've never really been one of the boys, so to speak, but Custer and Finnegan, you're the best lawn mowing comrades a man could hope for, and as for the rest of you, your names elude me."

He proposes a toast to his new wife, "Hazel, I have found you, and I do now believe you are what I have always been looking for, even though I never had it. In marrying you, the word "triumph" flashes through my head, even though I never use the word. But I know for certain that when we lay together in bed with our backsides pancaked together, I know we are meant to be man and wife. Your body of white hills and white thighs make you look like the world, and oh, the goblets of your breasts! The roses of your—"

*"THAT'S ENOUGH, HAZZARD!"*

Hazel rises like a mountain from her seat, turns to him, and says, "I have loved you for a short time. Until then, our courtship had been too bizarre to talk about—the sheer scope of its bizarreness makes me gasp...but you have grown on me lately. I don't understand you much at all, but I understand you better than other people...not the inside of your crazy head, but the inside of your big heart."

"God bless you both!" says Frieda Weatherby.

Before Pembrook sits down, he offers a few last words. "The eternal now of my life, for the first time, has a history. I am so grateful to you, Hazel. I'm happy that I'm not so crazy that I make no sense to you. I am certain that for as long as we are man and wife, our relationship will never descend into entropy—or is it atrophy, or is it apathy? Why you married me shall keep me in the dark for the rest of my life!" Everyone raises their champagne glasses in hearty agreement.

Louise Gnatkozski offers a toast of her own, "We're all darn good people—as good as they come!"

The newlyweds spend their first night in the Laura Bush Suite at The Grand Hotel on Mackinac Island. "Just think, Laura Bush slept here," Pembrook deduces. "Probably with George the Younger."

Pembrook surprises Hazel with a honeymoon trip to the Republic of Uganda, a land-locked country in East Africa. "I have always been an excursionist at heart," he says, "and I've heard that Africa is known wide and far for its awesome scenery...or was that New Zealand?"

They stay at a coffee farm in southern Uganda on a deep green lake ringed by volcanic mountains. Not surprising to anyone who knows him, while Hazel sleeps in, Pembrook takes a morning stroll, dressed in khakis with epaulets and a pith helmet. Squinting up into the morning sun, he walks into the middle of foraging gorillas. Drama always seems to shadow his footsteps.

Pembrook resolves to fight to the death, but the gorillas show little interest in him. However, the mere presence of the gorillas causes him to shake, and he scalds himself with the

## *The Lawnmower Club*

coffee he happens to be carrying. Even so, he manages to take pictures with his camera, mostly at the gorilla's silver backs, and later prepares a slideshow about gorilla trekking for the back-home service clubs. He adds a frontal view of three gorillas downloaded from Google Images, and photo shops himself standing among them. Except for the Musambya trees in the background, they look like a golf foursome.

Hazel feels out of place in her jodhpurs, thigh-high boots, scarf, and wide-brimmed hat, but Pembrook says she looks very Meryl Streepy. They visit a wildlife conservancy populated with desert lions, desert elephants, zebra, oryx, and black rhinos, all threatened by extinction. Everywhere she goes, Hazel sees the need for her nursing skills. After returning to Michigan, she joins Doctors Without Borders as a volunteer nurse. She returns to Africa every year, most often on her own. She finds that an annual Hazzard-free sabbatical, helps their marriage.

A few months later, Pembrook begins clerking at a local men's clothing store, hoping that he can someday turn dressing men into an upscale consulting business. He becomes a highly successful salesman. With his store discount, he buys more clothes, and turns one of CLINGSTONE's extra bedrooms into a closet. He plays the accordion once a week at Mallard Pond and performs duets with Mrs. Gnatkozski. He adores his new wife and wakes her up in the middle of most nights to tell her how much he loves her.

Hazel redecorates CLINGSTONE over the mild objections of Pembrook. Pal has returned to the house, but the dog regards Hazel as the alpha member of the family, not Hazzard.

Hazel has never had the luxury of domestic activities. She learns to cook and garden. Mysteriously, Pembrook turns out to be a good husband. He tries to follow what he refers to as the "honor your wife" clause in the Bible.

More former members return and join The Lawnmower Club loyalists, Custer, Finnegan, and Pembrook, who had already returned when Zitzelberger gave them the green light. The membership roster reaches its former levels. Zitzelberger convenes a membership meeting of the lawnmowerians, and, once again, he turns down Pembrook's request for a dress code.

"We will take a new hard look at your dress code proposal in five years," says Zitzelberger.

Undeterred, Pembrook designs his own line of lawn mowing outfits. He leaves nothing to chance—offers top-to-bottom matching sets along with steel-toed saddle shoes. Custer and Finnegan buy the whole line, including the saddle shoes, and straw hats woven out of plasticized grass cuttings. Finnegan, out of the goodness of his heart, promises Pembrook that he will never again mow shirtless. A year later, Pembrook establishes a

## The Lawnmower Club

successful internet clothing business for upscale grass cutters. He also displays his merchandise in a downtown store front next to the display case of his father's vintage golf clubs.

Zitzelberger invites Liza and Zach to build a cabin on the far edge of The Lawnmower Club property, near the woods. Within a year, they build a small log home with a large fireplace and adequate room for pets, including the rescued setter and Zach's pet skunk.

On a fine autumn Saturday, the following year, Frieda invites everyone over to the cottage for breakfast.

*"SHRUBBERY! FRIEDA, I CAN'T FIND THE COFFEE!"* says Zitzelberger. He's fully recovered from his encounter with the cougar and moves around the kitchen as smoothly as a big cat.

"Leo, dear, the coffee's where it always is—on the top shelf of the pantry."

"Oh, yeah. Do we need food for Baby Pembrook, or—"

"No, Haz has placed him on a special diet of some kind. He wants to supervise everything the poor child eats."

"I hope the little shit doesn't bring his toy squeezebox. It drives me nuts, especially the father-son duets. I hate accordion music, and I never did like babies. They're barely human."

"You be a good boy—we couldn't manage to live here on our own. If it weren't for Hazzard, Hazel, Liza, and Zach, I don't know what we'd do."

## Randy Evans

"Is this your day to volunteer at Mallard Pond?" he asks.

"Yep, I'm taking Pal over with me. I think the residents want to see the dog more than me."

"Well, I'm going out to mow with Custer and Finnegan this afternoon. I intend to break in the new Snapper. You're never too old for a new mower, and I'm going to talk to them about my new idea. I want to start a lawnmower museum here on the property. We'd need another building. I want to exhibit more than mowers—archives for manuals and handbooks, blueprints, and memorabilia, vintage spare parts, a restoration workshop—and a training program for future lawnmowerians."

Haz and Hazel enter the kitchen with little Pembrook and Pal. They had decided to adopt a child shortly after their marriage, a two-year old Ugandan boy.

"Well, this is marvelous of you to have us over for breakfast," says Pembrook. "Hope you still have some of your homemade strawberry preserves, Frieda. I love your preserves, all of them—blueberries, peaches, pears, salsa, tomatoes, pickles, relish, beans, asparagus, carrots, and peas. I have never seen so many bell jars in one place. Why do you make so much?"

With a mischievous smile, her chin in the air, her blue eyes round and shiny, Frieda replies, "Because I can."

"*BOY, STOP BITING MY HAND!* Sixteen teeth, last time I counted. He's going to be a big boy. You should see how he wolfs down his spinach! And his balls are the size of doorknobs! Oh, and what athleticism and physicality! He can do jumping jacks on his back when I poke him in the stomach. He doesn't say much yet, but I can tell, he often wants to say something that he doesn't have the words for."

"I smell coffee!" Liza pops in through the kitchen door. "Zach and I had business in town." Zach comes in. "We have an announcement!"

"Liza and I have found something we both want to do together," says Zach.

"Get married?" Hazel says.

"Well, not at the moment," says Liza, "but we have a new venture. We're starting up a dog and cat day care center in an old farmhouse next door to Mallard Pond. We plan to train therapy dogs and cats. We're calling the business, PAWS AND CLAWZ."

"I decided to sell my varmint control business to Felix Angler," says Zach. "Felix retired from the DNR and wants something to do that keeps him out of the house."

"Great idea!" Zitzelberger says. "I've also been thinking about a new enterprise, another good thing that may come out of the untidy mess of these past two years. Haz and I are going to talk with some people from Chicago about franchising lawnmower clubs across the country."

"Yes," says Pembrook. "I've been sitting on Daddy's trust fund all these years and haven't had the nerve to invest in anything other than U.S. Savings Bonds. But I just finished reading one of the books in my father's library, and one passage inspired me to do more: 'Thus the superior man encourages the people in their work and exhorts them to help one another'—this has inspired me to expand my work in many directions."

"What book would that be?" asks Frieda.

"Oh Frieda, you're testing my memory, but I believe the book was written by a sage named Lao Tzu, sounds like 'LOU-SY.' I think the book was titled ITCH-ING or KA-CHING...something like that. It was all about making change, and how if you don't change direction, you may end up where you are heading."

The three couples, along with little Hazzard Junior, sit down for what becomes a weekly Saturday breakfast. Together they grow into what each wish to be and help each other along the way.

On the edge of The Lawnmower Club property behind her log home, Liza plants a large garden. She weeds the long, thick beds of flowers and vegetables every day of the growing season. As she works, Liza often dreams of the cougar, her big cat with its big brain and big heart.

One October, Liza tends her garden in the subdued sounds of dusk. She looks up to the sky, because she hears distant thunder, but no lightening, and no signs of rain. Then she sees a pleasant-faced young girl standing at the border of the garden. She's dressed like a poor girl in boy's trousers and unlaced hightop shoes with feathery wings along her sides.

## *The Lawnmower Club*

"*Yoo-hoo how nice to see you,*" the *Whatshername Angel* says. She is holding something in her arms. Liza can't tell what it is at first, and she doesn't see what is standing behind the girl at the edge of the swamp. The girl comes up and speaks to Liza like a child saying prayers, with visible breath coming out of her little lungs.

"My name is *Whatshername*. I'm the guardian angel assigned to watch over people in this part of northern Michigan. Your cougar did not die. He stands over there, and you two are friends forever. We all choose our own kind of immortality, and yours involves animals. The cougar wants you to see this cub I hold in my arms."

Liza reaches out and rubs the ears of a baby cougar. She looks over the shoulder of the *Whatshername Angel* to see her beloved cougar, his face fixed and waiting.

"I always expected to see you again," Liza says to him.

"Yes," says the *Whatshername Angel*. "Art in heaven is like a magician with a full bag of tricks, who turns the bag upside down for us to enjoy *(hallowbehisname)*."

Liza smiles wide, and her mouth forms an unending curve of happiness. She looks at the cougar, and says, "Dear friend, why are you walking so wobbly? Your movements have always been so sure-footed."

"We all wobble when we ghost around without our skeletons," the angel says.

The cougar turns, and his feet pad back into the darkening woods. He looks back over his tail as he leaves. The cub follows.

"You didn't die," Liza says. *"MY KITTY IS ALIVE!* You came back to see me, and I know you'll come back to see me again."

"All beings are drawn by love," *Whatshername Angel says in a fading voice.*

For as many years as Liza keeps her garden, she finds imprints of the cougar's tracks in the soil, with the slender slit of a scar on the right forepaw. In the evenings, she goes to the garden, alone as an animal, and looks out into the immense hope of the universe. She looks for her cougar, and when she stops looking, he appears.

# ABOUT THE AUTHOR

Randy and Denise Evans live in Bay Harbor, Michigan with Little Traverse Lizzie, their English Setter. Randy graduated from Ohio University, Phi Beta Kappa, in English Literature. He earned an MBA from Columbia University in New York City, followed by a career as a human resources executive in manufacturing and high-tech industries. After retiring from business, Randy completed a Ph.D. in psychology at Saybrook University in San Francisco. He has taught developmental psychology at a local college, serves on community boards, and participates in Rotary International. Randy and Denise enjoy their blended stepfamily of five daughters and eight grandchildren.

*The Lawnmower Club* completes the fourth book in Randy's Red Sky Series—*Red Sky Anthology*, a border-crossing collection of poetry and short fiction, Book 1, *Out of the Inferno*, a memoir about how a high-achieving couple deal with breast cancer, Book 2, and *When Strangers Meet at Devil's Elbow*, a

## Randy Evans

novel about eight disparate strangers who meet at a cottage in northern Michigan, engage in collective adventures, and as a result, discover the meaning of love, home, and family, Book 3. Randy's poetry, essays, and fiction have appeared in Bear River Review, Dunes Review, Walloon Writers Review, and Whiskey Island Magazine. Randy seeks to bring joy to others through his writing. Please visit his blog: randyevansauthor.com.

# ACKNOWLEDGEMENTS

Thanks to readers and fellow writers who have continually supported my new life as a writer, including members of my writing groups in northern Michigan and students attending the Bear River Writers Conference. Thanks to Wade Rouse, Gary Edwards, the Lawler sisters, and other members of Wade's Writing Misfits. Stephanie Klosinski, David Thomas, my editors, provided invaluable feedback, as well as Bill and Lisa Hicklin, Dan Krull, Karen Langs, Bob and Lee Maldegan, and Al Sevener. Thanks to Tara Mayberry, TeaBerry Creative, for her interior and cover design. Special thanks to Cal Cook for advice on how large trees fall, and to Rabbi Sarah Adler for her recommendations about the contents of a rabbi's library. I am also thankful to Greg Schumacher, Wildlife Management and Nuisance Control, the real-life Skunk Whisperer, for his stories about varmints who love the great indoors. Admirations and appreciations would not be complete without mentioning the early and continuing support from all the folks at McLean

*Randy Evans*

& Eakin Booksellers on East Lake Street in Petoskey, Michigan. Above all, I am grateful for the loving support and gentle suggestions of Denise, my dear wife and first reader.

# READING GROUP GUIDE

1. Zitzelberger, Pembrook, and Liza, each with distinct personalities, are likeable and unlikeable in different ways. Discuss their differences.

2. By the end of the story, which of these characters changed the most?

3. What is Frieda Weatherby's role in the development of the story line?

4. Which of the secondary characters—Hazel Hertz, Willie Snowball, Frieda Weatherby, Zach Zuman—evoked your greatest empathy. Why?

5. In many ways, the cougar is the smartest protagonist in the novel. Of his physical, mental, and emotional gifts, which ones did you relate to most?

6. Pick a character and describe how cultural values influenced their behavior.

7. What did you learn or appreciate about personal resiliency by reading the book?

8. In what ways did a yearning for home drive the plot? How did the characters differ in how they defined and valued home?

9. Magical realism, a literary genre or style that presents elements of magic and the supernatural in a real-world setting, serves as the milieu for the story. As a reader, were there elements that were too strange, or were they true enough to believe?

10. Could you identify with the human failings of the characters as a source of humor? Which of their obsessions held the most comic value for you?

CPSIA information can be obtained
at www.ICGtesting.com
Printed in the USA
LVHW041218190123
737424LV00003B/427